American Horror Fiction

From Brockden Brown to Stephen King

Edited by
Brian Docherty

MACMILLAN

First published 1990

Published by
THE MACMILLAN PRESS LTD
Houndmills, Basingstoke, Hampshire RG21 2XS
and London
Companies and representatives
throughout the world

Typeset by Wessex Typesetters
(Division of The Eastern Press Ltd)
Frome, Somerset

Printed in Hong Kong

British Library Cataloguing in Publication Data
American horror fiction: from Brockden Brown
to Stephen King
1. Horror stories in English. American
writers, 1800—Critical studies
I. Docherty, Brian
813′.00916
ISBN 0-333-46128-2 (hc)
ISBN 0-333-46129-0 (pbk)

Contents

v

Acknowledgements

Thanks are due to Lesley Bloom for office services, to Frances and Leon Kacher for their invaluable assistance, and to Frances Arnold and Valery Rose for guiding the book to publication.

Notes on the Contributors

Clive Bloom is Co-ordinator of American Studies at Middlesex Polytechnic and General Editor of the Insights series. He is author of *The 'Occult' Experience and the New Criticism* and *Reading Poe, Reading Freud.*

Anne Cranny-Francis is a Lecturer in the Department of English at the University of Wollongong, Australia, and is an authority on Australian and Victorian literature.

Brian Docherty is co-editor of *Nineteenth-Century Suspense: From Poe to Conan Doyle,* editor of *American Crime Fiction: Studies in the Genre,* and is completing research on the Beat Poets.

Robert Giddings is a Lecturer at the Dorset Institute of Higher Education, and has edited *Literature and the Media* and *Literature and Imperialism* for the Insights series. He is editor of *The Changing World of Charles Dickens, Mark Twain: A Sumptuous Variety, Matthew Arnold: Between Two Worlds* and *J. R. R. Tolkien: This Far Land.*

Clare Hanson is a Lecturer in English and Humanities at the College of St Paul and St Mary, Cheltenham. She is author of *Katherine Mansfield* (with Andrew Gurr), *Short Stories and Short Fictions, 1880–1980* and *Virginia Woolf* (forthcoming), and has edited *The Critical Writings of Katherine Mansfield* and *Re-reading the Short Story.*

A. Robert Lee teaches English and American Literature at the University of Kent. He has edited the Everyman *Moby Dick,* and volumes on Afro-American fiction, Hawthorne, Hemingway, Melville, nineteenth-century American poetry, the nineteenth-century American short story, and Poe.

Odette L'Henry Evans is Principal Lecturer in Comparative Literature and French at the Polytechnic of North London, and has contributed to other volumes in the Insights series.

Judie Newman is a Lecturer in the Department of English Literature at the University of Newcastle upon Tyne. She is author of *Saul Bellow and History*, *John Updike* and *Nadine Gordimer*.

David Punter is Professor of English Studies at the University of Stirling. He is author of *The Literature of Terror*, *Blake, Hegel and Dialectic* and *The Hidden Script: Writing and the Unconscious*.

David Seed is a Lecturer in English and American Literature at the University of Liverpool, and is author of *The Fictional Labyrinths of Thomas Pynchon* and *The Fiction of Joseph Heller: Against the Grain*.

1

Introduction: Horror the Soul of the Plot

BRIAN DOCHERTY

Horror fiction, like detective and crime fiction, did not originate in America, but both genres were taken up early and with enthusiasm by both authors and readers. The name of Edgar Allan Poe, of course, is pre-eminent in both, although he was not the first American writer of horror. That distinction should probably go to the Puritan divine Michael Wigglesworth, whose long poem *The Day of Doom* (1662) achieved great popularity in Massachusetts as a warning to the elect of the consequences of religious backsliding. Nowadays, this turgid Calvinist doggerel probably has little to say to most people, since the theology is as unappealing as the verse.

Puritan hostility towards the novel and drama as forms of artistic production persisted throughout the eighteenth century, and thus the New World was behind the times in literary terms. Perhaps fittingly, the first American novelists appeared after the American Revolution, and, although there were American novels published before 1800, notably by Susanna Rowson and Hannah Foster, Charles Brockden Brown was America's first professional novelist, and is virtually the only one before Washington Irving whose name is remembered today. His first novel, *Wieland* (1798), was a Gothic tale which showed the influence of the English radical William Godwin, author of *Caleb Williams* and father of Mary Wollstonecraft Shelley, who wrote the classic *Frankenstein* (1818).

The Gothic tradition in English and German writing had been established for nearly forty years when Brockden Brown began publishing, and, indeed, its influence in Europe was diminishing rapidly, but it remained a powerful influence on American writers, especially horror and fantasy writers. In different ways, all the authors discussed in this volume have made use of, or reacted to, the Gothic tradition. This is appropriate, since America as a nation, if we date nationhood from 1776, is a product of the Romantic era, and Gothic writing is 'romance' in the broad sense. Terminology of course can be problematic, although it is to be hoped that a

1

sufficient degree of pluralism and open-mindedness exists today to make this a matter of secondary importance. We do not need to know whether a writer is a realist or modernist, or a suspense writer, before sitting down to enjoy the writing.

Some writers, evidently cause unease by their refusal to remain meekly in the cage allotted them: Poe, for example, has been labelled a crime writer, detective writer, horror writer, fantasy writer, science-fiction writer, and no doubt other things. The categories themselves are evasive and blurred at the margins: even though, for example, crime fiction and science fiction are formulaic types of writing. Because of this formulaic tendency, sub-genres such as 'police procedurals' (eg Ed McBain's 87th Precinct series) and 'sword and sorcery' (eg R. E. Howard's Conan the Barbarian novels) have appeared, but these are recognisably part of parent groupings, in turn related to fantasy, a broad category which includes all the modes of writing referred to here. For a detailed discussion of this area, readers are referred to Rosemary Jackson and David Punter.[1]

A. Robert Lee's essay on Brockden Brown (ch. 2) places him as a founding presence in American literature, though he, like Nathaniel Hawthorne, related his work to that of his European predecessors and contemporaries. The way in which Brown antici-pated some of the themes and concerns of Edgar Allan Poe is pointed to, while addressing both the successes and failures of the writing. Brown is treated as more than a Gothic sensationalist primarily concerned with titillating his audience, and his critique of traditional Gothic writing as 'puerile superstition' along with his conception of himself as a serious moralist is explored. Lee recognises that Brown employed the full panoply of late eighteenth-century enthusiasms in what are undoubtedly hastily written novels which have various defects according to modern criteria; but, in a detailed analysis of the four major works, he argues that Brown's concerns and ideas are sufficiently powerful and interesting to outweigh any lapses. Brown's persistent concern with darkness, literal and metaphorical, and his tacit influence on later American writers – notably Poe, Hawthorne, Faulkner, H. P. Lovecraft, Shirley Jackson and Stephen King – reveal him as a pioneer of American writing who tells a very modern tale.

Robert Giddings' essay on Edgar Allan Poe (ch. 3) outlines the history of the Gothic movement and analyses the Gothic elements in Poe's writing. The first half of the essay takes us back beyond the eighteenth century to ancient Greece, and Longinus's treatise *On the Sublime*. The concept of the 'sublime' became popular in France in the seventeenth century, as two opposing views of the nature of literature struggled for dominance. In the early eighteenth century, this struggle spread to England, and Alexander Pope, following Boileau, privileged a new type of writing based upon a rediscovery and reinterpretation of Greek and Roman writing. Contemporary opinion held that Pope had failed to achieve the sublime in his writing. Writers such as James Thomson and Edward Young, who were thought to have achieved the sublime, and who had a Gothic tone and a Romantic subjectivity, are quoted to show how particular subjects and states of being led away from neoclassicism towards the Gothic mode. The emphasis is placed on describing psychological states, while showing the danger of trusting to sense impressions. The relation of the sublime to Gothic writing is clearly shown in the quotation from Edmund Burke, and the link to the classic Gothic novels of Horace Walpole, William Beckford, Matthew Gregory Lewis and Ann Radcliffe is demonstrated; Gothic writing is not an aberration, but has identifiable sources and a history of development.

Poe undoubtedly drew on English and German Gothic writings, but he introduced his own peculiar interests to Gothic literature. Poe has often been considered an autobiographical writer, dramatising the workings of his own inner psychology, as if Roderick Usher was a representation of Poe himself. However, Giddings points out that Poe differed from other Gothic writers in that what interested him was not violence *per se*, or death itself, but the rituals of death and the boundary between life and death. In other writers, death and dying are not dealt with in detail, but are hurried over after the events and intrigues occasioning the violence. As an American, Poe could not exploit a medieval past, but he was able to deal with contemporary themes and obsessions. Poe's interest in ritual and ceremony, the product of nineteenth-century nationalism, is discussed, along with Egyptology and mesmerism, as one of the characteristic contemporary enthusiasms which influenced his writings. Note is also taken of the obsession with 'abnormal' mental states and the development of psychiatric practices in the nineteenth century. Giddings concludes that, instead of writing just about himself, Poe adapted a variety of contemporary material to his own use and incorporated it into his work.

Clive Bloom's essay on H. P. Lovecraft (ch. 4) moves us into the twentieth century, with a writer widely regarded as one of the classic authors of 'pulp' fiction of the inter-war period. However, Bloom argues that, while Lovecraft has influenced other horror and fantasy writers, he remains a cult figure rather than a popular writer. Lin Carter and August Derleth have defended and promoted Lovecraft and the 'Cthulhu Mythos', but they overlook his less attractive aspects. Bloom draws attention to the racist and anti-semitic views that underlie Lovecraft's work and pervade his letters. Lovecraft was a New England Yankee of English descent who was morbidly obsessed with his background, and had fascistic fantasies of himself as a Nordic superman. These are shown to be ludicrously inappropriate, but nevertheless central to an understanding of Lovecraft's writing. His personal and societal inadequacies, and his fears of the social changes occurring in America due to mass immigration from Southern and Eastern Europe during his early years, form the sub-text in his work. The fantasy nightmares involving Nyarlathotep and the Shoggoths reflect social fears of being swamped and invaded by an alien culture of racial degenerates who would overwhelm and obliterate the true Americans of Anglo-Saxon descent. It would be interesting to learn the views of the Native American nations, victims of a sustained policy of genocide by these same 'true Americans'.

However, it is not enough to simply condemn Lovecraft as a xenophobic racist, or to assume that the Ku-Klux Klan represent a fringe of mindless bigots who can safely be ignored. The Klan's populist rhetoric makes a substantial appeal to a dispossessed, declassed petit bourgeoisie who feel threatened on all sides. Bloom points out that Lovecraft came from precisely such a background, and he offers a materialist theory of the conditions of production of the insecurities, resentments and contradictions which manifest themselves in his writings. It is appropriate that these expressions of a disenfranchised social group should be consumed by another disenfranchised group, bourgeois intellectuals. Ultimately Lovecraft's writing centres on fears of and fantasies about social control. (Is this simultaneous fear of and desire for control the reason why this group tend to act against their own objective interest and vote for authoritarian populist demagogues?)

The people Lovecraft wrote about most often were, of course, poor whites – the very group on which William Faulkner concentrated his attention. David Seed's essay (ch. 5) focuses on *Sanctuary*, one of Faulkner's more lurid and controversial texts. Faulkner deliberately set out to write a horrific tale, with murder, rape and betrayal as the key elements. It is a sexual melodrama with a complex plot structure which resembles a detective novel in that revelation of key events is held back as long as possible. Notions of disclosure and concealment are central, building up suspense repeatedly as the reader strives to reconstruct the textual chronology into a linear narrative. Benbow, in fact, is used as witness or investigator, a procedure which further accentuates the text's affinity with the detective genre. (For a reading of *Sanctuary* as detective fiction see Peter Humm's essay in *American Crime Fiction: Studies in the Genre*.[2])

Faulkner employs the conventions of the popular novel to examine relations between men and women. Sex and violence are linked, with female sexuality seen as a threat, to be fled from, or confronted and punished. Benbow's journey is presented as a flight from sexuality only to end up in the hostile Gothic environment of the Old Frenchman place. The house is a Southern version of a Gothic ruin, and is peopled by grotesques. Here, Temple is imprisoned in darkness, after the car crash which strands her and Stevens in the wilderness. A familiar Gothic scene is thereby re-enacted, except that, instead of being threatened by one Byronic hero–villain, Temple has five men continually looking at or spying on her. The look becomes a deferred sexual threat, with her 'protector' Stevens disabled by moonshine liquor.

The nature of the horror – the rape of Temple and the lynching of Goodwin – is located within the social structure in the corruption and hypocrisy which underlie the codes of behaviour which govern Southern life. Popeye, who carries out the assault on Temple, is, as Faulkner makes clear, the representative of the town's men, who all desire to violate her. The language of the text, the descriptions, gestures, looks, all combine to deny the façade of bourgeois respectability. Ironically, the action of the plot denies the book's title; for Temple there is no sanctuary, and every man is a potential rapist.

David Punter's essay (ch. 6) deals with Robert Bloch's *Psycho*, source of one of the most genuinely frightening horror films. Like the Old Frenchman place in *Sanctuary*, the Bates Motel has Gothic attributes, and the story centres around violence towards women triggered by negative attitudes towards female sexuality. The act of violence is preceded by an act of voyeurism. In due course we learn that Norman Bates is a matricide and a transvestite who has kept his mother's decomposing corpse in the cellar for twenty years. Since Bloch's text employs the services of a psychiatrist to explain the story, this essay uses psychoanalytic theory, that of Karen Horney, to interrogate the text.

In one sense, we are returned to the characteristic Gothic concern with unusual psychic states, but, although the setting, especially in the film version, is outwardly Gothic, the Bates Motel should represent order and normality. This is where a large part of the shock value of the text resides. A motel should be a safe place to rest on a journey, exactly the same as the last and the next motel, a stronghold of stable bourgeois values. Although there is a rhetoric of individualism, America is in many respects a conformist, homogenised society where 'standardisers' such as Howard Johnson's and McDonald's promote societal security.

Of course, Bates, who displays a fear of women and female sexuality which leads to at least two murders (as well as that of the detective Arbogast) may not thereby exhibit an unusual psychic state. How unusual in men is fear of women? The problem arises through the splitting of Bates's personality into three fragments: the adult motel-keeper, the child dominated by his mother, and the mother herself. Because of this splitting, other people, especially women, can be treated as objects, and disposed of, and responsibility denied or shifted. Because of the multiplicity of personalities, boundaries are blurred, and Punter argues that the plot of the novel is concerned with the effort of Bates's psyche to reseal itself. Since the mother is, in one sense, in control at the end, this represents a successful strategy of the unconscious.

Odette L'Henry Evans' essay on Patricia Highsmith (ch. 7) – usually considered a crime writer but highly regarded by horror fans for *The Glass Cell*, *Those Who Walk Away* and *Eleven* – examines her work from a feminist point of view. The question of which genre Highsmith belongs to is seen as limiting and not helpful, especially since women's writing often refuses to fit neatly into the constructs of male critics. Since Gothic elements are noticeably absent in Highsmith's work, a narrowly specific examination of the horrific aspects of the texts is not undertaken. The essay concentrates instead on an explication of feminist theory, notably the work of French feminists such as Julia Kristeva, Hélène Cixous and Luce Irigaray.

The relation of women's language and women's writing to

women's experience has been a persistent concern of feminists since Virginia Woolf addressed this question, and there has been an important emphasis on not defining women's writing in relation to male cultural assumptions or male literature. Odette L'Henry Evans discusses the ways in which feminist critics have employed a variety of strategies to interrogate the language writers use, both at linguistic and formal levels and at deeper psychoanalytic levels, and then examines Highsmith's texts to determine the specific ways in which they can be identified as women's or feminine writing. The fruitful relationship between feminist theory and psychoanalysis is demonstrated, and it is concluded that, especially in its exploration of the unconscious, Highsmith's work does display features which identify it as part of a feminine corpus of production. In a more general way, of course, exploration of the unconscious, of states of mind and of motives for action, especially acts of violence, is characteristic of mystery and horror writers from Brockden Brown onwards.

Judie Newman's essay on Shirley Jackson (ch. 8) is a close reading of *The Haunting of Hill House*, employing psychoanalytic theory. The basic question of why we should find horror fiction so fascinating is asked, and an answer is found within Freud's theory of the 'uncanny'. Freud can be read as arguing that horror fiction is essentially a conservative, reassuring genre which allows us to exorcise real fears (the unknown, death, the natural world) by relegating them to an imaginary realm – 'It's all right, it's only fiction.' However, recent critics, notably Rosemary Jackson, have argued for the subversive nature of the fantastic (which includes horror fiction) and Newman argues that the writing of Shirley Jackson subverts Freud.

Appropriately, feminist revisions of Freud are used to interrogate Jackson's writing, and, after describing Freud's basic work on the unconscious and the uncanny, Newman outlines the theories of Nancy Chodorow. Attention is directed to the mother–daughter relationship and the way this differs from father–son relations; the importance of creating and maintaining relationships with others; the location of the sense of self in the ability to achieve and sustain relationships or affiliations; and the threat to female gender identity posed by separation.

The Haunting of Hill House, in which the landscape descriptions have an oddly English feel, is centrally concerned with mother–daughter relations and the theme of dissolution of ego boundaries.

Hill House is described in terms which recall Hawthorne's *House of the Seven Gables*, some of Lovecraft's New England houses, and Dracula's castle. Like Castle Dracula, it is isolated, accessible only by bad roads, has a bad reputation locally and is shunned by local people. Eleanor, like Jonathan Harker in *Dracula*, has to overcome local opposition – in this case the caretaker's – to enter the house. Thus Jackson indicates her relationship to the Gothic tradition by the setting, and the description of the house in which the action takes place. However, the novel clearly belongs to the 1950s, and the distance from previous generations of horror writers is indicated by the characters and the way they joke about Count Dracula as a weekend visitor and as a pantomime actor. Eleanor behaves like a rebellious teenager escaping from home for the first time (she is in fact thirty-two); Theo is a sophisticated bohemian lesbian, Luke an amoral gigolo unaffected by an expensive education, and Dr Montague a bearded, pipe-smoking academic who has chosen his area of interest in much the same way as other academics choose T. S. Eliot or the French Revolution. Like Highsmith's characters and unlike those of Lovecraft, Poe or Brockden Brown, Jackson's characters belong to the modern urban world, with nothing heroic about them.

They could fit into the plot of a regular mystery novel by, say, P. D. James or a later horror writer such as Stephen King, himself strongly influenced by Jackson. They are not Byronic figures with evil designs on others, or psychotics such as Norman Bates; they are 'ordinary' people to whom strange and inexplicable things happen. The mystery of Hill House is never explained; the text is circular, with the last paragraph echoing the first in a gesture of closure. The lack of an easy closure is characteristic of modern writing, and the implication is that the events at Hill House will be repeated as long as people are drawn to the house. Likewise, we shall continue to read horror fiction because it tells us what we do, and do not want to, know.

Clare Hanson's essay on Stephen King (ch. 9), probably the definitive modern horror writer, imitated by hordes and read by legions, also approaches the work from a psychoanalytic perspective. King's work is seen as gender-conscious in a specifically masculine way, concerned with origins and the construction of the self as a gendered social being. An account of Freud's theories on the development of the self is offered, with reference to some of the limitations of Freud's approach in relation to females, especially the account of the little girl's passage through the Oedipus complex. Hanson also considers the work of Jacques Lacan in revising Freud, Lacan's theories of language, and the problematics of Lacanian theory from a feminist point of view. Julia Kristeva's theories, which seek to recuperate the symbolic order from male domination, are outlined and are applied to King's fiction. Kristeva's theory of 'abjection', involving a specific turning-away from the mother, is particularly relevant to King, especially to his attitude to the female body.

Stephen King's novels, like those of Shirley Jackson, are set in contemporary New England and feature resolutely ordinary people. We find a setting which in many respects is as naturalistic as the work of Theodore Dreiser or Sinclair Lewis, although it would be wrong to read King purely as a latter-day naturalist. He has an eye for the detail of small-town life, including the hatreds and jealousies never far from the surface, as *Carrie* demonstrates. In King, the ordinary and the banal become monstrous, and latent tendencies are released with uncontrollable results. In *Carrie*, for example, the onset of menstruation, rite of passage into the adult world, becomes a terrifying demonstration of feminine power. Carrie's discourse, the result of the liberation of her unconscious after an assault in which she is drenched in pig's blood, destroys the town by fire. In nature, fire is a cleansing as well as a destructive force, but *Carrie* could be read as embodying King's fears of feminism, of an uncontrollable force which threatens to destroy society and patriarchal social order. Significantly, neither Carrie nor her mother has had a father in the home to impose order, and they die at the end of the book.

The Shining deals with the problems caused by the failure of father–son relationships. Like Carrie, Danny must also undergo a type of rite of passage – in his case through learning to control language and master the symbolic. Danny's entry into the dominant social and symbolic order depends on this, and much of the horror in the text derives from the dreams Danny has, and the threat represented there. Danny also has to contend with the change in his father, who has become a violent maniac by the end of the book.

Misery, the third text discussed, emphasises the self-conscious and self-referential tendencies in King's writing, and deals with a writer who is obliged to write for his very life. Conan Doyle, who was forced to bring Sherlock Holmes back from the dead, never suffered like this. *Misery* is perhaps indicative of King's attitudes towards women, as Annie Wilkes is a monstrous figure who functions as mother figure, muse and castrating female to the author Paul Sheldon. Paul has transgressed by killing off Annie's favourite character from his books – obviously a betrayal of the proper relationship between author and reader. Paul must give satisfaction or pay the price. (Does King feel persecuted by his readership, who put him through the misery of writing?) The essay concludes with an examination of the relationship between gender and genre, and the reasons why horror fiction appears to be largely written by and for men, often in misogynistic forms.

The final essay, by Anne Cranny-Francis (ch. 10), appropriately deals with a recent feminist reworking of the genre: Suzy McKee Charnas's *The Vampire Tapestry*. Charnas is a politically committed writer, as her assaults on the science-fiction genre, *Walk to the End of the World* and *Motherlines*, make clear; so this essay concentrates on her use of a popular genre to address political questions. If Stephen King represents the conservative aspect of the politics of fantasy writing, Charnas represents a radical alternative which does not abandon the conventions of the genre but revises and reinvigorates them. *The Vampire Tapestry* is written for a readership with a knowledge of horror texts from *Dracula* onwards, and of the numerous cinematic versions of *Dracula* and related stories.

Weyland is a very different figure from the archetype Count Dracula. Dracula is a medieval *boyar* commanding allegiance from the peasants who live in the surrounding area; Charnas's vampire, by contrast, is essentially anonymous, with Dr Weyland only the latest in a long series of temporary identities. Weyland is obliged to have a degree of empathy with his victims, and, when he is forced to undergo psychoanalysis, this proves to be his undoing. Weyland's research concerns the unconscious mind, precisely the territory of psychoanalysis, and after a public lecture he provides the audience with a description of his true nature. In this way, Charnas conducts a debate about the relation between fiction and reality.

In her text Charnas also deals with sexual politics. The figure of Katje de Groot is used to examine the issues of gender, class and race, and it is she who defeats the vampire by shooting him. No stakes or crucifixes are needed here: an ordinary automatic pistol suffices. Katje has been brought up as a hunter in South Africa, and she is able to empathise with Weyland because they are both constructed as 'other'. This difference is the source of Weyland's power, and significantly his victims are women and gay men. Weyland thus functions as a representative of an oppressive patriarchal social order where only heterosexual men are considered fully human. However, he can only function as a vampire by treating people as objects and victims; once he engages emotionally with Floria Landauer, he is no longer able to function as a vampire. The psychologist has attacked his subjectivity by proposing an alternative ideology, that of human relationships based on equality. Questions about the relationship between artistic production and the social function of art are raised when Weyland attends a performance of *Tosca*. In the opera, the heroine kills the evil Baron Scarpia, representative of state power and patriarchal order. Weyland empathises so completely that he confuses art and reality and is stimulated to kill needlessly. Weyland has become more human, and now begins to question his own practices. One of the characteristics of the fantastic, the decentred subject, is represented here by Weyland's increasingly fragmented consciousness which contains the possibility of change. Although he has to recall previous identities in order to defeat Reese, who represents male society at its most violent and exploitative, in doing so Weyland represents female opposition to patriarchy. It is argued here that the destruction of Reese represents the deconstruction of the ideology which engendered him.

Dracula and *The Vampire Tapestry* both represent responses to the women's movements of their times, and the generic conventions established in *Dracula* are self-consciously employed by Charnas to mount a radical critique of mainstream horror writing and of gender relations in contemporary society. The textual politics of such writing are exposed from within the castle walls, so to speak, positioning readers to engage in radical readings of these fictional structures. American horror fiction has come a long way since Brockden Brown and it is probably true to say that most writers in the genre are conservative moralists with a pessimistic view of human nature. However, the interests and preoccupations of modern writers are somewhat different from those of their predecessors, since many recent texts are really works of terror, concerned with gruesome physical destruction and lacking the moral overtones of Brockden Brown or Poe. King is undoubtedly the dominant member of the present horde of splatterhacks, and will be imitated *ad nauseam* until someone else has an idea. Charnas has demonstrated that energetic and inventive alternatives are possible, that there is nothing inherently conservative about the genre, and that feminist strategies can show a way forward for men as well as for women.

Notes

1. Rosemary Jackson, *Fantasy: The Literature of Subversion* (London: Methuen, 1981); David Punter, *The Literature of Terror: A History of Gothic Fictions from 1765 to the Present Day* (London: Longman, 1980).
2. Peter Humm, 'Camera Eye/Private Eye', in Brian Docherty (ed.), *American Crime Fiction: Studies in the Genre* (London: Macmillan, 1988) pp. 28–30.

2

A Darkness Visible: the Case of Charles Brockden Brown

A. ROBERT LEE

In niches and pedestals, around the hall, stood the statues or busts of men, who, in every age, have been rulers and demi-gods in the realms of imagination, and in kindred regions. The grand old countenance of Homer; the dark presence of Dante; the wild Ariosto; Rabelais's smile of deep-wrought mirth; the profound, pathetic humour of Cervantes; the all-glorious Shakespeare; Spenser, meet guest for an allegoric structure; the severe divinity of Milton; and Bunyan, moulded of homeliest clay, but instinct with celestial fire – were those that chiefly attracted my eye. Fielding, Richardson, and Scott, occupied conspicuous pedestals. In an obscure and shadowy niche was reposited the bust of our countryman, the author of Arthur Mervyn.

(Hawthorne, 'The Hall of Fantasy', 1842)[1]

All was astounding by its novelty, or terrific by its horror. . . . My understanding was bemazed, and my senses were taught to distrust their own testimony.

(Brockden Brown, *Arthur Mervyn*, 1799)[2]

Nathaniel Hawthorne's celebrated inclusion of Charles Brockden Brown (1771–1810) in 'The Hall of Fantasy' sets him, to be sure, infinitely among his betters, at first glance a truly discrepant name to be found in so august an assembly. But, if duly assigned a place at the periphery, 'an obscure and shadowy niche', Brown does have at least one legitimate cause for being named in this roll-call of the great and the good. Like Homer, Dante and Shakespeare, or any of the rest – especially his fellow novelists Richardson, Fielding and Scott – he was despite all his limits an essential founding presence, a figure of departure. For it fell to him to take his place as America's first fiction writer of consequence, a begetter of that line of 'romance' which begins at the turn of the nineteenth

13

century, and which, with key stop-overs at the likes of Poe, Melville and Hawthorne, evolves through to Faulkner and well beyond.[3]

But Brown's claims in fact go further. He was from the start possessed of his own substantial and truly singular imagination, one worthy of attention in terms which step outside mere antiquarian or historicist interest. To encounter him, at least, through his four Gothic – and best – novels, in turn *Wieland* (1798), *Ormond* (1799), *Arthur Mervyn* (1799) and *Arthur Mervyn . . . Second Part* (1800), and *Edgar Huntly* (1799), is to be faced with the recognition that, beyond all his 'horror', his shocks and melodrama, there lies a far subtler set of designs upon the reader, the upshot of Brown's nothing if not speculative turn of mind. In this he anticipates his fellow Gothic spirit of a generation later, Edgar Allan Poe. Not that, any more than in the case of Poe, such has protected him from the charge of being a 'bungler', the barest survivor of 'defects that would have wrecked an average writer'.[4] Yet whatever his excesses, the overdone plot lines, the proliferation of characters, the too-energetic fades and dissolves, even the suspicion that he has in mind to keep us reading no matter what the cost, he also manages to persuade that he is about altogether more consequential purposes. He may never quite have managed any single, decisive masterpiece, but the grounds are there for thinking that one never lay too far outside his imaginative grasp. However unlikely, in Hawthorne's terms, his elevation 'in the realms of the imagination' to a 'ruler' or 'demi-god', he compares favourably with more established adepts in the art of Gothic – with Horace Walpole, Monk Lewis, Ann Radcliffe and, of later vintage, Bram Stoker. And he does so, in large degree, because to confuse his Gothicism for the whole account does him a genuine disservice.

For Brown's 'Gothic' embodies an authentic force of ideas, his unremitting will to knowledge. Despite 1776, and its accompanying new-born American rhetoric of hope and belief in the perfectibility of mankind, he saw himself as looking out upon a world everywhere still beset by darkness – and a darkness as much within as without. Time and again he probes the otherness of much of human experience, the play of the unpredictable and random, the deceptiveness of appearance, the self as stranger or exile which without seeming reason can turn wilfully against itself and others. Brown's Gothic is thereby put to greater purpose than mere thrill or titillation. Indeed, in the preface to *Edgar Huntly*, 'To the Public', he actually takes it upon himself to castigate traditional Gothic as 'puerile superstition', 'exploded manners' and mere 'chimeras'. He speaks of favouring 'a series of adventures, growing out of the country', and of himself as a 'moral painter', an analyst both of 'the heart' and of 'the most wonderful diseases or affectations of the human frame'. Thus, as applied to Brown, Milton's 'darkness visible' does an additional duty. It directs us to the basic push behind his writing, the elucidation of nothing less than our own endemic mystery.

Which is hardly to say that a list of his key interests will necessarily warm the appetite of a first-time sampler of his wares. Among other things, Brown felt moved to explore religious mania, ventriloquism, the dangers of a reliance on sense data, secret international conspiracy, the spectacle of city life besieged by yellow fever, sleepwalking and the loss of mental self-control. Murders, both random and calculated, make a plentiful appearance, as does a full show of different phobias and frights. In addition, Brown borrowed much from the radical programmes of William Godwin, and in turn found himself borrowed from in the latter's novel of the English Civil War, *Mandeville* (1819). Not least of Brown's Godwinian leanings as a good Enlightenment American is his interest in feminism, especially in his first publication, *Alcuin: A Dialogue, Parts 1 and 2* (1798), a series of epistolary debates about the right of women to economic and sexual autonomy.

Forms of women's power, or its absence, also mark out his three other non-Gothic novels, works essentially of sentiment. *Memoirs of Stephen Calvert*, only recently made over from its original magazine form into a novel, tells a story of crossed loves, twinning, false claims to identity and appearance.[5] Yet, within its different reversals and masquerades, Brown keeps up a steady interest in the situation of women subject to male control. *Clara Howard; or, The Enthusiasm of Love* (1801) again treats women's sovereignty, but at the price of a weakly conceived and weakly written tale of courtship. *Jane Talbot* (1801) does marginally better, a work in which the 'issue' of women is linked to the clash of religious belief with agnosticism as embodied in the heroine and her suitor Henry Colden. All of these novels follow *Stephen Calvert* in using picaresque or epistolary style to explore not only sentiment but also manners and 'society'.

Brown's strongest suit, however, remains *Wieland* and his other Gothic work, even given the penchant for plot-making and digression. Godwinian ideas take on more vivid expression, as indeed does Brown's response to the current of changing ideas as the Age of Reason gave way to the Age of Romanticism. Hawthorne's placing of his bust in 'an obscure and shadowy niche' may have done justice to his place in literary history, but his language also speaks to key other aspects in Brown's achievement. 'Obscurity' and 'shadow' inscribe not only a reputation but also a body of themes and the actual workings of Brown's imagination. For his Gothic novels at their best seek to transform the darkness in the human make-up into the very grounds of narrative, being as in itself a plot to be unravelled and held up to the light.

Brown's interest in 'darkness' was not lost upon a run of early admirers on both sides of the Atlantic. In the English column John Keats was perhaps foremost. Writing to Richard Woodhouse in September 1819, he likens Brown both to German and to English contemporaries:

> And don't forget to tell Reynolds of the fairy tale Undine – Ask him if he has read any of the American Brown's novels that Hazlitt speaks so much of – I have read one called Wieland – very powerful – something like Godwin – Between Schiller and Godwin – More clever in plot and incident than Godwin – A strange American scion of the German trunk – Powerful genius – accomplished horrors . . . .[6]

Although Hazlitt did not in fact altogether share Keats's enthusiasm, he had no doubt of Brown's intensity of effect. A decade on, in the *Edinburgh Review* for October 1829, he spoke guardedly but with genuine respect of Brown's 'conclusive throes', his 'banquet of horrors'.[7] We also have Thomas Love Peacock's taste for Brown and, as importantly, his report of the impression Brown's novels made upon Shelley. In his *Memoir of Percy Bysshe Shelley*, Peacock testifies that 'nothing so blended with the structure of [Shelley's] interior mind as the creations of Brown'.[8] Not only Shelley's voyage and dream poems, but also his several early prose romances, confirm this affinity. Little wonder, too, that Mary Shelley, if not explicitly in *Frankenstein* (1818) then in her dystopian and futuristic plague novel *The Last Man* (1826), similarly acknowledged Brown's influence, or as she puts it 'the masterly delineations of the author of *Arthur Mervyn*'.[9]

In his own country Brown's fortunes were, initially, mixed: he was a figure always to be recognised but not always favourably. The first biography of him, commissioned by his widow, Elizabeth Brown, was drafted by Paul Allen and then rewritten by William Dunlop, the Connecticut wit and intimate friend of the novelist, as *The Life of Charles Brockden Brown: Together with Selections from the Rarest of his Original Letters, and from his Manuscripts before Unpublished* (1815). A second biography appeared in *Biographical and Critical Miscellanies* in 1865: this was a life-and-works hagiography by William Prescott, the Brahmin New England historian, entitled 'Memoir of Charles Brockden Brown, the American Novelist'. Prescott had earlier contributed an approving entry on Brown to Jared Spark's *American Biography* (1834). Although these versions of Brown differ (complicatedly in the case of the Allen–Dunlop *Life*, as Dunlop toned down a number of the unflattering observations made by Allen), they yield the necessary ground materials for the man behind the fiction, the Quaker-born, bookish Philadelphian whose *annus mirabilis* of 1798–9 brought forth so prodigious an amount of fiction. That he never again matched this output, in quantity or quality, hardly surprises, especially during his later years in which he found himself a reluctant businessman and struggling publisher of magazines and almanacs. Whatever else, then, the biographies direct us to Brown as a wonder of sorts: not only America's first would-be professional novelist, but also a figure of irrepressible personal energy.[10]

Typical of the mixed reactions he aroused in his literary countrymen is that of James Greenleaf Whittier, New England's veteran abolitionist poet and a doyen of the 'fireside' or 'domestic' style. While believing that Brown had not had his full critical due, Whittier nevertheless held back on too emphatic an endorsement – even of *Wieland* as Brown's best-known novel: '*Wieland* is not a pleasant book. In one respect it resembles the modern tale of *Wuthering Heights*: it has great strength and power, but no beauty.'[11] Whittier showed great canniness in bracketing *Wieland* with Emily Brontë's English moorlands drama of passions driven to the edge. But he clearly felt unease at the wildness, the show of extreme emotion, which no doubt jarred with his own ancestral gentility. Hawthorne, in one of his later sketches in *Mosses from an Old Manse*, 'P.'s Correspondence', is far less equivocal – he suggests that 'no American writer enjoys a more classic reputation on this side of the water'; and Poe, in his *Marginalia* for 1844, refers to

Brown and Hawthorne as 'each a genius'.[12] Likewise, other slightly later contemporaries looked back to Brown with admiration. R. H. Dana Sr preferred to set him in historical context, arguing, 'that Brown produced works at such a time shows clearly the power of his genius over circumstance'. James Fenimore Cooper, though in the Preface to *The Spy* (1821) a touch acerbic about Brown's Indian materials, wrote in his *Notions of the Americans* (1828) that 'This author . . . enjoys a high reputation among his countrymen.'

Brown also elicited two slightly askew tributes from lesser-known American contemporaries. Writing in *Blackwood's Edinburgh Magazine* in 1824, John Neale, author of *Logan, a Family History* (1822) and other nationalist stories, pictured Brown as 'a spirit absolutely crushed'. Leaning heavily upon this version of Brown, George Lippard, the Jacksonian radical author of *Quaker City; or, The Monks of Monk Hall* (1845), a Gothicly lurid and near-pornographic satire of the Philadelphia bourgeoisie, also alludes to him as an admired predecessor. In 'The Heart-Broken', a sketch he contributed to *Nineteenth-Century: A Quarterly Miscellany* for January 1848, Brown is seen as physically frail, a martyr to his age's unfeeling and neglect. Affecting though this is, it falls considerably short of the truth. Hardly less rhetorical but more accurate is the tribute of Margaret Fuller, the Transcendentalist poet and feminist. For her Brown holds sway as a 'man of the brooding eye, the teeming brain, the deep and fervent heart'.[13]

These reactions help place Brown in his time. But a far subtler measure of his importance lies in the way his pioneer conceptions of theme, type and setting have worked themselves into the grain of American fiction, as modern criticism, especially, has been quick to recognise, This applies particularly to accounts of a determinedly mythopoeic kind such as those by R. W. B. Lewis, Richard Chase and Leslie Fiedler.[14] For who, in truth, has a better claim to have inaugurated the American romance form, with its light and dark women (an adapted legacy from Richardson) and the allied stereotype of the Gothic male sexual adventurer, and with its emphasis upon the self as all, upon space either as untrammelled nature or as the regions within, and upon extremities of feeling?

Not that Brown's imprint can be said to have been other than largely tacit. Only occasionally, as in Poe's 'The Pit and the Pendulum', indebted to the powerful cave scene in *Edgar Huntly*, does Brown's influence show itself explicitly. More usually, his touch works quietly but unmistakably, a shadow presence.

Cooper's Leatherstocking novels, for instance, amplify materials also found in *Edgar Huntly*, especially the myth of the frontier and of the Indian as either Adamic or infernal 'savage'. Washington Irving's two best-known stories, 'Rip Van Winkle' and 'The Legend of Sleepy Hollow', in their envisioning of reality and even history as trance, stand at only one remove from the uses of delusion in *Wieland* or of sleepwalking in *Edgar Huntly*. Equally, Poe's 'The Fall of the House of Usher' and his only novel, *The Narrative of Arthur Gordon Pym* (1838), yield resemblances to Brown, whether in the theme of the double self or in that of the 'voyager' set down amid hitherto uncharted wilderness. Poe also joins Brown in foreshadowing the Symbolist preoccupation with the *moi intérieur*.

Key Hawthorne pieces, especially those, such as 'Ethan Brand' or 'The Birthmark' or *The Scarlet Letter* (1850), using versions of his vaunted Unpardonable Sinner, time and again bring Brown to mind. Indicative here is Hawthorne's interest in the man of intellect driven by the single or manic grand design, with an Esther, a Georgiana or a Hester Prynne as his victim. Melville, too, takes up kindred themes to Brown's, in his bitter Gothic pastiche, *Pierre* (1852), and in the best of his riddling *Piazza* stories, such as 'Bartleby' or 'Benito Cereno', in which a shadowy but utterly momentous play of deception lies at the core. Mention should also be made of the darker fiction of Henry James, *Doppelgänger* stories such as 'The Jolly Corner' and 'The Turn of the Screw', and the longer novels of psychological distress and conspiracy, such as *The Portrait of a Lady* (1881) and *The Wings of the Dove* (1902). Brown was the first American writer to explore 'psychology', the strange inward – or Gothic – turns of human behaviour under pressure, using an appropriately sombre or occluded setting.

If, too, one considers the varieties of modern Gothic, Brown's legacy is still much to be discerned, however attenuated. Is there not a Brownian residue (as assuredly there is of Poe) in Faulkner's Yoknapatawpha cycle, be it in his settings of the family mansion or in treating themes of obsession, violence or breakdown? Cannot something of Theodore Wieland be seen in Quentin Compson, whether the Quentin of *The Sound and the Fury* (1929) or *Absalom, Absalom!* (1936)? Similarly, cannot the resolution of a Carwin or an Ormond be seen in that implacable and thwarted maker of dynasty, Thomas Sutpen? A continuing set of affinities shows also in the Gothic of a subsequent Southern generation, whether the religio-comic Georgia parables of Flannery O'Connor, or the psychosexual dramas of Carson McCullers, or the wistful and Poe-like early stories of Truman Capote, or the operatic stir and passion of much of William Styron.

Links may be discerned between Brown and New England Gothic. One thinks here particularly of H. P. Lovecraft's spooky tales and novels, and his important essay *Supernatural Horror in Literature*, which explicitly acknowledges Brown's 'uncanny atmospheric power' and 'extreme vividness'.[15] We might further instance Shirley Jackson's *We Have Always Lived in the Castle* (1962), a regional tale of witchcraft, and, still more recently, John Updike's half tongue-in-cheek *The Witches of Eastwick* (1984). The latter also reminds us that Gothic often flies close to black humour and the comic, as Poe certainly knew and Brown seems to have recognised, on the evidence of some of his spoofier passages. It is this tradition which has yielded Nabokov's baroque fables, such as *Lolita* (1955) and *Pale Fire* (1962), or, at quite another remove, even the startling 'carnival' satires of William Burroughs, notably *The Naked Lunch* (1955). Yet another style of Gothic with Brownian undertones is to be found in the work of John Hawkes – for instance, in his early fantastical war novel *The Cannibal* (1949), and in the well-bred erotica of *Travestie* (1976) and *Virginie; her Two Lives* (1982).

Finally, what of pop Gothic, which has drawn not only from *film noir*, be it Alfred Hitchcock or Roger Corman, but also from the classic mystery fiction of Dashiell Hammett, Raymond Chandler, Cornell Woolrich and others? A generation of readers or movie-goers raised on the 'horror' of, say, Robert Bloch's *Psycho* (which began as two stories of menace, 'Lucy Comes to Stay' and 'The Real Bad Friend', became the Hitchcock screen landmark of 1960, and then got written up as the book of the film), of William Blatty's *The Exorcist* (1971), or Stephen King's *The Shining* (1977), would doubtless be considerably surprised at how much is prefigured in Brown. He, it hardly needs emphasising, wrote out of different values and in a different time as well as to his own period ends and revelations. But whatever his epoch, or even plentiful flaws, his work has had persistent and often unexpected reverberations. The darkness he took as his great theme in the Gothic novels continues to hold the imagination, both in high and in popular culture, as it continues to explore the 'obscure and shadowy' recesses of human behaviour.[16]

Towards the end of *Wieland; or, The Transformation, an American*

Tale – to give Brown's first novel its full title – the narrator–heroine, Clara Wieland, describes a dream she has had:

> Sometimes I was swallowed up by whirlpools, or caught up in the air by some half-seen and gigantic forms, and thrown upon pointed rocks or cast among the billows. Sometimes gleams of light were shot into a dark abyss, on the verge of which I was standing, and enabled me to discover for a moment, its enormous depth and hideous precipices. Anon, I was transported to some ridge of Etna, and made a terrified spectator of its fiery torrents and its pillars of smoke. (p. 264)

She could not have found an apter body of imagery to express the events which she has experienced. For hers is nothing if not a story of 'whirlpools', 'hideous precipices' and 'fiery torrents', in all and throughout 'a dark abyss'. Yet in the act of writing her narrative, done as a series of letters, she also indeed finds 'gleams of light', a way into and through an otherwise seemingly inexplicable round of calamity. And, as she writes herself out of puzzlement (though not sorrow), so she enables Brown's reader to establish his or her own 'light' for a drama which has been beset by the most violent and encircling dark.

This alternating pattern of darkness and elucidation begins early for Clara. In infancy, with her brother Theodore, she witnesses her father's seeming self-combustion in the summerhouse he has built by the Schuykill river just outside Philadelphia. Wieland Senior, a scion of aristocratic Saxony, has become the follower of an esoteric Protestantism, a would-be missionary to the Indians, and a man whose messianic delusions will be of dire consequence to his offspring. He dies almost literally blasted to a cinder, the very incarnation of a mystery. Theodore Wieland, after a peaceable upbringing and his marriage to Catherine Pleyel, also begins to yield to his father's example. He turns increasingly morose, secretive. Having read the same Albigensian text which held his father, he gives himself to the belief that he is commanded by God to murder Catherine, their young children and their adopted friend Luisa Conway. He also comes close to murdering Clara, after escaping the jail in which he has languished like a demented American prophet after his trial for butchering his family. That Clara survives, Job-like, to tell the tale, involves us in both 'horror' and her own uncertain attempts to understand its causes.

A sequence of voices, some real and others imagined, plays into these 'extraordinary and rare' incidents, as Brown calls them in his 'Advertisement'. Each one way or another connects to the wizardly figure of Carwin, a Hawthornian wanderer–scholar whose secret art is that of ventriloquism or, as it is termed in *Wieland*, 'biloquism'. To compound matters furthers, Clara finds herself unjustly accused by her would-be lover Henry Pleyel of a sexual liaison with Carwin. She is bereft of the very family she would preserve by her brother's actions. And from a world of almost blissful intimacy she is finally driven to exile in France. Her story, in other words, has all the same flux and displacement as dream itself, a kind of nightmare velocity.

But, summarised thus, *Wieland* can sound merely histrionic, merely an assemblage of effects. In fact, it reads with considerable agility, high drama for certain but also a story anything but formulaic or mechanical in its make-up. In the first place, Clara tells her 'narrative' as one who interrogates her own version of things even as she commits it to the page. The upshot makes for story-telling as itself a drama. 'Why should I protract a tale which I already begin to feel is too long?' she asks reflexively. She owns up to 'the hideous confusion of my understanding', implicating the reader as much as herself in the business of making order out of disaster. Then, too, the novel relies upon no merely arbitrary other world – 'chimeras', as Brown calls matters. Rather the novel keeps in view an actual Pennsylvania, a social hierarchy of gentry, country people, farms and hamlets, and at the centre of it the city of Philadelphia. The novel's 'horror' is so modulated, given a credible context and resonance. Most of all, *Wieland* deploys a strikingly figurative inner idiom, an inlaid language of lights and darks, which textures the main events. In Brown's fashioning, the 'dark abyss' of horror and chaos which eventually the 'gleams of light' will elucidate is actually built into the writing itself, story and story-telling fused to mutual good purpose.

Horror abounds. It begins with the death of Wieland Senior as witnessed by his wife, a veritable *son et lumière* explosion:

Her eyes were fixed upon the rock; suddenly it was illuminated. A light proceeding from the edifice made every part of the scene visible. A gleam diffused itself over the intermediate space, and instantly a loud report, like the explosion of a mine, followed. She uttered an involuntary shriek, but the new sounds that

greeted her ear quickly conquered her surprise. They were
piercing shrieks, and utterly without intermission. The gleams,
which had diffused themselves far and wide, were in a moment
withdrawn; but the interior of the edifice was filled with
rays. (p. 18)

The edifice in question is Wieland Senior's 'temple', his retreat. In
fact, as the language of the passage underscores, it serves as a
metaphor of the human mind, a site in which reason tussles with
unreason, illumination with darkness. The father's pursuit of some
godly 'right reason' has caused him, it seems, to implode, to
combust into a 'human cinder'. Goya's *The Sleep of Reason Produces
Monsters* lies not too far away. As a recurring point of reference,
the temple – and later Clara's own house – is transformed by
Brown into an image of the self as ever beset by its own inability
to separate the dark from the light. The point is taken up, neatly,
in the Socratic jousting that goes on between a 'grave', near-
Calvinist Theodore Wieland and Henry Pleyel as a 'champion of
intellectual liberty'. In the event, the pair of them will be deceived
by both 'religion' and reason, and also, it seems, by the evidence
of their senses.

The horror, the mystery, is throughout *Wieland* put in similar
terms. It may seem rather heavy-handed to have an actual ventrilo-
quist play a part in a novel which relies for its main plot upon
having a father and son hear 'voices'; but in fact Brown nicely
manages to merge the two. As to Carwin's voices, they again yield
a circuit of frights. First, Wieland hears, as he thinks, Catherine's
voice warning him of danger, a quite disastrous event as Clara
interprets it for a man 'of an ardent and melancholy character'.
Pleyel, in turn, imagines he hears his own sister announcing the
death of Theresa, his German fiancée. Clara, for her part, thinks
she hears a Macbethian voice warning of murder in her own house,
a voice which recurs when she strays too near a cliff-edge and
which calls up 'a train of horrors in my mind'. This same voice, in
turn, fools Pleyel, who thinks it Clara's in conversation with
Carwin. Lastly, it 'speaks' directly to the deranged Theodore
Wieland, causing him to mistake Carwin's ventriloquism for the
very voice of the God in whose name he has killed his family and
plans to kill Clara. In commanding Wieland to 'hold', Carwin's
false voice blends perfectly with the false voice that Wieland
believes himself bound to answer in his deluded role as God's

instrument on earth. In each of these instances, be the voice Carwin's or those which operate inside Wieland's madness, Brown situates things in a play of light and dark, a chiaroscuro of twilights and dusks or night-times irradiated if only 'sometimes' by 'shrieks', 'gleams' and 'rays'.

The point can be illustrated from a passage in which Carwin makes his final confessional appearance before Clara. Her house becomes the condition of her being, a self riven by 'ruin and blast' as she later calls it:

> I have said that the window-shutters were closed. A feeble light, however, found entrance through the crevices. A small window illuminated the closet, and the door being closed, a dim ray streamed through the keyhole. A kind of twilight was thus created, sufficient for the purposes of vision, but, at the same time, involving all minuter objects in obscurity.
>
> This darkness suited the colour of my thoughts. I sickened at the remembrance of the past. The prospect of the future excited my loathing. I muttered, in a low voice, 'Why should I live longer? Why should I drag a miserable being? All for whom I ought to live have perished. Am I not myself hunted to death?'   (pp. 217–18)

'This darkness' is at once hers, the narrative's 'horror', and the overall mystery which has brought on Wieland's madness and Carwin's own meddling. Lights, rays, vision, obscurity, darkness, all yet again make up the texture of Clara's account – right through to her view of herself as a creature 'hunted to death', an outcast and wanderer from a world hitherto unobscured by mystery or horror.

Even Carwin, the very spirit of 'transformation' in the novel (born an Englishman, he has turned Spanish and Catholic before settling in America), emerges as other than Clara has thought. 'Darkness rests upon the designs of this man', she says before he explains that it has been 'curiosity', a passion for 'mystery' and 'imposture', which has led him to play the part he has. This Brown will confirm in his *Memoirs of Carwin the Biloquist* (published in Dunlop's *Life* in 1815 and as a separate 'fragment' in 1822). Carwin serves less as the villain than as a figure of 'restless', 'unconquerable' curiosity, and 'experimentalist' in human actions and emotions. Hawthorne's Roger Chillingworth or Ethan Brand can be seen not far ahead. Carwin, too, speaks of lights and darks in the human make-up, and of his own tension in dealing with both: 'I saw in a stronger light than ever the dangerousness of that instrument which I employed, and renewed my resolutions to abstain from the use of it in the future; but I was destined perpetually to violate my resolutions' (p. 231).

Wieland, then, tells at the very least a double story. Ostensibly it offers horror fiction *par excellence*: a man's murder of his family in answer to the imagined voice of his God – no flight of fancy given the case (in Tomhannock, New York) on which Brown based his story, or in our own time the Charles Manson and the Jonestown killings or the recent 'religious' slayings in Texas and Utah. But within the horror, the delusion, lies Brown's greater story, that of the 'perversions of the human mind', to use a further phrase from his 'Advertisement'. For, if Brown is indeed best thought a horror writer, a Gothicist, it ought to be recognised that *Wieland* tells of dangers and failings very much still with us. It tells, and at its best most memorably, the story of the darkness within, the ineradicable will to destruction and death.

Ormond, or The Secret Witness, Brown's second novel, more than anything offers intrigue, the pursuit by the unscrupulous, hypnotic Ormond, a member of the malign utopian alliance known as the Illuminati, of Constantia Dudley, a young woman in the mould of Clara Wieland and in whom the author once more expresses his feminist commitment. The plot turns upon the ruination of the Dudley family by Thomas Craig, embezzler and devil's apprentice to Ormond, and then upon Ormond's dark resolve to conquer Constantia sexually whatever the cost. A 'chase' melodrama ensues, but not without genuine pace and its own brand of eroticism. The story, as told by Constantia's friend Sophia Westwyn Courtland, thus fuses a number of elements. It depicts conspiracy, a trail of killings and criminal manoeuvres, an intellectual villain and a varied gallery of women, in which Constantia contrasts with the fey, quiescent mistress of Ormond, Helena Cleves, and his quite opposite sister, Martinette de Beauvais, a veteran combatant in nothing less than the French Revolutionary War. The novel's several mysteries each possess their own 'darkness', not least the hints and pointers to Ormond's role in a conspiracy of international proportions.

But, as in *Arthur Mervyn* (Brown's next novel), the main operative image of horror in the novel has to do with plague, a 'darkness' altogether more convincing than nearly all Ormond's talk of his 'adventurous and visionary sect' or the allegations against him of 'excesses of debauchery'. Lively scenes there are in plenty: Ormond's different schemes and circlings; the suicide of Helena; the death of Constantia's father, Stephen; the closing drama as Ormond descends upon his prey, a figure at once 'singular' and beset with an 'incomprehensible evil'. Brown keeps his plot turning well enough, though one has to show a certain tolerance in places where it creaks and groans. It best serves him, however, in his early scenes of yellow fever in Philadelphia, site of a double contagion: that of Ormond and that of the literal pestilence.

The drama of the plague is registered early, as Constantia witnesses the following:

> Night was the season usually selected for the removal of the dead. The sound of wheels thus employed was incessant. This, and the images with which it was sure to be accompanied, bereaved her of repose. The shrieks and laments of survivors, who could not be prevented from attending the remains of an husband or child to the place of interment, frequently struck her senses. Sometimes urged by a furious delirium, the sick would break from their attendants, rush into the streets, and expire on the pavement, amidst frantic outcries and gestures. By these she was often aroused from imperfect sleep, and called upon to reflect upon the fate which impended over her father and herself. (p. 58)

As elsewhere, Brown here blends the actual plague with the moral one which threatens to destroy Constantia. Each plague scene in the novel (mainly its opening sequences) is sharp and often gruesomely well-observed. But it is always shrewdly linked to the Ormond–Constantia equation, the one a darkness working to give emphasis to the other.

Ormond may disappoint readers who compare it to vintage mystery in Dickens or even Wilkie Collins. Brown's Philadelphia is no fog-bound, unreal city. His plot line can be laboured and his effects too stagy. But he does establish a powerful and credible connection between his surface plot and the enclosing yellow fever. When Constantia observes that 'Every day added to the devastation and confusion of the city', she also senses the parallel in the 'devastation' and 'confusion' of her own life, subject as it has become to 'the incredible reverses' visited on her and her family by Ormond. The plague, thereby, adds its 'witness' to that of Ormond, its own mode of keeping Constantia from the light.

'Astounding by its novelty', 'terrific by its horror': appropriate as these phrases are to much of *Arthur Mervyn*, they do not encapsulate the entire two-part narrative. For *Mervyn* can justly also be thought a story of intrigue and initiation, even a fully fledged *Bildungsroman*. Arthur's departure from his country roots, his maze-like progress through any number of scrapes and turns, his considerable experience also of the yellow fever in Philadelphia, his apprenticeship to the conspirator Welbeck (a criminal intelligence in the line of Carwin, Carwin's mentor Ludloe, and Ormond), and even his eventual suit for the Jewish widow Mrs Achsa Fielding all bespeak picaresque of sorts. If again decidely sub-Dickensian, however, the novel does not fail to engage. Not that the plot helps: it zigzags about infuriatingly and almost beyond summary. Told in the voice of one Dr Stevens, it relies upon long interpolations by Mervyn himself and others. But, against these odds, and more even than in *Ormond*, Brown does depict a real horror, his further reworking of the pestilence which descended upon Philadelphia in the 1790s. In this, again more so than *Ormond*, *Arthur Mervyn* merits comparison with Defoe's *A Journal of the Plague Year* (1722), Poe's spoof story 'King Pest' and Camus's *La Peste* (1948), all related portraits of fever as a kind of invading darkness.

In calling attention to the plague scenes in *Arthur Mervyn*, there is no intention to play down the importance of the multiple lesser plots: the story of Welbeck, whose stalking of the city calls up a rich tradition of underworld activity; the various love stories and courtships, such as the case of Clemenza Lodi, which reflect Brown's continuing interest in women placed unfairly under pressure; and the depiction of Quaker life in the Hadwin family. But the novel best secures its effect in the plague material, Brown's quite startling ability to portray a city under siege and the yellow fever as a virtually animate presence in its own right. The liveliness of his writing can be judged from the following account of Mervyn's return to Philadelphia. As in *Wieland*, the patterns of light and dark are of the essence:

The market-place, and each side of this magnificent avenue were illuminated, as before, by lamps; but between the verge of the Schuykill and the heart of the city, I met no more than a dozen figures; and these were ghost-like, wrapt in cloaks, from behind which they cast upon me glances of wonder and suspicion; and, as I approached, changed their course, to avoid touching me. Their clothes were sprinkled with vinegar; and their nostrils defended from contagion by some powerful perfume.

I cast a look upon the houses, which I recollected to have formerly been, at this hour, brilliant with lights, resounding with lively voices, and thronged with busy faces. Now they were closed, above and below; dark, and without tokens of being inhabited. From the upper windows of some, a gleam sometimes fell upon the pavement I was traversing, and shewed that their tenants had not fled, but were secluded or disabled.

These tokens were not new, and awakened all my panicks. Death seemed to hover over this scene, and I dreaded that the floating pestilence had already lighted on my frame . . .   (pp. 139–40)

This passage, with its clear, vivid story-telling in the first person, represents Brown at his best (a few pages later, Mervyn actually finds himself by accident 'inclosed in a coffin' – black-farcical horror, yet too close for comfort). The account approaches early fiction of fact, documentary witness persuasively made over into narrative. Widening the vista, Brown depicts the city at large as 'effluvia', its households stained by 'gangrenous or black vomit'. Infected himself and then carried off to the hospital, Mervyn gives graphic witness to the further horrors of waiting coffins, wasted death's-head victims, predatory hearse-carriers, even though he acknowledges the heroism of certain doctors and the city's Committee of Health.

But, if the plague embodies one kind of malignancy, the city harbours others. Brown depicts Philadelphia as also a deadlock of special interests, cadres of the rich and powerful, manipulators in property and money. This brand of 'darkness' involves acts of forgery, cheating, financial connivance, the concealment or destruction of important wills and letters. Night-time stealth and robbery become almost normal. These aspects of *Arthur Mervyn*, mainly in the second part, move the novel on from horror into the kind of intrigue at work in *Ormond*. Mervyn himself, a no-doubt too-knowing neophyte, is transformed from a seeming innocent abroad into a veteran in the ways of the city's inner energies. Brown's plot in these later scenes unquestionably grows tiresome, overspun and even contradictory. But the novel's finest achievement, its anatomy of a city at once literally and figuratively a huge fever hospital, is not to be denied. In so depicting his 'yellowish and livid' Philadelphia, Brown conveys genuine menace, an urban 'darkness' both medical and political yet also symptomatic of a more general human condition.

Like Brown's other fiction, *Edgar Huntly; or Memoirs of a Sleepwalker* is not easily summarised. Huntly, in the guise of letter-writer to his fiancée, tells how he has come upon Clithero Edny by the graveside of her murdered brother Waldegrave. An Irish immigrant servant, Edny in fact is also a deeply disturbed somnambulist acting out his past life, unaware of his actions. But, in telling this story, Huntly reveals another – that of his own breakdown, his own sleepwalking and seeming recovery. Set in eighteenth-century frontier Delaware, and given a due admixture of encounters with the wild, and Indian–settler conflict (apart from the memorable squaw Queen Mab, the Indians are mostly stock savages), the novel makes use of new American material but hovers at times close to parody. Further, it exhibits the usual Brownian encumbrances: the stories-within-stories, the coincidences, and the lengthy flashbacks and interpolations. Nor have matters been helped by the assumption that *Wieland* is the natural front runner in Brown's repertoire.

So much said, it remains arguable that *Edgar Huntly* contains some of Brown's most original work, a novel which actually belies and transcends its ostensible plot. Leslie Fiedler, at least, unhesitatingly pronounces it 'the most successful and characteristic of [Brown's] gothic romances'.[17] For, beyond all the show of adventure, the novel offers a striking portrait of psychosis, catatonia even, the darkness of a self spiralling down into madness and an inability to make the world cohere. Time after time, Huntly misreads both himself and the signs about him. He proves wrong to think he can cure Edny. He deceives himself in thinking the Irishman Waldegrave's killer (a renegade Indian is responsible). He supposes, again wrongly, that his own family and friends have been massacred by Indians. He thus 'sleepwalks' as much when sane as when unhinged, signalling a self which is beginning to fracture and separate. Brown's touch may not always be secure in depicting this double self, or the double plot which contains it; but the use of Huntly and Edny as each other's *alter ego*, a twinned other, anticipates far better accounts of the divided self. Poe's 'William Wilson', Wilde's *Dorian Gray* and Conrad's *The Secret Sharer* come readily to mind.

Opening his story Huntly proclaims, 'What light has burst upon my ignorance of myself and mankind! How sudden and enormous this transition from uncertainty to knowledge!' The irony deepens with each page of his account. To achieve this light, the price has indeed been heavy. Not only has Huntly's 'benevolism' been misplaced, but Edny has turned truly mad, dangerous, a would-be murderer and a suicide. Huntly has risked the life of his friend Sarsefield's wife, Mrs Lorimer, who belongs not only to his own story but also to Edny's. He gives the insane Edny her address in New York, causes her to miscarry, and can write only a feeble letter of warning about his actions. He is mistaken, too, when he thinks Waldegrave's papers (and his own) have been purloined and hidden by others. But the larger price, supremely ironic in a narrator who boasts his rationality and his certainty of the world's order, is that of the stunning breakdown he suffers, the sleep-walking which leads him into the wilderness cave first found by Edny. The topography is made by Brown to serve also as a landscape of mind or dream, not least in Huntly's assertion that 'I love to immerse myself in shades and dells' and his talk of the forest wilderness as a 'maze' and 'labyrinth'.

For the cave, Poe-like to a degree, oneiric, hidden, could not be a more arresting image of a darkness visible, of the inner psyche lost and turned in on itself.[18] Huntly undergoes a symbolic death and rebirth, a necessary new envisioning of all that is about him:

> The first effort of reflection was to suggest the belief that I was blind; that disease is known to assail us in a moment and without previous warning. This, surely, was the misfortune that had now befallen me. Some ray, however fleeting and uncertain, could not fail to be discerned, if the power of vision was not utterly extinguished. . . .
>
>   The utter darkness disabled me from comparing directions and distances.   (p. 160)

Light as against dark, rays which may or not illuminate: we

cannot but recognise a familiar idiom. As Huntly works his way, uncertainly, out of this 'utter darkness', there emerges a yet greater emphasis to Brown's overwhelming theme. The true 'power of vision' visits us only in moments, oddly, unpredictably. More often, on Brown's reckoning, ours is a 'dark' world, whose show indeed keeps us off-balance, at a loss to know its many and contradictory 'directions and distances'. In this, as in some other respects, Brown tells a very modern tale.

Notes

1. *Mosses from an Old Manse*, in *The Works of Nathaniel Hawthorne*, Centenary Edition, vol. x (Kent, Ohio: Kent State University Press, 1974) pp. 173–4.
2. *The Novels and Related Works of Charles Brockden Brown*, Bicentennial Edition, vol. iii (Kent, Ohio: Kent State University Press, 1980) p. 107. Subsequent quotations from Brown's novels are taken from this edition (page references in the text). *Wieland* is vol. i, *Ormond* vol. ii, *Arthur Mervyn* vol. iii and *Edgar Huntly* vol. iv of the edition.
3. Here and elsewhere in this essay, I have benefited from the following works: Arthur Hobson Quinn, *American Fiction, an Historical and Critical Survey* (New York: D. Appleton-Century, 1936); Alexander Cowie, *The Rise of the American Novel* (New York: American Book Company, 1948); R. W. B. Lewis, *The American Adam: Innocence, Tragedy and Tradition in the Nineteenth Century* (Chicago: University of Chicago Press, 1955); Richard Chase, *The American Novel and its Tradition* (New York: Doubleday, Anchor, 1957); Harry Levin, *The Power of Blackness* (New York: Alfred A. Knopf, 1958); Leslie A. Fiedler, *Love and Death in the American Novel*, rev. edn (New York: Criterion, 1966); and Richard Brodhead, *Hawthorne, Melville, and the Novel* (Chicago: University of Chicago Press, 1976).
4. These terms are used by Cowie in *The Rise of the American Novel* to characterise the case against Brown.
5. *Memoirs of Stephen Calvert* was initially serialised in Brown's *Monthly Magazine and American Review* in 1799–1800. Its reconstitution as a novel in its own right has been as a work of German scholarship: *Memoirs of Stephen Calvert*, ed. with an introduction and notes by Hans Borchers, Studien und Texte zur Amerikanistik (Frankfurt-am-Main: Peter Lang, 1978). Though I discuss the fiction, I do not wish it to be thought that I underrate Brown's other literary endeavours: essays such as 'The Rhapsodist' in the *Columbian Magazine* (1789); his contributions to the Philadelphia *Weekly Magazine* (1798); his editorship of the *Monthly Magazine and American Review* (1799–1800) and of *The Literary Magazine and American Register* (1803–6); his various political and nationalistic pamphlets; his translation in 1804 of Volnay's *A View of the Soil and Climate of the United States*; and his semi-annual *The*

American Register, or General Repository of History, Politics, and Science (1807–10).

6. John Keats to Richard Woodhouse, 21–2 Sep 1819, in *Letters of John Keats*, ed. Robert Gittings (Oxford: Oxford University Press, 1970) p. 297.

7. 'Sermons and Tracts . . . by W. E. Channing', *Edinburgh Review*, L (Oct 1829) 125–8.

8. *Memoir of Percy Bysshe Shelley*, in *The Works of Thomas Love Peacock*, vol. III (London: Richard Bentley, 1875).

9. This is taken from the preface. Missing from this list is Sir Walter Scott's appreciation of Brown's 'wonderful powers', though he thought the American had given way to 'unwholesome' subjects (see Cowie, *The Rise of the American Novel*, p. 99).

10. There are also two modern biographies of Brown: David Lee Clark's *Charles Brockden Brown: Pioneer Voice of America* (Durham, NC: Duke University Press, 1952); and, far more definitive, Harry R. Warfel's *Charles Brockden Brown: American Gothic Novelist* (Gainesville, Fla: University of Florida Press, 1949). To call Brown America's first *professional* novelist is in no way to ignore the importance of other pioneer Americans, notably Susanna Rowson with her *Charlotte Temple* (1791).

11. *The National Era*, 1 June 1848; repr. in *The Prose Works of John Greenleaf Whittier*, vol. VII (Boston, Mass.: Houghton Mifflin, 1888–9).

12. For a complete bibliographical listing of reviews and essays on Brown see Patricia L. Parker, *Charles Brockden Brown: A Reference Guide* (Boston, Mass.: G. K. Hall, 1980).

13. All of the remarks quoted in this paragraph, plus those of R. H. Dana Sr, Hazlitt and Whittier cited earlier, may be found in Bernard Rosenthal (ed.), *Critical Essays on Charles Brockden Brown* (Boston, Mass.: G. K. Hall, 1981). Rosenthal's introduction offers a full, most helpful account of Brown's early reputation.

14. Lewis, *The American Adam*; Chase, *The American Novel and its Tradition*; and Fiedler, *Love and Death in the American Novel*.

15. Howard Phillips Lovecraft, *Supernatural Horror in Literature* (New York: Dover, 1973).

16. In my account of Brown's fiction I have benefited particularly from the following works: Larzer Ziff, 'A Reading of *Wieland*', *PMLA*, LXXVII (1962) 51–7; Donald A. Ringe, *Charles Brockden Brown* (New York: Twayne, 1966); Arthur G. Kimball, *Rational Fictions: A Study of Charles Brockden Brown* (McMinnville, Ore.: Linfield Research Institute, 1968); Norman S. Grabo, *The Coincidental Art of Charles Brockden Brown* (Chapel Hill: University of North Carolina Press, 1981); and Alan Axelrod, *Charles Brockden Brown: An American Tale* (Austin: University of Texas Press, 1983).

17. Fiedler, *Love and Death in the American Novel*, ch. 6: 'Charles Brockden Brown and the Invention of American Gothic'.

18. A helpful colloquium on the Gothic as darkness is to be found in *Emerson Society Quarterly: A Journal of the American Renaissance*, 18, no. 1 (1972). See esp. Robert D. Hume, 'Charles Brockden Brown and the Uses of Gothicism' (pp. 10–18).

3

Poe: Rituals of Life and Death

ROBERT GIDDINGS

I trembled not – I stirred not – for a crowd of unutterable fancies connected with the air, the stature, the demeanor of the figure, rushing hurriedly through my brain, had paralysed – had chilled me into stone. I stirred not – but gazed upon the apparition. There was a mad disorder in my thoughts – a tumult unappeasable. Could it, indeed, be the living Rowena who confronted me? Could it indeed be Rowena at all?

(Poe, 'Ligeia'[1])

Poe's art is rightly celebrated for its obsession with horror and with death, and may justly be ranked very high in 'Gothic' literature, yet there are some important qualities which set it apart and make it uniquely the art of Edgar Allan Poe. By all means let us regard Poe as one of the most distinguished heirs of the Gothic movement, which clearly began with the work of the Graveyard School in the early eighteenth century, following the rediscovery of Longinus, but let us also see the peculiar qualities of Poe's treatment of horrific subjects. The most important striking thing is that at moments of supreme horror, such as that in 'Ligeia' quoted above, the dead live and the living are struck dead. Writers of Gothic horror before Poe had made death the culminating horror, but had concentrated on making the moment of death itself the ultimate horror. For Poe the horror lies in the animation of death itself. In his imagination, and in his hands as a writer, the terror lies in the vitality of death.

It is curious that the work known to literary criticism as Longinus's *On the Sublime* (the attribution to 'Longinus' is a misunderstanding) should have had the influence on literary taste that it undoubtedly has. The date and true authorship of this work, known to us from a Greek manuscript of the first or second century AD, are uncertain. It is no accident that it had such an appeal to Dryden, Pope, Gray and Burke as it became fashionable during the period when the battle between the Ancients and the Moderns

33

raged at its height. Battle commenced in 1657 with the publication of Jean Desmarets de Saint-Sorlin's long poem *Clovis ou la France chrétienne*. The poet's theme was the history of France during the Carolingian period. He furthered his case in the preface to *Marie-Madeline* (1669), and his assertion of native French literary genius was answered by Nicolas Boileau in *L'Art poetique* (1674), which championed Greek and Roman authors as the true models to be imitated. Charles Perrault's poem *Le Siècle de Louis le Grand* (1687), which the poet himself read to the Académie Française, favourably compared the arts and culture of modern France with the great period of Rome under Augustus. This in effect was an official declaration of war, and the conflict between the Académie – commanded by such writers as Perrault and Phillipe Quinault, with supporting battalions from the Cartesians – and the Ancients, led by the Duc de Richelieu, lasted for three decades. Longinus's *On the Sublime* became fashionable at this moment, and it was attacked by Boileau in *Réflexions sur Longinus* (1694). But, as we have learned, there is nothing quite so powerful as an idea which occurs at the right time.

In the opening years of the new century the conflict spread across the Channel to Britain, and Sir William Temple's *Essay on Ancient and Classical Learning* (1690) led Swift to write one of his finest satires, *The Battle of the Books* (1704). Read in the context of this debate, Longinus's theories of the sublime could be interpreted as an invitation to write a new kind of literature buttressed and supported by 'classical' authority. Longinus's treatise is in the form of an address to a friend – Postumius Terentianus – which attempts an exegesis on the nature of the sublime in literature. The author commends good, clear style, noble emotion, dignity and elevation of subject matter, and the avoidance of lapses of taste and tone; his arguments are underpinned with several worthy illustrations from the *Iliad*, the *Odyssey*, the writings of Demosthenes, Plato and Cicero, and the opening of the book of Genesis.

In no European culture did 'classicism' mean simply a return to the standards of ancient Greece and Rome and a rejection of contemporary culture in the search for truth, meaning and values. Each culture, on its exposure to the rediscovery of the past during the rebirth of learning, reinterpreted and in fact distorted the past in the very processes by which it creatively responded to it. The Italian Renaissance was in essence a national movement, involving the rehabilitation of ancient Roman relatives and predecessors.

French classicism had the ambition of constructing a national French literature comparable with some supposed (or assumed) Greek ideal, the rich fulfilment of the influence of the Pléiade, who swept away French medievalism and realised the theories of Joachim Du Bellay's *La Défense et illustration de la langue française* (1549). In England, classicism reached its high-water mark in Augustanism, the endeavour to produce a perfect, polished, poised and sophisticated literature based on an assumed set of principles inherited from the noblest civilisation of the past. French classicism was the product of an aristocratic society in which high art was the consumer product of a limited elite, whereas English classicism was at bottom a bourgeois affair, strongly rooted in Locke's philosophy of middle-class rights and Dryden's common sense. In place of the French tendency towards grandeur and grandilo-quence, the English sought for what was correct, reasonable and harmonious.

The key work here is Alexander Pope's *An Essay on Criticism* (1711), which rehearses the leading critical ideas of the moment and comes down on the side of the classics to the extent that the soundest theory of art is to work from the principles of the ancients as the best guarantee against failure in literature:

> Those RULES of old discover'd, not devised,
> Are nature still, but nature methodized;
> Nature, like liberty, is but restrain'd
> By the same laws which first herself ordain'd.

The appeal made here (in book I of the *Essay*) is significantly not just to the laws of the ancients but also to the fact that these classical ideals are linked with the ideals of bourgeois politics – nature and liberty are one and the same thing. Interestingly enough, Pope finds ample space, when holding up examples of the ancients we should follow, to number Longinus among his other heroes – Homer, Quintilian and Horace:

> Thee, bold Longinus! all the Nine inspire,
> And bless their critic with a poet's fire.
> An ardent judge, who, jealous in his trust,
> With warmth gives sentence, yet is always just:
> Whose own example strengthens all his laws;
> And is himself that great sublime he draws.

Pope attempted to achieve the classical ideal in England in his translations of Homer, but academic opinion held that he had failed to realise the sublime. Joseph Warton had this to say:

> I revere the memory of POPE, I respect and honour his abilities; but I do not think him at the head of his profession. In other words, in that species of poetry wherein POPE excelled, he is superior to all mankind: and I only say, that this species of poetry is not the most excellent one of the art. . . .
> The SUBLIME and the PATHETIC are the two chief nerves of all genuine poesy. What is there very Sublime or very Pathetic in Pope? In his works there is indeed 'nihil inane, nihil arcessitum; – puro tamen fonti quam magno flumini propior' ['Nothing irrelevant or far-fetched. Nonetheless I would compare him to a clear stream rather than a mightly river.' *Institutio Oratorio*, x.i.78] as the excellent Quintilian remarks of Lysias. And perhaps because I am ashamed or afraid to speak out in plain English, I will adopt the following passage of Voltaire, which, in my opinion, as exactly characterizes POPE, as it does his model Boileau, for whom it was originally designed: 'INCAPABLE PEUTÊTRE DU SUBLIME QUE ÉLÈVE L'ÂME, ET DU SENTIMENT QUI L'ATTENDRIT, MAIS FAIT POUR ÉCLAIRER CEUX À QUI LA NATURE ACCORDA L'UN ET L'AUTRE, LABORIEUX, SEVÈRE, PRÉCIS, PUR, HARMONIEUX, IL DEVINT, ENFIN, LE POÈTE DE LA RAISON' ['incapable, perhaps, of the sublime which lifts up the soul, and of the feeling which softens it, but made to enlighten those upon whom nature bestowed the one and the other, hard-working, stern, precise, pure, harmonious, he becomes, finally, the poet of reason.' 'Discours à sa reception a l'Académie française, prononcée le lundi 9 Mai 1746', Oeuvres (1748) XLVII, 12].
> Our English poets may, I think, be disposed in four different classes and degrees. In the first class, I would place, first, our only three sublime and pathetic poets; SPENSER, SHAKESPEARE, MILTON; and then, at proper intervals, OTWAY and LEE . . . .[2]

By the theories applied by the Augustans themselves, then, Alexander Pope had failed to achieve the sublime. At the time when the literary world was relishing the publication of Pope's translation of the *Odyssey*, the Scottish poet James Thomson published 'Winter' (1726), the first part of his popular work *The Seasons*, which was destined to remain in vogue well into the

Romantic period. This first poem is particularly interesting, and its literary interest far outweighs its possible poetic merits. Thomson is clearly attempting something in the manner of the sublime. He has chosen a season of the year to write about which will offer him opportunities to describe the punishment of a cruel season and scenes of terror and desolation:

> See, WINTER comes, to rule the vary'd Year,
> Sullen, and sad, with all his rising Train;
> *Vapours*, and *Clouds*, and *Storms*. Be these my Theme,
> These, that exalt the soul to solemn Thought,
> And heavenly Musing. Welcome, kindred Glooms!
> Congenial Horrors, hail!

In Thomson's view the subject matter is obviously inherently sublime, and in order to handle the material in the appropriate register he elects to use the Miltonic tone of voice.

Early in the century the poet and dramatist John Dennis had stressed the importance of passion as the lifeblood of poetry, and had pointed the way to the sublime through imitation of Milton. In *The Advancement and Reformation of Modern Poetry* (1701) he had written, 'Passion is the Principal thing in Poetry.' Several leading poets of the period sought their own routes to the sublime, which, though sundry and various, when examined begin to display a certain similarity in their landscape features and topographical detail.

Edward Young's *Night Thoughts on Life, Death, and Immortality* (1742–5) was extremely popular and influential in its time, and, although much of its rambling and didactic reflections on the deaths of Lucia, Narcisa and Philander (supposedly the poet's wife, stepdaughter and her husband) somewhat tax a modern reader's patience, the iconography and locations are often quite striking, and seem to point towards a style and manner more familiar later in the century:

> The Bell strikes *One*: We take no note of Time,
> But from its Loss. To give it then a Tongue,
> Is wise in man. As if an Angel spoke,
> I feel the solemn Sound. If heard aright,
> It is the *Knell* of my departed Hours;
> Where are they? With the years beyond the Flood:

It is the *Signal* that demands Dispatch;
How Much is to be done? My Hopes and Fears
Start up alarm'd, and so o'er life's narrow Verge
Look down – on what? A fathomless Abyss;
A dread Eternity! how surely *mine!*
And can Eternity belong to me,
Poor Pensioner on the bounties of an Hour?

The heavily self-conscious Gothic tone seems to foreshadow the mode of Romantic melodrama, and the striking of poses over matters of life and death are almost Dickensian – it is no accident that Micawber's catchphrase about procrastination as the thief of time is actually a quotation from Young's *Night Thoughts*.

At the same time Robert Blair led the stampede into the darkening graveyard with *The Grave* in 1743:

See yonder Hallow'd Fane! the pious Word
Of Names once fam'd, now dubious or forgot,
And buried 'midst the Wreck of Things which were:
There lie interr'd the more illustrious Dead.
The Wind is up: Hark! how it howls! Methinks
Till now, I never heard a Sound so dreary:
Doors creak, and Windows clap, and Night's foul Bird
Rook'd in the Spire screams loud: The gloomy Isles
Black-plaster'd, and hung round with Shreds of 'Scutcheons
And tatter'd Coats of Arms, send back the Sound
Laden with heavier Airs, and from the low Vaults
The Mansions of the Dead. Rous'd from their Slumbers
In grim Array the grizly Spectres rise,
Grin horrible, and obstinately sullen
Pass and repass, hush'd as the Foot of Night.
Again! the Screech-Owl shrieks: Ungracious Sound!
I'll hear no more, it makes one's Blood run chill.

The subject matter has become familiar from numerous imitations, but this solemn, overtly blood-curdling blank-verse poem by the minister of Athelstaneford set the tone and almost prescribed the ingredients of graveyard poetry for generations (significantly, it was illustrated by William Blake in 1808). Thomas Warton (brother of the distinguished critic and editor of Pope, Joseph Warton), who was Poet Laureate and Professor of Poetry at Oxford, was an enthusiast for medieval and Elizabethan literature. He, too, tried his hand at something in the graveyard manner, *The Pleasures of Melancholy* (1747):

> Beneath yon' ruin'd Abbey's moss-grown piles
> Oft let me sit, at twilight hour of Eve,
> Where through some western window the pale moon
> Pours her long-levelled rule of streaming light;
> While sullen sacred silence reigns around,
> Save the lone Screech-owl's note, who builds his bow'r
> Amid the mould'ring caverns dark and damp,
> Or the calm breeze, that rustles in the leaves
> Of flaunting Ivy, that with mantle green
> Invests some wasted tow'r. Or let me tread
> Its neighb'ring walk of pines, where mus'd of old
> The cloyster'd brothers: thro' the gloomy void
> That far extends beneath their ample arch
> As on I pace, religious horror wraps
> My soul in dread repose.

A certain group of feelings is obviously beginning to be selected time after time and selected together, and these feelings are ones for which neoclassicism had found little room – admiration, transport, enthusiasm, vehemence, awe, terror. Poets sought to locate their musings at a time and in a location where these emotions might most readily be evoked – at that mystery-laden moment, midnight, when day merges into night, and in scenes of ruin, decay and religious feeling, where the dread imponderables of life and death are more likely to impose themselves on our thinking. In William Collins's 'Ode to Evening' (1747) we find the mood well evoked, but to little meditative effect; in fact, feelings so dominate thought that syntax breaks under the weight of emotion and sense evaporates:

> If ought of oaten stop, or pastoral song,
> May hope, chaste Eve, to soothe thy modest ear,
>   Like thy own solemn springs,
>   Thy springs, and dying gales,
> O Nymph reserv'd, while now the bright-hair'd sun
> Sits in yon western tent, whose cloudy skirts,

With brede ethereal wove,
   O'erhang his wavy bed:
Now air is hush'd, save where the weak-ey'd bat,
With short shrill shriek flits by on leathern wing,
   Or where the Beetle winds
   His small but sullen horn
As oft he rises 'midst the twilight path,
Against the pilgrim born in heedless hum:
   Now teach me, Maid compos'd,
   To breathe some soften'd strain,
Whose numbers stealing thro' thy darkening vale,
May not unseemly with its stillness suit,
   As musing slow, I hail
   Thy genial lov'd return!

Collins suffered from severe depression and may well have been certifiable in terms of modern psychiatric medical practice (he was certainly confined in an asylum for a while). What we get in this ode is an ostensible attempt to address Evening, here personified; but in his attempts to create the appropriate atmosphere of twilight, gloom and mystical religiosity the poet loses track of what it is that he actually wants to say to Evening. He is actually more interested in the mood than in the message. In Thomas Gray's 'Elegy Written in a Country Church-yard' (1750), the finest poem produced by the Graveyard School, mood and message exist in perfect harmony. Taking the meaning of the poem from the whole text, instead of rubbing, polishing and admiring each individual striking image (a temptation easily indulged in this of all poems), we can see that it is an extended series of reflections on life and death in modern society, prompted by the feelings which arise in a sensitive mind at the close of day in a country churchyard. The by-now expected apparatus of graveyard poetry is all duly present in Gray's poem – the time of day, the tolling bell, the droning beetle, the shrieking owl in its ivy-clad tower, the mossy graves – but the attention is focused on the inner psychology of the mind through which we perceive these images and unravel the disturbing thoughts associated with them.

These thoughts are Gray's thoughts, these fears are Gray's fears, but we all admit to them as we read this poem and enter Gray's mind; we observe our own mortality in Gray's fearful account of the death of the subject of the poem, who began it by musing

about the tolling curfew and the lowing herd. The celebrated praise
of Samuel Johnson is wholly justified:

> In the character of his Elegy I rejoice to concur with the common
> reader; for by the common sense of readers uncorrupted with
> literary prejudices, after all the refinements of subtilty and the
> dogmatism of learning, must be finally decided all claim to
> poetical honours. The *Churchyard* abounds with images which
> find a mirror in every mind, and with sentiments to which every
> bosom returns an echo.[3]

The emphasis on the feelings, which Johnson acknowledges with
his memorable references to the mirror in every mind and the echo
returned by every bosom, is significant, and indicates a notable
advance in the psychologising of literature, towards subjectivism.
The eighteenth century constructed the notion of the 'original
genius', and here, in Gray's 'Elegy', we have the famous notion
that those who lie in their graves under the greensward in this
country churchyard and hear no more the bustle of daily life
include not only the rustic dead but perhaps also some who might
have been great persons, had they only had the opportunity:

> Can storied urn or animated bust
> Back to its mansion call the fleeting breath?
> Can Honour's voice provoke the silent dust,
> Or Flatt'ry sooth the dull cold ear of Death?
>
> Perhaps in this neglected spot is laid
> Some heart once pregnant with celestial fire;
> Hands, that the rod of empire might have sway'd,
> Or wak'd to ecstasy the living lyre.
>
> But Knowledge to their eyes her ample page
> Rich with the spoils of time did ne'er unroll:
> Chill Penury repress'd their noble rage,
> And froze the genial current of the soul.

These might have been men of towering genius – a Hampden, a
Milton or a Cromwell – Gray suggests. Long before William
Wordsworth was a twinkle in his father's eye, we are looking at
the beginnings of Romanticism. Appropriately, Gray's masterly

poem was a work chosen by Horace Walpole to be printed on his Gothic press in Strawberry Hill, that instant monument and shrine to the Graveyard School and Gothic revival which was Walpole's home from 1747.

In fact the embryo of 'original genius' is discernible in a poem by a leading master of the Graveyard School – the somewhat neglected 'Ode on the Poetical Character' (1746) by William Collins, which bodies forth the idea of the blind, inspired bard, personified in the creator of *Paradise Lost*:

> such bliss to one alone,
> Of all the sons of soul was known,
> And Heaven, and Fancy, kindred powers,
> Have now o'erturned the inspiring bowers,
> Or curtained close such scene from every future view.

The theme of this poem is clear: just as the girdle of Venus may be worn only by the chaste, so the girdle of Fancy may only be worn by the truly creative – the poets. And a poet may only be born as a result of the union of God and the imagination: Milton is here put forward as the ideal poet to wear the girdle of Fancy. The mid-eighteenth-century concept of 'original genius' further developed the idea of the poet–prophet, suggesting that, if genius depended upon nothing but the individual's inspiration, then those who were so inspired would owe nothing to anything outside themselves, nor depend upon the world of ordinary humanity – such poets would therefore resemble gods, elevated above the rest of mankind. It is clear from the evidence that this revolutionary theory alarmed and distressed such orthodox Christians as Samuel Johnson, who in his biography of Cowley in *The Lives of the Poets* argued that a true genius was no special divinity but a man among men: 'a mind of large general powers, accidentally determined to some particular direction'. Sir Joshua Reynolds asserted in his Sixth Discourse (1774) that genius and imitation, like nature and art, may be one and the same: 'Invention is one of the great marks of genius; but if we consult experience, we shall find, that it is by being conversant with the inventions of others, that we learn to invent; as by reading the thoughts of others we learn to think.'

It was William Blake who finally cut genius free from all bonds, and the process may be observed in his marginalia (c. 1808) to Reynolds' Discourse: 'The man who says that the Genius is not

Born, but Taught – Is a Knave . . . .' Reynolds Thinks that Man Learns all that he knows;

> I [Blake] say on the Contrary that Man Brings All that he has or can have Into the World with him. Man is Like a Garden ready Planted and Sown. This World is too poor to produce one Seed. He who can be bound down is no Genius. Genius cannot be Bound; it may be Render'd Indignant and Outrageous.[4]

The same ground was fought over in the famous conversations (1826–30) between William Hazlitt and the painter James Northcote, a distinguished student of Reynolds.

The Satanic–Byronic hero now hoves into sight. Blake made the claim that Milton had unconsciously taken the part of the Devil against God.[5] Blake was writing in the closing decade of the eighteenth century, but in fact his argument in *The Marriage of Heaven and Hell* locates a tendency in Gothic horror writing which dates from the middle of the century. The hero–villain figure, with his oddly attractive flawed grandeur, makes his appearance in fiction fifty years before Byron's Lara and Manfred. Edmund Burke, in his *A Philosophical Inquiry into the Origin of our Ideas of the Sublime and Beautiful* (1756) found that anything which was capable of exciting the idea of pain and danger was a source of the sublime:

> Whatever is fitted in any sort to excite the idea of pain and danger; that is to say, whatever is in any sort terrible, or is conversant about terrible objects, or operates in a manner analogous to terror is a source of the sublime; that is, it is productive of the strongest emotion which the mind is capable of feeling.[6]

The poets of the Graveyard School had sought terror in the contemplation of tombs and churchyards in the darkening gloom of twilight, but the writers of Gothic fiction began very early to explore the possibilities of terror in hero–villain figures who were not simply evil or sinister, but who mixed a fatal, almost attractive, charm with their villainy. These tendency certainly seem to anticipate Blake's famous dictum about Milton's Satan. Horace Walpole printed his Gothic novel *The Castle of Otranto* (1764) on his black-letter press at Strawberry Hill, and, even though his leading character, Manfred, is undoubtedly the villain of the piece, he is not described as dark, sinister, ugly or deformed. Quite the contrary:

> Manfred was not one of those savage tyrants who wanton in cruelty unprovoked. The circumstances of his fortune had given an asperity to his temper, which was naturally humane; and his virtues were always ready to operate, when his passion did not obscure his reason.[7]

This epoch-making novel does not end with the death of the villain: Manfred is exposed and abdicates his principality. The horror, the terror of the piece lies in its splendid Gothic locations and in the romantic–sinister personal qualities of Manfred himself.

William Beckford's extravagant Gothic story *Vathek* (1786) carries these tendencies a stage further. The caliph Vathek, like some oriental Faust, is sated with earthly pleasures and experiences, and in his search for an extension of his power and curiosity makes a pact with the Devil figure Eblis. Terror is provided in full measure; the sacrifice of fifty children tops the list of Vathek's crimes. The terror of the scene is increased by the exploration of Vathek's initial unwillingness to go through with his pact, and his capitulation as he realises this is the price he must pay for what he wants. He calls the children to him, promising them rewards of diamonds, emeralds and rubies.

> This declaration was received with reiterated acclamations. . . . The Caliph, in the meanwhile, undressed himself by degrees, and, raising his arm as high as he was able, made each of the prizes glitter in the air; but whilst he delivered it with one hand to the child who sprang forward to receive it, he with the other pushed the poor innocent into the gulph . . . .[8]

The punishment for Vathek's ghastly crimes is 'an eternity of unabating anguish'. It is important to note that Vathek too does not conform to the Richard of Gloucester villain-stereotype; like Manfred, he is princely and handsome:

> Vathek, ninth Caliph of the race of the Abassides, was the son of Motassem, and the grandson of Haroun al Rashid. From an early accession to the throne, and the talents he possessed to adorn it, his subjects were induced to expect that his reign would

be long and happy. His figure was pleasing and majestic; but when he was angry one of his eyes became so terrible, that no person could bear to behold it . . . .[9]

Vathek has that flawed grandeur so noted in the Satanic-hero figure.

Another impressive example of the genre is to be found in Matthew Gregory Lewis's novel *The Monk* (1796), which features the dreadful deeds of the 'saintly' Superior of the Capuchins of Madrid:

> He was a man of noble port and commanding presence. His stature was lofty, and his features uncommonly handsome. His nose was aquiline, his eyes large, black and sparkling, and his dark brows almost joined together. His complexion was of a deep but clear brown. . . . Tranquillity reigned upon his smooth unwrinkled forehead; and content, expressed upon every feature, seemed to announce the man equally unacquainted with cares and crimes . . . there was a certain severity in his look and manner that inspired universal awe. . . . Such was Ambrosio, abbot of the Capuchins, and surnamed 'The Man of Holiness'.[10]

This outwardly saintly young man embarks on a series of sexual and murderous exploits which bring him eventual doom. He is seduced by the fiendish Mathilda, who gains access to him in male guise as a novice. Once on the slippery slope of vice and corruption, Ambrosio takes advantage of one of his penitents and pursues her with the aid of necromancy. He is tortured by the Inquisition, but makes a pact with the Devil for his escape. The Devil tricks him, and, although he saves him from the authorities, he carries him high into the air and hurls him into the wilderness, where his body is shattered and broken on the rocks, he suffers the torments of dreadful thirst, and he is finally washed away by a river in flood. The mixture of fascinating attractiveness and evil of soul is exploited throughout the novel to inspire horror and terror. Father Schedoni, the villain–hero of Ann Radcliffe's *The Italian, or The Confessions of the Black Penitents* (1797), is similarly outwardly striking – tall, dark, melancholy, severe and outwardly penitent – but inwardly deeply villainous. The type reached its apotheosis in the hands of Byron, whose Conrad, Lara and Manfred are exemplary treatments of the figure of the handsome–sinister Satanic hero.

The Gothic achieved its effect by inverting the values of the classical: in place of ancient Greece and Rome, it sought its haven in the Middle Ages; in place of order, harmony and the light of reason we have darkness and chaos; and in place of moral certainties we have evil and confusion. Poe draws considerably on this well-established tradition, but adds some very important ingredients of his own. Since Marie Bonaparte published her Freudian study *The Life and Works of Edgar Allan Poe* (1949), the tendency in assessing and explicating Poe's work has been to concentrate on his inner psychology, rather than to consider the impact of the outside world on his imagination. This is the inner-directed Poe, so well categorised by A. Robert Lee, the Poe who was in real life like something out of his own work:

> Poe the dweller among the undead and their crypts, the would-be necrophiliac or vampire, the madman, the drug-taker, the alcoholic, the husband of a child-bride, the gambler and celebrant of 'the perverse', in effect none other than his own tormented figure of Roderick Usher . . . .[11]

If we examine the textual evidence it seems clear that Poe was fascinated not by death itself (as the Graveyard School and Gothic romance writers had been) but by the rituals of death, and by the terrors implicit in prolonging a form or manifestation of life after the moment of bodily death. These are themes endlessly rehearsed in Poe's horror stories. If we move the focus of our attention away from the subject-centred Poe which Marie Bonaparte and her followers have more or less succeeded in making obligatory, we shall see that the intellectual furniture of the period in which Poe spent his creative life offers several possible sources for his preoccupations.

If we look first at Poe's horror stories as a group, we shall see that certain themes are very strong and frequently recur, in varying forms. One theme is death and dying, given an elaborate, ceremonial treatment. This is new in horror fiction: the early English writers of Gothic fiction may have dealt in terrible goings-on, but they did not linger over death and showed little interest in its rituals. A second theme is the mistaking of life for death: Poe was obsessed with the catatonic condition in which life imitated death – a condition dealt with in morbid seriousness in 'The Fall of the House of Usher', and given the joke-in-the-tail treatment in 'The Premature Burial'. A third theme is that of the continuing dialogue between the living and the dead. The most famous example of this is 'The Facts in the Case of M. Valdemar', and the theme receives comic treatment in 'Some Words with a Mummy'. These recurring themes suggest to me that, besides drawing (whether consciously or unconsciously) on his own inner psychological tensions, Poe was deftly handling some of the leading ideas of his generation, and exploiting them to create some of the most exciting and dramatic horror writing of the nineteenth century. This, in my view, makes Poe a great American writer: unlike the European masters of horror writing, he belonged to a society of comparatively recent origin, with little of a past to which he could have recourse. A Southerner, too, so far as the cast of his mind was concerned, he was not drawn to exploit the Puritan past of New England, as Hawthorne did. One of the unifying qualities of European Gothic was the exploitation of the Gothic/medieval past. Poe frequently attempts to associate his horror stories with the 'Gothic' past through copious references to Joseph Glanvill (author of *Lux Orientalis*, 1662, and *Saducismus Triumphatus*, 1667), Sir Thomas Browne (author of *Hydriotaphia, Urne-Burial*, 1658) and other older authorities, but in fact his most brilliant effects are achieved in his exploitation of contemporary themes, concepts, obsessions and ideas.

Poe's interest in rituals and ceremonies associated with death is very striking. Several of the stories deal with a death very elaborately planned, staged and executed. In 'The Cask of Amontillado' the narrator plans to revenge the thousand insults he has borne at the hands of Fortunato. He lures him to his death with the bait of a favourite bottle of wine, but does not kill him immediately he has him in his power in the cellars. The victim is slowly bricked up, after having been rendered drunk by the wine which has brought him to his fate. The atmosphere of the story is generated not so much by the darkness, the damp and the scattered bones down below, as by the punctilious and time-consuming ritual of his entombment. Fortunato is treated to a personal funeral ceremony all on his own in which the references to the brotherhood of the Masons has its own ghastly irony:

At the most remote end of the crypt there appeared another less spacious. Its walls had been lined with human remains, piled to the vault overhead. . . . . It was in vain that Fortunato, uplifting his dull torch, endeavoured to pry into the depth of the recess. . . . 'Proceed,' I said, 'herein is the Amontillado. . . .'[12]

Fortunato is easily manipulated into the cavity and is chained to the interior wall and then carefully bricked up. The murderer then re-erects the old rampart of bones to mark the grave and resting place. The tale ends with the admission that this occurred fifty years ago and that the place has not been disturbed: *'In pace requiescat!'*

'The Pit and the Pendulum' involves the attempted killing of a victim by highly elaborate machinery which would render his death into a ritual. The religious context of this story of the tortures of the Inquisition is not a piece of accidental colour. 'The Tell-Tale Heart' concerns the murder of an old man, the careful, almost ritualistic dismembering of his corpse, and its concealment between the floorboards. 'The Oblong Box' is the study of a man's obsessive desperation in taking his wife's body from Charleston to New York by sea. In 'Hop-Frog' the King and his seven counsellors are ritualistically slain by burning, and swing in chains 'a fetid, blackened, hideous, and indistinguishable mass'. 'The Masque of the Red Death' concerns the attempt by Prince Prospero and his court to take refuge from the Red Death which has ravaged the country, but Death intrudes into the elaborately prepared masque they have been enjoying. Death appears dramatically like the chief dignitary at a public ceremony: 'And now was acknowledged the presence of the Red Death. He had come like a thief in the night. . . . And Darkness and Decay and the Red Death held illimitable dominion over all.'[13]

Poe's preoccupation with ritual and ceremony is a very nine-teenth-century one. National consciousness was something fostered and encouraged by modern societies, in the New World no less than in Europe, and protocol, ceremony and ritual were part of the outward show of national identity. It was the age of the national anthem, the national emblem, the national flag. This century saw the construction of most of those public ceremonials which media commentators always unctuously claim reach back into the mists of time – royal weddings, state funerals, trooping the colour, coronations, inaugurations, state openings of legislative bodies – but which really only began to assume their present form during the last century.[14]

Another very important influence was the establishment of archaeology as a respected academic discipline and the wide popular interest in Egyptology which resulted from the translation of the Rosetta Stone by Jean-François Champollion in 1822. The fashion for the Egyptian style in costume, architecture and furniture design had been triggered by Napoleon's expedition to Egypt in 1798, which resulted in the publication of the influential *Description de l'Egypte* and focused world attention on Egypt. This was part of the much wider fascination with the East and the Arab world which inspired Mozart's *Die Entführung aus dem Serail* (*The Abduction from the Seraglio*, Vienna, 1782), Boïeldieu's *Le Calife de Bagdad* (Paris, 1800), several of Rossini's operas, the enduring craze for *The Arabian Nights*, and endless poems and fictions featuring Arab steeds, tribesmen, mysterious sheikhs and innocent English governesses exposed to wickedness and temptation after being shipwrecked on the shores of Algeria. The cult of the East (including the Arab world) entered military music and iconography.[15] Champollion was sent by royal command to Egypt on a scientific expedition in 1828–9, and a chair of Egyptology was founded for him at the College de France in 1830. The revelations of the early Egyptologists (including also Sir John Gardner Wilkinson, Karl Richard Lepsius, Samuel Birch and Heinrich Karl Brugsch) aroused popular interest in funeral rites, mummification and the disposal of the dead in ancient Egypt.

In America, the first to lecture publicly on these discoveries (during the 1830s) was G. R. Gliddon, who appears in person in Edgar Allan Poe's amusing little story 'Some Words with a Mummy'. In this tale Poe himself is present at a scientific gathering where an Egyptian mummy is brought to life by the application of electrical power in much the same way as Dr Frankenstein brings his creature to life. Gliddon is there to explain scientific matters and add the insights of Egyptology to proceedings. He is also able to communicate directly with the mummy in its own language.

Looking beneath the comic surface of this tale, we can recognise that it is a satiric treatment of another favourite theme in Poe's horror stories: communication with the dead. Here Poe shows himself familiar not only with the great craze for Egyptology but also with mesmerism and animal magnetism. Probably the most famous example of his interest in mesmerism is the ghastly little story 'The Facts in the Case of M. Valdemar'. The narrator is an expert mesmerist who is allowed by Valdemar to experiment at maintaining communication with him as he crosses the borders of life and death during the final stages of a mortal illness. He talks with Valdemar as the latter's body dies:

> While I spoke, there came a marked change over the countenance of the sleep-walker. The eyes rolled themselves slowly open, the pupils disappearing upwardly; the skin generally assumed a cadaverous hue . . . and the circular hectic spots which . . . had been strongly defined in the centre of each cheek, *went out* at once. . . . The upper lip, at the same time, writhed itself away from the teeth . . . while the lower jaw fell with an audible jerk, leaving the mouth widely extended, and disclosing in full view the swollen and blackened tongue. . . .[16]

Poe reinforces the horror of this moment by adding that, when the patient's face assumed this set of expressions, there was a general shrinking-back from the region of the bed by those in the room. Various tests demonstrate that the man is physically dead, and yet the mesmerist is able to continue to communicate with him, and Valdemar, in his turn, is able to reply by means of a ghastly disembodied voice. This manner of communication continues for seven months after death. When attempts are made to awake the patient, his whole frame immediately shrinks, crumbles and rots away upon the bed into a loathsome mass of detestable putridity.

What Poe does here is to take the known state of the mesmerist's art and apply it in an extreme context. Friedrich Anton Mesmer was born in 1733 and, after studying medicine in Vienna, developed an interest in astrology. He believed that the stars exerted a direct influence upon living creatures here in earth, and he developed various theories about the 'life force', which he associated with electricity. He published his first work, *De Planetarum Influxu*, in 1766. In Switzerland ten years later he made the acquaintance of the priest J. J. Gassner, who effected impressive cures by means of manipulation. Mesmer, who previously had sought to cure illness by using magnets, now began to assert that he possessed an occult force that he could exert to heal the sick. This force, he claimed, permeated the entire universe, and more especially influenced the nervous system of men. He himself, naturally, was particularly well-endowed with its power and able to use it. He held séances in Vienna but was asked to leave by the authorities. In 1778 he moved to Paris, where his consultations became the vogue. (Mesmerism is satirised in Mozart's opera *Così fan tutte*, first produced in Vienna in 1790.) The Parisian medical profession was furious at his social success and a commission of scientists and physicians was appointed to investigate his claims. They were forced to admit to Mesmer's frequent successes, but would not concede that he possessed the occult powers of animal magnetism which he claimed. He was offered 20,000 livres for his secret, but refused. After the publication of the commission's report in 1785, Mesmer retired to obscurity in Switzerland, where he died in 1815. But he had started a vogue for hypnotism, mesmerism and spiritualism which became one of the great social fads of the nineteenth century.

The success of Mesmer's theories had much to do with the growing fascination with electricity. Scientific knowledge of the subject was advanced by Michael Faraday, who was apprenticed to Humphry Davy in 1812 and travelled as his amanuensis in France, Switzerland and the Tyrol in 1813–15. Faraday went on to make important discoveries in electro-magnetism and his ideas were spread not only by his publications but also by his celebrated public lectures. Poe was clearly fascinated by the connection between developments in electrical science and the supernatural. Here again he is to be seen as part of an existing tradition, as these connections had been made previously by Konrad Dippel (1673–1734) and popularised by Mary Shelley in her Gothic novel *Frankenstein* (1818).

After their elopement in 1814, Mary and the poet Shelley sailed down the Rhine and probably stayed near Castle Frankenstein, which is not far from Darmstadt. This castle dates from the thirteenth century and was sold by the Frankenstein family in 1662. Konrad Dippel was born and brought up there. During his childhood the castle was used as an army hospital, so he grew up among wounded and disfigured soldiers, some of whom had lost limbs. Dippel went on to study alchemy and was employed by the Landgrave of Hesse. He believed that the body was an inert substance which was inhabited by an errant spirit that could leave it at any time and infuse life into another substance. Dippel was convinced that he could reproduce this spirit by distilling the blood and bones of human remains, and thought that he could animate a body assembled from various bodily parts. He died without having completed his work, but this phantasmagoric story was turned into a Gothic classic by Mary Shelley.[17]

It may or it may not be paradoxical, but the phenomenal interest in spiritualism during the early ninteenth century seems to have gained energy and stimulus from developments in the natural sciences, almost as if it were a logical consequence of them. Modern spiritualism seems to be an American phenomenon and appears to date from the opening decades of the nineteenth century. Spiritualistic episodes are found in all cultures and in all periods, and are well recorded from the time of the Hebrew patriarchs right down to the time of John Wesley. David and the other kings of Israel often consulted seers, and Samuel (among other prophets) experienced what is now called 'direct voice' communication. The ancient Greeks and Romans placed some faith in omens and oracles, and there was a craze for ghosts in the late seventeenth and early eighteenth centuries. The age which produced Shakespeare was rich in supernatural lore, to the extent that it might be said that an alternative theology existed. At Hyndesville, near Rochester, New York, in the mid 1840s intelligent table-rapping was first reported, and the celebrated spiritualist and medium Daniel Dunglas Home (1833–86) first began to practise what was in effect his profession in the United States, beginning with demonstrations of telepathy in Connecticut. His séances were attended by such eminent Americans as William Cullen Bryant and Judge Edmonds, and it was at the house of Ward Cheney that Home first levitated. He came to England in 1855 and demonstrated his powers before Bulwer Lytton and the Brownings. Robert Browning immortalised him as Mr Sludge the medium.[18]

Communication between the living and the dead, which is the essence of spiritualism, is a recurring theme in Poe's fiction, and invariably the message from that other side of the grave is a frightening one. In 'The Black Cat' the feline who denounces the narrator and exposes his crime is undoubtedly his own conscience personified, but he reacts like one who hears a voice from the other side:

> Swooning, I staggered to the opposite wall. For one instant the party upon the stairs remained motionless, through extremity of terror and of awe. In the next, a dozen stout arms were toiling at the wall. It fell bodily. The corpse, already greatly decayed

and clotted with gore, stood erect before the eyes of the spectators. Upon its head, with red extended mouth and solitary eye of fire, sat the hideous beast whose craft had seduced me into murder, and whose informing voice had consigned me to the hangman . . . .[19]

In 'The Tell-Tale Heart', it is the loud beating of the concealed victim's heart, rising in a crescendo, which, like a sign from the other world, betrays the guilt of the murderer:

No doubt I now grew *very* pale; – But Talked more fluently and with a heightened voice. Yet the sound increased – and what could I do? It was *a low, dull, quick sound – much such a sound as a watch makes when enveloped in cotton*. I gasped for breath . . . but the noise steadily increased. . . . O God! What *could* I do? . . . I felt that I must screen or die – and now – again – hark! louder! louder! *louder*!

'Villains!' I shrieked, 'dissemble no more! I admit the deed! – tear up the planks! here, here! it is the beating of his hideous heart!'[20]

Another theme that is very strong in Poe's work is that of the similarities between life and death, such that the one state can be mistaken for the other – as in 'The Premature Burial'. This theme is deployed in those tales which deal with the catatonic condition of schizophrenia: 'The Fall of the House of Usher', 'Ligeia' and 'Berenice'. Here, too, Poe was drawing on current ideas and discoveries in medical science, as he was contemporary with the beginnings of modern psychiatric medicine. Up to this time, medical treatment of the insane had been based on restraint: the insane were regarded with fear and abhorrence, and frequently were chained or imprisoned. The founding father of modern psychiatric medicine was Philippe Pinel (1745–1826), who became head of the Bicêtre and later held senior staff positions at the Salpêtrière clinic in Paris. In place of the old barbaric methods of torture, punishment and restraint, he recommended a psychological approach. He published his theories in his influential *Traité médico-philosophique sur l'alienation mentale* (1801). By 1838 in France the insane had been transferred from the larger institutions of restraint – workhouses and prisons – and placed in asylums constructed specially for their treatment.

One major result of Pinel's work was that the recognition that treatment of the insane was only possible if it could be discovered what was wrong with them. Thus began the diagnosis and classification of mental illnesses.[21] The men who laid the foundations of modern psychiatry were John Haslam (1764–1844), a medical writer who was apothecary to Bethlehem Hospital in London and later qualified as a physician, and James Cowles Pritchard (1786–1848). Haslam has a particularly important place in the history of psychiatry as being probably the earliest physician to publish proper clinical descriptions of the various kinds of mental ailment. These appeared in his *Observations on Insanity* (later *Observations on Madness and Melancholy*, 1798) and *Illustrations of Madness* (1810). His work contains what is probably the first clinical description of schizophrenia, and it has been claimed that Haslam's clarity is such that he still provides a sound basis for diagnosis.[22] Another physician who advanced the diagnosis and treatment of the insane was John Conolly (1794–1866), who worked in Warwickshire asylums and became Professor of Medicine at University College, London in 1828. He was resident physician at Hanwell Asylum, Middlesex, from 1839 to 1844, and has earned a worthy place in medical history for his advocacy of the humane treatment of the insane. His *Indications of Insanity* (1830) and *Croonian Lectures* (1849) are landmarks in clinical psychiatry.[23]

The theory and practice of psychiatric medicine in America were certainly influenced by these developments. In his *American Notes* (1842) Charles Dickens refers to the mental institution in South Boston as being 'admirably conducted on those enlightened principles of conciliation and kindness, which twenty years ago would have been worse than heretical and which have been acted on with so much success in our own Asylum at Hanwell.'[24] The first well-organised and well-appointed hospitals for the treatment of the insane in America were private institutions: the New York Hospital, the Massachusetts General and the Pennsylvania Hospital, and special foundations such as the Hartford Retreat, the Butler Hospital and the Sheppard and Enoch Pratt Hospital. As a new nation, the United States was relatively free of the old, harsher methods of 'treatment' that were common in Europe up to the end of the eighteenth century.

Insanity was a subject of considerable interest to Romantic writers and poets – not only because of the extreme imaginative activity and bizarre behaviour of the insane, but also because insanity was the polar opposite of reason, supposedly the guiding principle of classicism. The controversy and debate that surrounded the diagnosis and treatment of the insane, as new and more scientific methods came to the fore, also excited interest. Poe seems to have been particularly fascinated by the schizophrenic group of illnesses, marked by a disintegration of thought processes, hallucination, and an unrealistic and wholly subjective relationship with the outside world, based on fantasy. The various kinds of schizophrenia are difficult to define, but they all involve disturbances of thought, emotions and contacts with reality.[25] Andrew Crowcroft divides the schizophrenic disorders into four main groups.

1 *Simple:* characterised by lack of emotional depth, otherworldliness, isolation and a lack of activity, a gradual diminution of the use of inner resources and a retreat into increasingly stereotyped patterns of behaviour.
2 *Hebephrenia:* characterised by shallow and incongruous emotional responses which seem foolish, bizarre and often involve illusions and hallucinations, voices and strange visual experiences.
3 *Catatonia:* characterised by striking and unpredictable motor behaviour, trances, rigidity of posture, and loss of speech.
4 *Paranoia:* manifested in feelings of persecution, of being watched and plotted against.

What unites these terrible mental illnesses is the occurrence of hallucinations, of mental impressions of sensory vividness which occur without external stimulus. The schizophrenic illnesses were first categorised by Emil Kraepelin (1856–1926), who was the first to distinguish schizophrenia (which he called dementia praecox) from the manic-depressive group of mental disorders.[26] Hallucinations and catalepsy – the conditions which seem most to have interested Poe – were well-known centuries before this time and had already been well-documented and frequently brilliantly described and exploited by writers, poets and dramatists.

Poe's 'William Wilson' has frequently been analysed as largely autobiographical,[27] but it may also be seen as a brilliant account of a subject afflicted with hallucinations. Wilson is always pursued by his double, he hears whispering, and, when he kills the other

William Wilson, he sees in the mirror his own pale, blood-stained person:

> A large mirror, so at first it seemed to me in my confusion, now stood where none had been perceptible before; and, as I stepped up to it in extremity of terror, mine own image, but with features all pale and dabbled in blood, advanced to meet me with a feeble and tottering gait. Thus it appeared, I say, but was not. It was my antagonist – it was Wilson, who then stood before me in the agonies of his dissolution. . . . Not a thread in all his rainment – not a line in all the marked and singular lineaments of his face which was not, even in the most absolute identity, *mine own!*[28]

'The Fall of the House of Usher' also employs the theme of the divided personality, as Roderick and Madeline are twins and seem to be intended to represent two sides of a single personality. The theme of catalepsy so severe that it may well be mistaken for death itself is treated with grisly humour in 'The Premature Burial' and with full attention to its horrific potential in 'The Fall of the House of Usher', in which Madeline Usher is put living into her tomb, from which she escapes to terrify her brother.

It has long been almost uncontested that Poe invariably wrote about himself. Julian Symons speaks on behalf of a considerable body of critical opinion when he says, 'He had no subject except himself.'[29] It is my contention that Poe wrote as much about his own time as about himself: the leading themes of his tales of horror and terror reflect ideas current in the early nineteenth century. The problem lies in the way in which we read Poe. We read him as a nineteenth-century writer, and his Gothic fiction takes on a quaint spooky quality that has come to be associated with the period in which he wrote; yet his fiction was once modern and contemporary. And, if we make the effort to see it like that, we shall have to concede that, like many great creative artists before and since, Edgar Allan Poe took the things he found to hand and worked them into the stuff of his art.

Notes

1. Edgar Allan Poe, *The Complete Stories and Poems* (New York: Doubleday, 1966) p. 108.
2. Joseph Warton, *An Essay on the Writings and Genius of Pope*, vol. I (1756), quoted in John Barnard (ed.), *Pope: The Critical Heritage* (London: Routledge and Kegan Paul, 1973) pp. 381–2. The material in square brackets is taken from Barnard's notes.
3. Samuel Johnson, *The Lives of the Poets* (1783), ed. John Wain (London: Dent, 1953) II, 392.
4. William Blake, *Complete Writings*, ed. Geoffrey Keynes (London: Oxford University Press, 1968) pp. 470–2.
5. Cf J. and A. J. Aikin, *On the Pleasure Derived from Objects of Terror, and Enquiry into Those Kinds of Distress Which Excite Agreeable Sensations. Miscellaneous Pieces of Prose* (London, 1773); David Irwin, *English Neoclassical Art* (London: Faber, 1966) pp. 135ff.; Robert Rosenblum, *Transformation in Late 18th Century Art* (Princeton, NJ: Princeton University Press, 1967) pp. 11–19.
6. Edmund Burke, *A Philosophical Enquiry into the Origin of Our Ideas of the Sublime and Beautiful* (1757; Gloucester: Bryant and Jeffries, 1841) p. 40.
7. *Three Gothic Novels*, ed. Peter Fairclough (Harmondsworth: Penguin, 1975) pp. 66–7.
8. Ibid., p. 173.
9. Ibid., p. 15.
10. Matthew Gregory Lewis, *The Monk* (1796; New York: Grove Press, 1959) p. 45.
11. A. Robert Lee (ed.), *Edgar Allan Poe: The Design of Order* (London: Vision Press, 1987) p. 7.
12. Poe, *The Complete Stories and Poems*, pp. 194–5.
13. Ibid., p. 260.
14. Eric Hobsbawm and Terence Ranger (eds), *The Invention of Tradition* (Cambridge: Cambridge University Press, 1983) pp. 110ff.; and Jeffrey L. Lant, *Insubstantial Pageant: Ceremony and Confusion at Queen Victoria's Court* (London: Hamish Hamilton, 1979) pp. 17ff.
15. Robert Giddings, 'Listen to the Band', *New Society*, 8 May 1978.
16. Poe, *The Complete Stories and Poems*, p. 260.
17. Alan Bold and Robert Giddings, *Who Was Really Who in Fiction* (London: Longman, 1987) pp. 131–2.
18. Ibid., pp. 306–7.
19. Poe, *The Complete Stories and Poems*, p. 70.
20. Ibid., p. 124.
21. See Denis Leigh, *The Historical Development of British Psychiatry* (Oxford: Pergamon Press, 1961) I, 94–202.
22. Ibid., p. 118.
23. Conolly was satirically portrayed in Charles Reade's novel *Very Hard Cash* (1863).
24. Charles Dickens, *American Notes* (1842; London: Macmillan, 1932) p. 38.

25. David Stafford Clark, *What Freud Really Said* (Harmondsworth: Penguin, 1968) pp. 136ff.; and J. S. Kasanin (ed.), *Language and Thought in Schizophrenia* (Berkeley, Calif.: University of California Press, 1944).
26. Andrew Crowcroft, *The Psychotic: Understanding Madness* (Harmondsworth: Penguin, 1967) pp. 34–46.
27. Julian Symons, *The Tell Tale Heart: The Life and Works of Edgar Allan Poe* (London: Faber, 1978) p. 215.
28. Poe, *The Complete Stories and Poems*, p. 170.
29. Symons, *The Tell Tale Heart*, p. 240.

4

This Revolting Graveyard of the Universe: the Horror Fiction of H. P. Lovecraft

CLIVE BLOOM

The twentieth century has had two major sources of inspiration for the horrific imagination. The first is Hollywood, where modern cinematographic technology has been used to reproduce the Romantic Gothic worlds of Mary Shelley's *Frankenstein*, Gaston Le Roux's *Phantom of the Opera* and Bram Stoker's *Dracula*. The work of Universal and other studios creating horror movies has been widely distributed and is well known, appearing nowadays regularly on television. The second major influence is the work of Howard Phillips Lovecraft, a pulp-fiction writer whose short life ended before the Second World War. Where the studios were motivated by publicity and commercialism, Lovecraft was motivated by horror of publicity and by a disgust with commercial enterprise. Lovecraft remains, fifty years since his death, an enigmatic writer and a strange and stranded personality. He wrote 'popular fiction' which was never and is still *not* popular; he considered himself a man of letters who wrote exclusively for pulp magazines; he instinctively felt that he was a gentleman but was actually the son of a commercial salesman; and he was a writer in the early twentieth century who owed nothing to the work of James, Eliot, Pound or Lawrence. His output was small, consisting of two novellas (one published after his death) and some short stories, many of which were completed by others after his death. In many ways Lovecraft has been an influence on film makers (especially Roger Corman) and on other writers (Robert Bloch, Ray Bradbury, Colin Wilson and Stephen King), but Lovecraft himself remains locked away – a cult interest for fantasy fanatics (who are rare) and academics or intellectuals (who are rarer).

Who was H. P. Lovecraft and what did he do? He was born to parents of British stock on 20 August 1890 in Providence, Rhode Island.[1] We are told that

> Lovecraft was of predominantly British stock on both sides of his family. His father was the son of an Englishman who had lost his fortune and emigrated from Devonshire to New York in 1847 and married a girl of British descent – an Allgood from Northumberland, descended from a former British officer who remained in the United States after what Lovecraft himself, ardent Anglophile that he was, would term 'the disastrous Revolution'. On his mother's side, Lovecraft was, in his own words, 'a complete New-England Yankee, coming from Phillipses, Places, & Rathbones'.[2]

In 1898 his father, named after the hero Winfield Scott, died of a serious and lingering illness. Lovecraft was eight. For some time his father had been a paretic, muscularly paralysed and mentally incompetent. Winfield Scott Lovecraft died insane, perhaps from untreated syphilis, but, before he did, he and his small son spent time together on the father's occasional visits from the hospital to which he had been sent.[3] After his father's death, Lovecraft was brought up in the exclusive home company of the Lovecraft women – mother, aunts and grandmother.

After his father's death Lovecraft began to suffer from terrifying nightly disturbances and nightmares, which lasted until his own death in 1937. In order to deal with these unresolved nightmares Lovecraft wrote them into his letters or wrote them up into short stories. Although he hated Freud's concepts, which he considered paltry and inconsequential, his attempts at fiction and at verse can be seen to be a prolonged working-through of his unsatisfactory relationship with his father – a man whose insanity was accompanied by periods of hallucination.[4] One of Lovecraft's later pantheon of 'gods', the terrifying and imbecile Nyarlathotep, may owe his origin, many years later, to the period of the elder Lovecraft's madness, for everything leads 'me on even unto those grinning caverns of earth's centre where Nyarlathotep, the mad faceless god, howls blindly in the darkness to the piping of two amorphous idiot flute players' ('The Rats in the Wall'). Indeed, this imbecile god is *the* impulse of the universe:

And through this revolting graveyard of the universe the muffled, maddening beating of drums, and thin, monotonous whine of blasphemous flutes from inconceivable, unlighted chambers beyond Time; the detestable pounding and piping whereunto dance slowly, awkwardly, and absurdly the gigantic, tenebrous ultimate gods – the blind, voiceless, mindless gargoyles whose soul is Nyarlathotep.[5]

But this terrifying and significantly 'faceless' entity was not always a god, for Lovecraft transformed dream material of another kind, a kind much closer to the commercial traveller that was his father:

Nyarlathotep is a nightmare – an actual phantasm of my own, with the first paragraph written *before I fully awaked*. I had been feeling execrably of late – whole weeks have passed without relief from head-ache. . . . I had never heard the name NYARLATHOTEP before, but seemed to understand the allusion. Nyarlathotep was a kind of itinerant showman or lecturer who held forth in publick [*sic*] halls and aroused wide spread fear and discussion with his exhibitions. These exhibitions consisted of two parts – first, a horrible – possible prophetic – cinema reel; and later some extraordinary experiments with scientific and electrical apparatus. . . . I seem to recall that Nyarlathotep was already in Providence; and that he was the cause of the shocking fear which brooded over all the people. I seem to remember that persons had whispered to me in awe of his horrors, and warned me not to go near him. . . . The terror [has] become a matter of conscious artistic creation.[6]

This was a nightmare Lovecraft could not exorcise, and it created a form of self-punishment which he wrote into his story *The Case of Charles Dexter Ward*:

From a private hospital for the insane near Providence, Rhode Island, there recently disappeared an exceedingly singular person. He bore the name of Charles Dexter Ward, and was placed under restraint most reluctantly by the *grieving father* who had watched his aberration grow from a eccentricity to a dark mania involving both a possibility of murderous tendencies and a peculiar change in the apparent contents of his mind. Doctors confess themselves quite baffled by his case, since it presented

oddities of a general physiological as well as psychological
character.　(Emphasis added)

It is clear that Lovecraft brought deeply personal material to his
work, and this may account for his low output of stories and high
output of confessional letters.

Another area of 'neurosis' for him was his relationship with the
ordinary modern world in the United States of the 1920s and
1930s. Lovecraft's background was essentially Anglophile and of
provincial New England. As a young man he published a magazine
called *The Conservative*.[7] Self-educated and outside the New England
college world, Lovecraft yearned for a past age into which he could
escape. In 1923 he wrote,

> Nothing must disturb my undiluted Englishry – God Save the
> King! I am naturally a Nordic – a chalk-white, bulky Teuton of
> the Scandinavian or North-German forests – a Viking – a berserk
> killer – a predatory rover of the blood of Hengist and Horsa – a
> conqueror of Celts and Mongrels and founder of Empires – a
> son of the thunders and the arctic winds, and brother to the
> frosts and the auroras – a drinker of foemen's blood from new-
> picked skulls –[8]

And in 1929, in another letter, he tells us, 'my writing soon became
distorted – till at length I wrote only as a means of re-creating
around me the atmosphere of my 18th century favourites'.[9] After
his marriage, he moved to Brooklyn and travelled, in a limited
fashion, visiting the older colonial USA: Philadelphia, Richmond,
Williamsburg and Yorktown. When his marriage failed he returned
to Providence and the world of his aunts. Indeed, when previously
offered the editorship of *Weird Tales*, then published in Chicago,
Lovecraft refused to commit himself on the grounds of having just
arrived in New York (which he refers to as 'venerable New-
Amsterdam').[10] Moreover, his stories are usually set in a just-
surviving seventeenth-century America. For instance, in his tale
'The Survivor' his narrator tells us,

> I came to Providence, Rhode Island, in 1930, intending to make
> only a brief visit and then go on to New Orleans. But I saw the
> Charriere house on Benefit Street, and was drawn to it as only
> an antiquarian would be drawn to any unusual house isolated

in a New England street of a period not its own, a house clearly of some age . . . indefinable aura that both attracted and repelled. . . . I saw it first as an antiquarian, delighted to discover set in a row of staid New England houses a house which was manifestly of a seventeenth-century Quebec style, and thus so different from its neighbours as to attract immediately the eye of any passer-by. I had made many visits to Quebec, as well as to other old cities of the North American continent, but on this first visit to Providence, I had not come primarily in search of ancient dwellings.

'The Peabody Heritage', too, is architecturally specific: 'the dwelling itself was the product of many generations. It had been built originally in 1787, at first as a simple colonial house, with severe lines, an unfinished second story, and four impressive pillars at the front.'

Lovecraft's desperation for a gentlemanly existence was set against a background of rapid social change. Although married to a Jew, he continually poured vitriol on the incoming waves of immigrants, reserving a special hatred for the new Jewish immigrants, whom he called 'beady eyed rat-faced Asiatics'.[11] Moreover, his wife Sonia recalls that, when he actually came face to face with them in New York, 'Howard would become livid with rage. He seemed almost to lose his mind.'[12] This distinctly unusual behaviour Lovecraft could not deal with in direct terms choosing rather a 'black magic' science fiction which transformed social fears into fantasy nightmares.[13] New York is also suitably transformed into a fantastical realm of historical and 'species' degeneracy:[14]

I saw a vista which will ever afterward torment me in dreams. I saw the heavens verminous with strange flying things, and beneath them a hellish black city of giant stone terraces with impious pyramids flung savagely to the moon, and devil-lights burning from un-numbered windows. And swarming loathsomely on aerial galleries I saw the yellow, squint-eyed people of that city, robed horribly in orange and red and dancing insanely to the pounding of fevered kettle-drums. . . . I have gone home to the pure New England lanes up which fragrant sea-winds sweep at evening.   ('He')

Elsewhere this becomes more explicit, and a New York police

detective finds himself amid the degenerate hoards of the metropolitan heart:

> He had for some time been detailed to the Butler Street station in Brooklyn when the Red Hook matter came to his notice. Red Hook is a maze of hybrid squalor near the ancient waterfront opposite Governor's Island, with dirty highways climbing the hill from the wharves to that higher ground where the decayed lengths of Clinton and Court Streets lead off towards the Borough Hall. Its houses are mostly of brick, dating from the first quarter to the middle of the nineteenth century. . . . The population is a hopeless tangle and enigma; Syrian, Spanish, Italian, and negro elements impinging upon one another, and fragments of Scandinavian and American belts lying not far distant. It is a babel of sound and filth.   ('The Horror at Red Hook')

In his long tale 'At the Mountains of Madness', a 'fetid black' monster which Lovecraft called a 'Shoggoth' is likened to the 'Boston–Cambridge tunnel' subway train. Yet the Shoggoths 'whatever they had been . . . were men'.

This is evidence enough of Lovecraft's peculiar brand of horror – a transposition of his social fears about new immigrant groups into a cosmic battle in which the evil *Untermenschen* are constantly defeating the less numerous *Übermenschen*. Many critics stop at this point, believing Lovecraft's horror to be purely racist, but this is perhaps only half the story, for the majority of Lovecraft's tales depict Anglo-Saxon degeneracy among the rural white poor, not the newly arrived passengers of the steerage. Two examples must suffice:

> He paused exhausted, as the whole group of natives stared in a bewilderment not quite crystallized into fresh terror. Only old Zebulon Whateley, who wanderingly remembered ancient things but who had been silent heretofore, spoke aloud.
>
> 'Fifteen year' gone,' he rambled, 'I heered Ol' Whateley say as haow some day we'd hear a child o' Lavinny's a callin' its father's name on the top o' Sentinel Hill. . . .'
>
> But Joe Osborn interrupted him to question the Arkham men anew.
>
> '*What was it, anyhaow*, an' haowever did young Wizard Whateley call it aout o' the air it come from?'

Armitage chose his words very carefully. . . . I'm going to burn his accursed diary, and if you men are wise you'll dynamite that altar-stone up there, and pull down all the rings of standing stones on the other hills.   ('The Dunwich Horror')

Or:

Sir William, standing with his searchlight in the Roman ruin, translated aloud the most shocking ritual I have ever known; and told of the diet of the antediluvian cult which the priests of Cybele found and mingled with their own. Norrys, used as he was to the trenches, could not walk straight when he came out of the English building. It was a butcher shop and kitchen – he had expected that – but it was too much to see familiar English implements in such a place, and to read familiar English *graffiti* there, some as recent as 1610.   ('The Rats in the Wall')

On one side Lovecraft was faced with an invasion of 'Asiatics', but on the other he witnessed another form of degeneracy – that of his own race. In 1926, when Lovecraft produced his largest body of work, he would have been witness to an amazing growth of rural religious fervour. In 1925 an article on the rise of the 'Holy Rollers' painted this picture of rural enthusiasm:

The song became a dirge and the dirge became a fiendish thing, rising in howls and wails and moanings that stilled the wild things of the night. Preacher Joe Leffew preached. 'Some folks thinks as how as we-uns are funny people. They come here, poor sinners that they are, to mock an' revile us. Here's our word of Scripture. "An' Christ reeled to an' fro, as a drunken man." Now, children, dear children, some folks think that means the Lamb was a drunkard. T'aint so at all. It says "as a drunken man". You cain't tell me God's son ever went home all soused up.'
    Preacher Joe Leffew assailed education. 'I ain't got no learnin' an' never had none,' said Preacher Joe Leffew. 'Glory be to the Lamb! Some folks work their hands off'n up 'n to the elbows to give their young-uns education, and all they do is send their young-uns to hell.'[15]

This needs to be added to the growth of the 'know-nothing'

intolerance of the Ku-Klux Klan, which had been recently 'revived' in the 1920s. In 1926, the year of Lovecraft's most prolific outpouring, Hiram Wesley Evans, Imperial Wizard of the Klan, had this to say about Americanness:

We are a movement of the plain people, very weak in matter of culture, intellectual support, and trained leadership. We are demanding, and we expect to win, a return of power into the hands of the everyday, not highly cultured, . . . but entirely unspoiled and not de-Americanized, average citizen of the old stock. Our members and leaders are all of this class – the opposition of the intellectuals and liberals. . . .

The Klan . . . has now come to speak for the great mass of Americans of the old pioneer stock. . . .

These are . . . a blend of various peoples of the so-called Nordic race . . . the Klan does not try to represent any people but these. . . .

[Now] we [have] found our great cities and the control of much of our industry and commerce taken over by strangers. . . .

So the Nordic American today is a stranger in large parts of the land his fathers gave him.[16]

In 1928 the Klan's rise in Indiana was described by Morton Harrison in terms reminiscent of Lovecraft's monster gods. The Klan is addressed by its leader:

Here in this uplifted hand, where all can see, I bear an official document addressed to the Grand Dragon, Hydras, Great Titans, Furies, Giants, Kleagles, Exalted Cyclops, Terrors, and All Citizens of the Invisible Empire of the Realm of Indiana. It is done in the executive chambers of His Lordship, the Imperial Wizard, in the Imperial City of Atlanta.[17]

This side of Lovecraft's fears is not mentioned by any critics who deal with his work. That Lovecraft pictured himself as a barbarian Nordic type was purely ironic given his frailty and lack of physicality; that he was a rationalist materialist, whose hobby was astronomy, added to his distaste for cults based on ignorance (he was, after all, an eighteenth-century gentleman).

In order to cope with racial alienation from both directions Lovecraft turned his social fears into nightmare fantasies. His *real* nightmares then returned upon themselves and fictional fantasy returned to its origins. To suggest, as most critics do, that Lovecraft's social fears were simply translated into fantasy ignores the fact that Lovecraft's fantasy life (his dreams) ran parallel to his social experience and was not just an internalisation of that social experience: Holy Roller, Ku-Klux Klan Grand Wizard, Nyarlathotep, Father trace Lovecraft's concern with origins – origins in family and in America that literally paralysed him. Unable to cope with marriage, with city life, with work of any sort, Lovecraft finally could not exist in temperatures lower than 80°F, actually fainting when the heat dropped to 60°. In his stories the seeker after origins either is destroyed or goes mad; the 'Old Ones', for example, are decapitated ('At the Mountains of Madness'). Indeed, in 1929 Lovecraft wrote of his inability to escape the literary influence of either Poe or Dunsany: 'where', he asks, 'are my Lovecraft pieces?'[18] During March 1937 he died of cancer. Lin Carter's 1972 biographical obituary remarks,

> He lived like a hermit, a recluse, in self-imposed exile from his own world and his age, neither of which he enjoyed. Far rather would he have been born a cosmopolitan Roman of the late Empire, or an English squire in his beloved 18th century, or a colonial gentleman of the days before the Revolution. Alas, he was none of these things, except in his extraordinarily vivid dreams.[19]

After Lovecraft's death August Derleth made it a lifelong work of love to keep the master's writings available; yet the collections of Lovecraft work did not sell well. *Weird Tales* also went into decline. Stephen King drily comments,

> During and after the war years, horror fiction was in decline. The age did not like it. It was a period of rapid scientific development and rationalism – they grow very well in a war atmosphere, thanks – and it became a period which is now thought of by fans and writers alike as the 'golden age of science

fiction' . . . . *Weird Tales* plugged grimly along, holding its own but hardly reaping millions (it would fold in the mid-fifties after a down-sizing from its original gaudy pulp size to a digest form failed to effect a cure for its ailing circulation).[20]

Nevertheless, Lovecraft's pantheon of gods steadily grew as other writers embellished the 'Cthulhu mythos', as it is called. The cult status of Lovecraft was becoming an inescapable fact. For many who loathed his excesses and 'poverty' of style, but for whom Lovecraft stories were an addiction there was also a problem. Stephen King says that Lovecraft

> Has been called a hack, a description I would dispute vigorously, but whether he was or wasn't, and whether he was a writer of popular fiction or a writer of so-called 'literary fiction' (depending on your critical bent), really doesn't matter very much in this context, because either way, the man himself took his work seriously.[21]

David Punter confesses, 'perhaps little more needs to be said about Lovecraft: his writing is crude, repetitive, compulsively readable, the essence of pulp fiction'.[22]

In order to understand this ambivalence over Lovecraft's work it is necessary to see that Lovecraft's personal traumas are, in fact, the *social traumas* of the group from which his work emerged and to which his work is addressed. While that group of readers has evolved over the years since his death and the specific milieu in which he wrote his tales belongs to the past, it is, nevertheless, still possible to identify some broader cultural issues which stop his work from being of purely historical interest.

We may speculate theoretically that Lovecraft's work emerges at a certain point: the moment of the emergence of mass literacy based upon self-educative values. Mass-production techniques opened the way for the mass consumption of cheaply available literature. So-called pulp magazines, and in particular *Weird Tales*, met this need following the period of mass readership for dime novels. The petit-bourgeois class that had emerged during this period looked to magazines which included petit-bourgeois writers who represented the world of a class *without a voice* – a class that saw itself as neither proletarian nor fully bourgeois and that felt itself *exploited* by bourgeois cultural requirements (Lovecraft emerged from such a class, being self-educated, aspiring to be an eighteenth-century gentleman yet the son of a travelling salesman). This petit-bourgeois-generated antagonism left it feeling bewildered and *disenfranchised* (hence Lovecraft's hatred of *others*, especially *aliens*). The readership of one class unknowingly united with another readership of fantasy tales – the bourgeois intelligentsia, who also felt (and feel) disenfranchised. In both classes a desire for a period before technological specialisation (the very period from which these classes emerge) led to an alliance among the pages of *Weird Tales*. Such an alliance manifests itself in a distaste for money (Lovecraft's disinterest in publishing fiction or editing magazines) and a paradoxical love of ostentatious consumption (Lovecraft's taste for the life of a gentleman and, in his tales, for 'empires' and for prehistoric gods and 'heroes', who do not have to earn a living). This paradox is represented in the fiction by a 'revival' of a mythic past, a romanticised past of Gothic or feudal origins and a whole mythology of warring gods being a rewriting in fantasy terms of the myth of Genesis.

This construction of *another* (quite separate) *history to the world* other than the official bourgeois history reflects the petit-bourgeois belief in a conspiracy by 'those at the top'. This conspiracy involves the translation of social forces into black magic and occult forces which because they are about to *return* suggest forces outside human (therefore bourgeois) control. The immanence of *archaic elements* about to irrupt into modern life always brings the bourgeoisie near to defeat, but they can always recover and this allows the petit-bourgeoisie also to survive, for total defeat of the bourgeoisie would lead to total dissolution of the petit-bourgeoisie. These dangerous archaic elements represent anti-bourgeois forces, *but* they embody petit-bourgeois ideas about the bourgeoisie controlling everything. Hence Lovecraft's 'good' monsters have pyramidal heads covered with all-encompassing tentacles. Being buried under pyramids of power ('Imprisoned with the Pharaohs') suggests social pyramids, but, again, paradoxically, the monsters are always at the very bottom of the pyramid, *beneath history* and therefore *outside* it. What is seen to be at the top is represented as being underneath.

Such a representation of life also involves (despite Lovecraft's distaste for Holy Rollers) a strongly religious notion, but one that has become scientifically objectified: a materialist belief system. The class to which Lovecraft belonged had 'liberated' itself from an old-style religion, but was unable to go back to the superstitious beliefs of the *Lumpen-proletariat* or rural peasantry. Lovecraft instead turned to his hobby of astronomy in order to create stories about *astrology* and black magic bringing *real* monsters from the stars as star-spawn. Moreover, this quasi-religiosity which is fatalistic and deterministic rests on a scientific understanding of phenomena, at once upholding the incredible but defeated by it ('At the Mountains of Madness'). Objective, materialist science is used to defeat itself: it recognises what it cannot control – the other, the Absolute, ultimately the gods or God (but the gods are mad).

We return to the question of origins – of the cosmos, of man, of the petit-bourgeoisie. The identification of those origins is bound to the textual unravelling of a riddle, which once deciphered offers Truth – not merely a set of truths, but an absolute reassurance of the impossibility of *change*, both capitalist and bourgeois; for the Truth is that the 'Old Ones' and their enemies will always exist and battle for the universe. Hence, history stops in eternal recurrence. In order to stop history it is necessary to travel back in time to find it and to *disturb* it, thereby discovering that it exists not merely as the past but also *in the present* as a *threat*. For the return of the past reassures us of permanence even as it acts to threaten the very class representatives (and hence the whole class) who go in search of it. Indeed, the *other place* for history fantasised by the petit-bourgeoisie is actually the place of archaic feudal relations, the relations of autocrat to peasant – the very class relationships that must not return if the petit-bourgeois (servants of the bourgeoisie) are to survive. Questioning the cosmic order (the social order) may lead to destruction, but it also leads to an answer: there is a need for order and a need to 'know one's place'. Hence, hatred of the *new* coincides with hatred of the *old* and ends in personal and class paralysis.

This paralysis is the result of the nature of the quest and the quester. It is not a metaphysical quest, but a materialist quest for metaphysical certainties. The hero is a loner, disenfranchised in the modern world by his desire for *lost* knowledge. He is character-ised by physicality and a distaste for psychology. His actions *are* character, as introversion by extension implies the bourgeois notion of individual control and the privacy of thought. The petit-bourgeois hero is always a man who acts *publicly* in the arena of activity allowed him (Lovecraft hated Freud). Yet this lone quester is, paradoxically, removed from socialised activity: he avoids

women, and hates blacks and Jews (who are deeply socialised).
His actions are public, but they are not the property of the group
from which he emerges (he prefers communion with dead masters)
or of aliens (whom he avoids and whose alienation, ironically,
destroys him). In Lovecraft's tales public action is public only
because it indicates *private* motives which are *openly* represented
by a character's hostility or withdrawal from public life.

Like the heroes of his tales, Lovecraft's life was public but always
anonymous (conducted with many people but only by letter). Like
his characters, the pulp-fiction author has no biography: his cult
is that of a name to a text only. The author's authority is ensured
by the repetition of his name on the cover of a work or magazine –
a name without personality. Hence, like the tales of the fabulous
that he produced, the author himself becomes fabulous, and this
fabulousness is both projected away from and determined by his
ordinary existence.

This fabulousness accords well with Lovecraft's lack of and
distaste for professionalism (bourgeois work). Remaining anonymous Lovecraft imposes no bourgeois ethic of the artist: any writer
can join in with the mythology and create new monsters. Lovecraft's
name on his stories stands for a *type* of story which anybody can
create and which allows a tradition to emerge: even in his lifetime
he rewrote other people's stories, and August Derleth completed
Lovecraft's unfinished works after the author's death. The essential
element thus emerges which constitutes the industrial processes
within which Lovecraft tales exist. Always different, 'Lovecraft's'
stories (whoever writes them: Colin Wilson, Robert Bloch, August
Derleth) are, at the same time, always the same: they reflect the
need for a production-line process and an unchanging product in
an unchanging world – a world whose unchangingness reassures
as it terrifies. But it is a world where the production process is
always out of control. For Lovecraft it invaded his dreams:

> The death of my grandmother plunged me into a gloom from
> which I never fully recovered. . . . I began to have nightmares
> of the most hideous description, peopled with *things* which I
> called 'nightgaunts' – a compound word of my own coinage.[23]

Lovecraft's monsters enjoy a horribly easy reduplication of bodily
parts which are animal but function unnaturally. Lovecraft's
nightmare was of 'things' which had a life of their own – things

which act quasi-humanly in his stories. Lovecraft's nightmares are about the products of the production line – things with their own history: a production line that he exorcised and reproduced in his fiction.

Notes

1. Lin Carter, *Lovecraft: A Look behind the Cthulhu Mythos* (London: Panther, 1975) p. 21.
2. Ibid.
3. Colin Wilson, Introduction to George Hay (ed.), *The Necronomicon* (London: Corgi, 1980) p. 22.
4. Ibid., p. 149.
5. Quoted in David Punter, *The Literature of Terror* (London: Longman, 1980) p. 285.
6. Carter, *Lovecraft*, pp. 35–6.
7. Ibid., p. 23.
8. Ibid., pp. 52–3.
9. Ibid., p. 82.
10. Ibid., p. 56.
11. Ibid., p. 57.
12. Ibid., p. 58.
13. Punter, *The Literature of Terror*, p. 285.
14. Ibid., p. 282.
15. Quoted in George E. Mowry (ed.), *The Twenties* (Englewood Cliffs, NJ: Prentice-Hall, 1963) p. 155.
16. Ibid., pp. 137–9.
17. Ibid., p. 146.
18. Quoted in Carter, *Lovecraft*, p. 82.
19. Ibid., p. 129.
20. Stephen King, *Danse Macabre* (London: Futura, 1986) p. 45.
21. Ibid., p. 17.
22. Punter, *The Literature of Terror*, p. 288.
23. Carter, *Lovecraft*, p. 25.

5

The Evidence of Things Seen and Unseen: William Faulkner's *Sanctuary*

DAVID SEED

When a new edition of *Sanctuary* was published by Random House in 1932 it carried a new introduction by Faulkner in which he claimed that he had written the novel hastily as a pot-boiler. This cynical claim has now been disproved in every detail by subsequent Faulkner scholarship, but one assertion made in the Introduction still gives us a clue to the effects Faulkner was aiming for: '[I] invented the most horrific tale I could imagine'.[1] The means he chose for evoking this horror was a sexual melodrama based partly on symbolism and partly on a complex plot structure which retards the revelation of key events (rape and murder) for as long as possible. *Sanctuary* plays constantly on the notions of disclosure and concealment, building up suspense through a series of narrative surges towards revelation. Not only is the chronology of the plot reordered from a simple linear sequence, but narration is built into the plot to such an extent that in virtually every episode a character has a story to tell. This urge is nowhere more plain than in the first major character we meet in the novel, the lawyer Horace Benbow.

Benbow's notional role in the novel as lawyer enables Faulkner to place him in scenes as either witness or investigator. In other words he acts as a structural convenience in being the 'man who links the different milieux in his attempt to impose order on a lawless and corrupt society'.[2] From a professional point of view his actions in taking care of Ruby and defending Goodwin are suicidal: they alienate the townspeople and his sister, and end in failure. It is much more important to note that Benbow has a novelist's interest in the characters, seeking to draw out the 'irony that lurks in events' and using the elongated participial sentences characteristic of Faulkner's other narratives. When Benbow describes Ruby to his sister, the descriptive phrases mime his sympathy but without conclusion: 'Asking nothing of anyone except to be let alone, trying to make something out of her life when all you sheltered chaste women – .'[3] Benbow's Quixotic belief in honour is offset by an inability to bring himself to denounce the sexual hypocrisy of the socially chaste, and leaves unresolved a tension between observation and involvement. His tortuous sentences contrast strongly with the narrator's deadpan notation of action and appearance, and suggest a self-involvement brought out in the opening chapters.

Benbow is the precursor. The first three chapters take him through a sequence which anticipates Temple Drake's, since he is in flight from his wife, finds himself quite by chance at the Old Frenchman place and spends a night there. He establishes his credentials through literary comparison (linking Popeye with Emma Bovary's death agony) and a literary talisman (he is carrying a book and therefore is identified by Popeye as a 'professor'); more importantly, Benbow uses the occasion to narrate the story of his unsuccessful relationship with his wife Belle. This story charges Nature itself with sexuality in an annual cycle of 'conspiracy between female flesh and female season'. The image haunting his memory is a hammock, which – like the swing in *The Sound and the Fury* – functions as a sexual trysting-place for his stepdaughter, Little Belle. She dresses in innocent white but has many relations with the opposite sex. On the basis of this implied hypocrisy and the supposed duplicity of his wife, Benbow projects his sexual fears into Nature, which he identifies as the feminine root of all evil. His journey across the delta country is thus a flight from sexuality itself, though he finds some relief by telling his story to the uncomprehending bootleggers at the Old Frenchman place. The only person to pay attention to it is Ruby the ex-prostitute, who responds first with disgust and then, as he addresses her directly, with gestures of revelation (of her hands, her baby, and so on), which come to nothing. An explanatory mannerism used repeatedly by Benbow – the phrase 'you see' – draws our attention unobtrusively to a major theme in the novel: what is seen and what isn't, and how far seeing is related to comprehension.

When *Sanctuary* was first published the reviewer Philip E. Wheelwright noted that the most dominant character was Popeye and that 'his primary symbol is the eye'.[4] Eyes receive particular attention by Faulkner as stylised objects: Popeye's are compared to rubber knobs, the blind old man's to clots of phlegm, and so on. The eye is thus thrown into prominence as an object of no visual depth, an object to be looked *at* rather than *from*. In traditional Gothic fiction the hero–villain's Miltonic power is signalled through eyes which flash with power and which exert a mesmeric force over those with whom they come in contact. In *Sanctuary* eyes function, rather, to render ambivalent what is seen. Tommy's eyes, for instance, glow in the dark as if to indicate an animal-like sexual excitement; and Temple's are compared to 'holes burned with a cigar', in an analogy which reduces her entirely to the victim of sadistic assault.

The novel opens with one man covertly observing another, and this image sets the keynote for the book's exploitation of concealment and observation. In this way Faulkner brilliantly manages the suspense of the critical chapters leading up to Temple's rape (4–13). Temple herself is defined as a public spectacle, a figure watched enviously by the town boys with a consciousness which dilates her pupils until her eyes are all black. When the car carrying her and Gowan Stevens crashes onto its side, her first impression is of two men watching her from behind a screen of cane. From this point onwards looking becomes a sexual act, a prelude to more aggressive physical appropriation. Predictably, the one character at the Old Frenchman place who does not gaze at Temple is Ruby, who, on the contrary, attacks her appearance. By calling her a 'doll-faced slut' Ruby obliterates the literary image of Temple as a suffering innocent. Elizabeth M. Kerr has rightly called Temple a 'modern [i.e. inverted] version of the Persecuted Maiden'.[5] This is yet another way in which Faulkner diverges from the pattern of Gothic fiction. Instead of categorising Temple as an innocent victim he repeatedly hints at a coquettish self-consciousness on her part, a consciousness of being seen as a sexual object which she simultaneously rejects (pulling her skirt down, for example) and invites (her key piece of personal equipment is her powder-compact and mirror). Ruby – referred to repeatedly as 'the woman', to contrast her with the child-like Temple – angrily senses this and attacks Temple's exploitation of appearance.

As dusk falls and the house darkens, Temple's fears increase and her behaviour becomes outwardly more ambivalent: she adopts a fixed grin (placatory?) or freezes her features into an expression of coquetry. Once again Faulkner weaves variations on traditional means of evoking terror. Temple finds a momentary refuge in a corner: 'Immediately she stopped [crying] and ceased breathing. Something was moving beyond the wall against which she leaned. It crossed the room with minute, blundering sounds, preceded by a dry rapping. It emerged into the hall and she screamed . . .' p. 213). By limiting the perspective to Temple's, Faulkner builds up a suspense where uncertainty (the repeated pronoun 'it' keeps the creature's identity open) blends powerfully with threat, building up to a climactic moment of exposure signalled by the release of Temple's scream. It is only after the figure passes that it can be revealed as the old man and thereby defused as a threat. Darkness disables Temple into a state of utter helplessness, rendering her as blind as the old man and introducing Ruby's temporary role as saviour. Chapter 9 positions her in the bedroom, where Temple is lying beside the drunken Stevens. Once again attracting an audience, Temple – unknown to herself – is being observed by Ruby, Popeye and Tommy, although the room is in total darkness. Ruby's consciousness registers the arrival of the two men through tenuous physical hints – smell and a luminous quality in Tommy's eyes. It is she who decides to move Temple outside to the barn, to another room in total darkness, where she has to guide her step by step. Darkness heightens Temple's shrinking terror of the rats in the barn and, more importantly, gives her (and the reader) a margin to imagine what is going to happen next. In other words, darkness maximises our sense of imminence, our sense of impending rape.

At this point we need to note how carefully Faulkner manipulates our expectations of a climax, which are set up partly by our sense of the familiarity of Temple's situation – vulnerable young girl isolated in a ruined house – and partly by the repeated references by characters to whores and sex in general. Instead of having one figure of threat, Faulkner introduces five (Tommy, Van, Goodwin, Popeye and the old man), so that Temple's panic is compounded by an uncertainty over whom to fear most. The surges in her panic correspond approximately to the local climaxes which conclude chapters 5, 6 and 9. Again and again Faulkner leads us towards the expected rape only to defuse the tension. In the passage quoted above, the old man is introduced as possible assailant and then ruled out just before the conclusion of the chapter, where Goodwin discovers Temple. At the beginning of chapter 8, Van makes his first sexual approaches to her during supper; he follows them up when the men bring the drunken Stevens to her room. Finally, in chapter 9 Popeye and Tommy come to the forefront as candidates. Traditionally the gaps between the chapters of novels are used for implying action of no great significance to the main plot. Thus between chapters 2 and 3 of *Sanctuary* Benbow travels to his sister's house. Chapter endings, however, are also traditionally used to arrest action at a point of maximum suspense and to exploit the reader's sense of what is likely to happen next. So at the end of chapter 7 Goodwin's discovery of Temple *might* be a prelude to rape. In fact it is not. In the gap between chapters 9 and 10 (the night) once again Temple *might* be attacked, but once again she is not. Darkness and confinement do introduce the rape of Antonia in Matthew Lewis's *The Monk*, for example, but Faulkner varies the generic pattern, setting up scenes nearer and nearer to rape while deferring the event itself.

The visual shift from night to day, from darkness to visibility, defuses the tension in Temple's situation, but prematurely. Threat has not disappeared; its expression has simply become more complex. Whereas previously we noted examples of characters looking at others, we now encounter intersecting angles of vision, as in the following passage (with emphasis added):

> Before he reached the house Popeye left the road and followed a wooded slope. When he emerged he *saw* Goodwin standing behind a tree in the orchard, *looking* toward the barn. Popeye stopped at the edge of the wood and *looked* at Goodwin's back. He put another cigarette into his mouth and thrust his fingers into his vest. He went on across the orchard, walking gingerly. Goodwin heard him and *looked* over his shoulder. Popeye took a match from his vest, flicked it into flame and lit the cigarette. Goodwin *looked* towards the barn again and Popeye stood at this shoulder, *looking* towards the barn.   (pp. 246–7)

By this stage in the novel looking has been firmly established as an expression of sexual purpose. The narrator scrupulously refuses to comment on this scene, assembling converging perspectives on a sexual focus (Temple in the barn) and describing physical attitude in such a way that the reader's angle of vision (already implicated in watching Temple) includes Popeye's and Goodwin's. First we look *at* them; then we look *from* them. And the visual direction expresses the purpose of the narrative at this point. Just as all eyes are directed towards the barn, so the plot seems obviously to be taking Temple towards assault. Tantalisingly, the long-expected climax comes but is left undescribed, in the hiatus between chapters 13 and 14. Similarly, when Temple later leaves Miss Reba's and goes to a dance hall with Popeye, her sexual activity leads up to another climax and that too occurs in a gap, between chapters 24 and 25.

The tension in the chapters just discussed grows out of the shock effect of sudden sights and playing off the seen against the unseen. Temple is repeatedly described as a visual sexual object, especially in the scene where Tommy peers through the window at her while she undresses. Does she like him? The text is ambiguous and, besides, it is more important that Temple takes off her dress and then puts on not just one coat but two. This scene defines a characteristic rhythm in the sections of the book dealing with Temple – an alternation between revelation and concealment. The obvious purpose in the men's gaze is to unclothe her, to expose her; and the equally obvious purpose in most of Temple's actions is to resist this. By putting on two coats and drawing the bed quilt up to her chin she is multiplying concealment, but the direction of the plot is to strip the layers away. When she receives medical attention at Miss Reba's in Memphis, Temple is exposed; when Benbow presses her to tell her story, she is exposed again; and, when she has to tell it yet again in open court, the exposure is complete. Her attempts at resisting this process (pressing her legs together, hiding under bedclothes, speaking in a very low voice) are all ineffectual and, as we shall see, ambivalent. By leaving her rape undescribed Faulkner does not collude with Temple's privacy, since each new exposure is tantamount to a re-enactment of the initial deed. The symbolism of doors and rooms plays a part in this issue and draws attention to the possible meanings in the novel's title. The Old Frenchman place functions as a sanctuary to its inhabitants, but during her stay there Temple is seen in almost constant flight. The characteristic verbs attached to her movements ('sprang', 'whirled', 'ran') suggest panic and shock as she hunts for safety in different rooms. Doors can either shut out or shut in, and we alternately see Temple closing them in self-defence (she repeatedly bolts her door at Miss Reba's) or scrabbling frantically to open them. Again and again rooms prove to offer a spurious sanctuary and Temple is constantly looking for adequate means of self-protection. Ironically, the very details of her appearance which give her a feeling of security – the mask-like make-up, the 'savage' bow of her lipstick, and her flimsy dress – stimulate the sexual attraction which threatens that security. The title suggests a dimension of meaning in Temple's name which renders the self a spatial area liable to sexual invasion.

As Temple comes under threat, panic leaves her speechless. This is a perfectly plausible physical reaction but one which bears on Gothic fiction's engagement with the inexpressible. E. K. Sedgwick has explained it as a linguistic lapse: 'The unspeakable here is an interpersonal barrier where no barrier ought to be – language is properly just the medium that should flow between people, mitigating their physical and psychic separateness – but once this barrier has come into being, it is breached only at the cost of violence and deepened separateness.'[6] Faulkner's use of grotesque characters emphasises their physical differences to the extent that they scarcely seem to be members of the same species, and he increases this impression by stylising the dialogue between the men at the Old Frenchman place into short Hemingwayesque exchanges repeatedly marked out by 'he said . . . he said'. Only the woman Ruby is verbally articulate. In the case of the men, words repeatedly give way to a language of gesture. Even Tommy's body becomes energised with an expressive force: his eyes glow, his feet 'whisper', his hands 'writhe'. At the climactic point where Temple's rape begins, her frenzy is articulated through impotent verbalisation:

> She could hear silence in a thick rustling as he moved toward her through it, thrusting it aside, and she began to say Something is going to happen to me. She was saying it to the old man with the yellow clots for eyes. 'Something is happening to me!' she screamed at him, sitting in his chair in the sunlight, his hands crossed on the top of the stick. 'I told you it was!' she screamed, voiding the words like hot silent bubbles into the bright silence about them until he turned his head and the two phlegm-clots above her where she lay tossing and thrashing on the rough, sunny boards. 'I told you! I told you all the time!' (p. 250)

Whereas Ruby earlier could tell her story to Temple, Temple now reaches new heights of terror because she lacks an audience. This moment represents one of the many nightmare effects identified by William Rossky, who locates the novel's power in the 'dreamlike images and scenes in which the principals – and the readers – are caught in a clotting motion, in a paralysis, or near-paralysis, of helpless terror'.[7] For Rossky, this effect of stasis helps to explain the inevitability of the plot and the characters' helplessness. In contrast to Faulkner's comment that 'life is motion', these early chapters of *Sanctuary*, appropriately set in an inert ruin, repeatedly arrest movement so as to prolong suspense.[8] As Popeye gradually penetrates the space between himself and Temple, she begins to 'explain' her experience to a blind deaf-mute whose placid immobility makes a travesty of human communication. Temple's words sink to the purely physiological level of bubbles, linking in anticipation with a beheaded negro's wife whose 'bubbling throat' grotesquely expresses her doom. While words collapse as an efficient means of communication, 'blood' intermittently takes over as an alternative sub-language with its own syntax, suggesting not, as in many of Faulkner's novels, inheritance but rather the compulsions of sexual energy. Hence the significant detail that the syphilitic Popeye's face has a 'bloodless' colour.

Temple's loss of voice at a point of crisis is only a temporary problem, since by chapter 23 she has become capable of telling her own story with an astonishingly impersonal gusto. This narrative not only confirms some of the reader's suspicions (although the part played by the corn cob is not made absolutely explicit until Goodwin's trial), but also takes Temple through a series of psychic transformations as she seeks for ways to avoid the present. She imagines herself variously as a boy, as wearing a chastity belt, as a dead bride and as a middle-aged teacher, until finally she lapses into unconsciousness. More evidence is thus given to the reader of Temple's ambivalence about her age and gender. At some points in the novel Faulkner takes pains to stress that she is not quite a woman, and she confirms this by regressing into child-like behaviour. Miss Reba's comment that 'Temple' is a man's name anticipates her own gender fantasy, and she even starts making sexual overtures to Popeye, calling him 'Daddy'. Ruby's description of Temple as 'putty-face' now becomes indicative of a sexual identity as yet inchoate and unformed.

It should be obvious by now that the sources of horror in *Sanctuary* are insistently sexual. The novel sets Temple's rape within the broad context of a social system which tries to maintain a hard-and-fast separation between gentility and wickedness. Faulkner implies that such a separation is unfeasible, repressive and hypocritical; and establishes these implications through a process of reduction. Temple's escort, Gowan Stevens, adopts the pose of a Virginia gentleman, a pose which is rudely shattered as he turns into a drunken, dishevelled wreck over the weekend when Temple is raped. His speech becomes as fragmented as his self-image reflected in the surface of the spring, at which point he leaves the action and the novel. His mock-Homeric fate on drinking the local home brew is to be turned into a 'pig'. Other characters are compared to animals, and Temple at one point finds herself on all fours confronting a rat. The stress on animal appetites deromanticises the action and makes it impossible to read the plot as the corruption of an innocent. To reinforce this effect Faulkner repeatedly compares Temple to a mechanical doll, showing how little conscious control she has over her own movements and making her the marionette of her own physical impulses. The coda to the novel places her and her father in the Luxembourg Gardens; as she passively watching the passers-by, her immobility reflects her inability to take decisive action.

The houses of *Sanctuary* also question the maintenance of gentility. The Old Frenchman place is not just a hired setting but is reverting back to jungle, and therefore seems to make a sharp contrast with Narcissa's house. When Benbow tries to accommodate Ruby in the town house which he owns jointly with his sister, Narcissa sees this as a pollution, a sexual defilement, so that Ruby has to find refuge first in the jail and then in the ruinous hovel of a woman who sells magic charms. *Sanctuary* inverts decorous social values so that, the more disreputable the dwelling, the more likely hospitality is to be found in it. When Benbow remembers how recently the streets of Jefferson were paved, he is in effect reminding the reader of how precarious is the division between the cultural and the natural. In fact the very term 'house' becomes totally ambiguous. Miss Reba's brothel is in a street of 'equivocal' appearance, and the interior of Temple's room is described entirely in terms of tawdry disguising surfaces. The enclosed stagnant space of this room resembles the 'dead pools' in Benbow's Jefferson house, where every detail of the furnishing suggests an attempt to imitate the decorous and, when this attempt breaks down, to patch up appearances. If even the terminology of dwelling becomes ambiguous, appearances may be misread – as they are, to comic effect, in chapter 21. Two Snopes brothers, two country hicks, arrive in Memphis and absurdly misinterpret the appearance of Miss Reba's, concluding that it is a hotel. Whereas

Temple, staying in the same building, bolts her door against the sexual activities going on around her, the brothers lack the necessary social awareness to interpret correctly what they see.

A much grimmer form of comedy characterises an episode where social decorum should be at its height – the funeral of the bootlegger Red. At the beginning Faulkner is careful to stress the mimicry of the respectable: the older women (presumably former prostitutes) are matronly figures resembling housewives on a Sunday afternoon excursion. As the drink is consumed the decorous surface slips and the occasion breaks down into a rough-house in which the corpse is knocked over:

> When they raised the corpse the wreath came too, attached to him by a hidden end of wire driven into his cheek. He had worn a cap which, tumbling off, exposed a small blue hole in the centre of his forehead. It had been neatly plugged with wax and was painted, but the wax had been jarred out and lost. They couldn't find it, but by unfastening the snap in the peak, they could draw the cap down to his eyes.   (p. 351)

This grotesque image brilliantly exploits an apparently neutral prose style which carefully enumerates its descriptive details with impassive accuracy. Within the context of looking, however, this image takes on extra significance as an exposure. The wreath, plug and cap are exactly those objects used to disguise the corpse and give it an appearance of peaceful slumber, and their removal mimes out in miniature the process which spreads through chapter 25 and for that matter the whole novel. Faulkner forces the reader to confront an image of violent death, to see beneath the corpse's 'dress'. The exposure of the bullet hole in this way corresponds to the gradual collapse of decorum at the funeral and at Miss Reba's, an episode which drew grudging praise from Henry Seidel Canby for its 'prosaic horror'.[9] Temple Drake is a member of one social world suddenly placed in a quite different context, and Faulkner satirically undermines the distinction between the two worlds by showing how the one imitates the other and how the 'reputable' world tries to put the 'disreputable' out of sight. Senator Clarence Snopes leeringly articulates this point of view when he tells Benbow that it is quite understandable for a man to have one house for his wife and another for sexual 'exercise'. The particular targets of this satire are the town Baptists, but Faulkner implies that they have no monopoly on hypocrisy.

Temple's rape then turns out to be tactical, since it takes her and the reader into 'unacceptable' areas of Southern society and enables Faulkner to question the values of that society. The polarities of purity and corruption collapse together as he establishes a context where casual obscenity surcharges actions and objects with a heightened sexual symbolism. Horace Benbow's lone voice of honour is virtually smothered by the minor characters who pass in and out of the novel only to make ribald jokes about Temple and other women. These comments are so insistent that it becomes impossible to read the narrative with innocence. There is no hard evidence of a direct influence from any of Freud's works here, but indirect influence is possible: Faulkner has gone on record as stating that 'everybody talked about Freud when I lived in New Orleans, but I have never read him'.[10] Also, in the original version of *Sanctuary* Benbow's wife Belle levels an accusation against him which confirms some familiarity with psychoanalytical theory: 'you're in love with your sister. What do the books call it? What sort of complex?'[11] The constant discussion of sex within the text and these external corroborations justify us in identifying a heavily sexual symbolism in the novel. The following examples are attached to specific symbols listed in Freud's writings on dream work (in *Introductory Lectures on Psychoanalysis* and *The Interpretation of Dreams*). Any erect or mechanical object represents the penis: when Popeye begins his assault on Temple he 'waggles' his pistol at her – like the corn cob, the pistol, which Temple herself later 'reads' as an erotic object, is a penis-substitute. A hill similarly can have phallic significance: Benbow is explicitly searching for a hill and at one point fingers his (unlit) *cob* pipe while reading Temple's name on the wall of a lavatory. Shoes and slippers can represent the female genitals: on the way to the house Tommy takes one of Temple's shoes and thrusts his fingers inside. Rooms can represent woman and therefore doors suggest the genital orifice: Temple is repeatedly trying to bolt doors for self-protection, but, when Popeye finally catches her alone, the door of the room 'yawns' open as if to underline her sexual vulnerability. Finally blossoms are, Freud reminds us, the 'genitals of plants' and arouse a particular disgust in Benbow and Temple; as the latter walks through undergrowth the weeds are 'slashing at her with huge, moist, malodorous blossoms' (p. 242).[12]

This list could be extended considerably, and the introduction of such symbolism at points of sexual intensity suggests some familiarity with Freud's descriptions of psychic processes. Indeed Temple's naïvely honest narration to Benbow resembles the confession of a patient to her therapist. Faulkner had already used such symbolism in *The Sound and the Fury*, where Quentin's suicide is motivated by a horror of having committed incest with his sister Caddy. In his section of the novel he attempts to walk back into his childhood, progressively uncovering deeper and deeper levels of repressed memory until, at the point of maximum emotional pressure after being accused of assaulting a little girl, he remembers a suicide pact with Caddy. This transparently sexual action with his knife/phallus comes to nothing as he impotently drops it, but it is enough for him to have mimed out incestuous desire. Three characters in *Sanctuary* receive this kind of pathological attention – Temple, Popeye and Benbow. Temple's rape is presented partly as a sexual awakening which frees her uncontrollable appetite so that she indulges in incestuous flirting with Popeye and tries to play him off against Red, with the result that the latter is shot. Faulkner clearly establishes that Popeye is a psychopath, but holds back until the very end of the novel the information about his childhood which would explain his behaviour. It seems, then, that Faulkner was less interested in diagnosing origins than in investigating consequences. Temple's rape is the harshest consequence that could follow from the socially ritualised flirtations of her outings from college. It is even implied that she and Popeye 'fit' together, since they are both insistently identified through similar physical signs – their clothes and their hats worn aslant.

Horace Benbow represents a more complex case, because he both states and embodies the contagion of sexuality. He attempts to maintain distances between the images of his experience by seeing them as texts: Temple and Ruby impress him as narrators; the students he encounters on the train to Oxford are like 'printed pages'; and the photograph of his stepdaughter Little Belle refuses to remain a flat representation and takes on uncomfortably erotic attractions which Benbow tries to suppress. The most complex instance of sexual imagining occurs at the end of chapter 23, after Benbow has heard Temple's story. A variety of factors combine to induce a crisis of nausea: the sexual symbolism of the lush honeysuckle near his house (the 'voice of the night'), the 'invitation and voluptuous promise' of Little Belle, and an undigested coffee. The nausea triggers off a sequence of images:

> Then he knew what that sensation in his stomach meant. He put the photograph down hurriedly and went to the bathroom. He opened the door running and fumbled at the light. But he had not time to find it and he gave over and plunged forward and struck the lavatory and leaned upon his braced arms while the shucks set up a terrific uproar beneath her thighs. Lying with her head lifted slightly, her chin depressed like a figure lifted down from a crucifix, she watched something black and furious go roaring out of her pale body. She was bound naked on her back on a flat car moving at speed through a black tunnel, the blackness streaming in rigid threads overhead, a roar of iron wheels in her ears. The car shot bodily from the tunnel in a long upward slant, the darkness overhead now shredded with parallel attenuations of living fire, toward a crescendo like a held breath, an interval in which she would swing faintly and lazily in nothingness filled with pale, myriad points of light. Far beneath her she could hear the faint, furious uproar of the shucks. (p. 333)[13]

Benbow re-enacts Temple's rape through a travesty birth, a multiple voiding, both physical and sexual, which nightmarishly combines inner and outer dimensions to her experience. The stark colour-coding (white against black) and the figurations of Temple as helpless victim or holy icon suggest that Benbow is persisting in his attempts to idealise her away from co-operation in her rape, and contrast ironically with her rampantly sexual behaviour in the next chapter. Bizarre though it may seem, vomiting is a repeated action in *Sanctuary* which delights in juxtaposing sacred or idealised references with the profane. In spite of the physical immediacy of Benbow's nausea, he is double distanced from the original deed in re-enacting a re-enactment. Here we need to turn to the complex structure of the novel.

The original version of *Sanctuary* presents the action through a series of flashbacks in Horace Benbow's consciousness, complicating the plot by an intricate series of recalls. The first chapters firmly establish Benbow's as the main point of view, but then Faulkner shifts awkwardly to a neutral third-person narrative to recount Temple's story and the subsequent trial. The critic Noel

Polk has explained Faulkner's subsequent revisions as acting on the 'felt need to get us outside of Horace Benbow's cloyingly introspective, narcissistic personality' but then has argued elsewhere that the changes repress important material.[14] It is difficult to see what distinction there is between 'repress' and 'delete' here, since Faulkner firmly reduces Benbow's status to one perspective among others. This crucial change confirms the formal logic of the novel and makes it impossible to read it as dealing with one consciousness, thus raising a possible objection to proposing a Freudian symbolism. As the narrative perspective shifts temporarily from Benbow to Gavin Stevens, Popeye, the townsfolk and others, the novel develops a more social emphasis and turns its attention to society's half-admitted preoccupation with sex. From the very beginning, appearances have sexual implications: for instance, the locals glimpse Temple's underclothes on her regular evening outings, and she is seen as 'predatory' on these occasions (although the blankness of her eyes would deter us from inferring self-consciousness on her part). Redeploying Freud's distinction between the manifest and latent content of dreams, we may distinguish between explicit and implicit areas of significance in the text. If we take the example of Tommy's handling of Temple's shoe, on the most superficial level it shows curiosity. As we move away from the superficial, the action becomes progressively more erotic. The shoe is, after all, an item of dress, and Faulkner constantly stresses that clothes and make-up constitute Temple's erotic appeal (her actual body is 'match-like'). While the shoe can function metonymically without damaging the naturalistic surface of events, it also symbolises the ultimate goal of the sexual attraction which Temple stimulates – her genitals – and this symbolism helps to build up the narrative suspense before her rape. In anticipation, Temple is raped several times through metaphorical figures of penetration and opening-out (Tommy's fingers in the shoe, Popeye looking through a hole into the barn loft, and so on). Thus, when Van tears open her coat and is then fought off by Goodwin, the initial action constitutes one such assault and the sequel signifies the precarious maintenance of a decorum which is constantly on the verge of breaking down.

Faulkner repeatedly plays on the puns of sexual slang ('slit', 'punch', and so forth) to draw the reader's attention to erotic metaphor. Since these metaphors are all bawdy, it seems that in *Sanctuary* the surface levels of linguistic meaning correspond to the decorous gloss society attempts to apply to sexual activity, and deeper metaphorical levels reveal the crude workings of that appetite which society imperfectly recognises. The subsequent trial of Goodwin and his lynching show society acting collectively to suppress consciousness of the anarchic energy betokened by the blood-stained corn cob. Needless to say, this does not end the novel, or is it an efficient action, since it is directed against the wrong person. Even more importantly, it does not begin to cope with the attraction the trial holds for the townsfolk. Faulkner's indignation at their hypocrisy emerges through the novel's persistent association of sexuality with disease, waste and death; and this perhaps realise in fictional terms a feeling of disgust he had registered in 1925 when comparing French and American sexual *mores*:

> After having observed Americans in Europe I believe more than ever that sex with us has become a national disease. The way we get it into our politics and religion, where it does not belong anymore than digestion belongs there. All our paintings, our novels, our music, is concerned with it, sort of leering and winking and rubbing our hands on it. But Latin people keep it where it belongs, in a secondary place.[15]

We have already seen how the narrative voice of *Sanctuary* adopts a deadpan tone to avoid commenting on events, thereby distinguishing its attitude from that of the townsfolk. But on the other hand the novel obliges us to develop an awareness of sexual implication which prevents us from maintaining a detachment from the narrative.

If the novel's focus becomes more and more social, then we should note that Faulkner is conflating at least two different genres in *Sanctuary*: the novel of horror and the detective story. Joseph Blotner has shown that Faulkner was reading mystery stories during the period when he was working on the novel, and concludes that it is an exercise in the same genre. The changes which were made to the manuscript were thus designed to 'heighten suspense and emphasize action'.[16] We have already seen examples of Faulkner diverging from the Gothic pattern, though after setting up enough resemblances for the divergences to be identifiable as such. The emphatic association of Popeye with blackness and death, for instance, is traditional enough; and the use of a victim–heroine who turns into an aggressive vamp is reminiscent of *Dracula*. The use of hiatuses in the narrative and of limited points of view (perhaps influenced by Conrad, whom Faulkner read and admired) both heigthen suspense, as Blotner suggests, and invite the reader to fill those gaps retospectively. On the publication of *Sanctuary* Granville Hicks noted that it 'forces the reader to reconstruct from piecemeal evidence the actual nature and sequence of events'.[17] In this respect it follows the method of Faulkner's earlier novels, but Hicks noted with approval that the process of reconstruction was much easier in *Sanctuary*. Hicks's use of the term 'evidence' and my own forensic title are relevant here, because the novel may be read on one level as a mystery thriller. It is as if Faulkner combined the two sides of Poe, the melodramatic and the ratiocinative, to produce a novel which straddles the two genres. A considerable part of the action shows the working-out of the due process of law in the trials of Goodwin and Popeye, but in each case a wrong conviction results.

Once again Horace Benbow has a role to play in establishing a naïve perspective on events which those events actually under-mine. Goodwin's trial becomes a spectacle to which the townsfolk flock to hear the sordid details of the rape. Largely on Temple's evidence (which we know to be false) Goodwin is convicted and the jail is burnt to the ground. At the height of this fire, when Benbow is seized and almost lynched, he registers a hallucinatory sense of panic as the fire burns with a 'voice of fury like in a dream, roaring silently out of a peaceful void' (p. 384). The imagery of chaos (containing perhaps a glance at Faulkner's earlier novel *The Sound and the Fury*) paradoxically combines opposites in another usurpation of human linguistic activity. The fire has a voice which feeds on itself, articulating the collapse of a legal process which has already gone awry in the trial verdict and which will ironically misfire again when Popeye is tried and convicted for the wrong murder. The fire at the jail signals Benbow's failure in his search for truth and his submissive return to his wife and domestic conformity, but more is involved here than an individual's fate. One purpose of a trial is to put together partial information to assemble a coherent narrative of a crime. In other words, the trial of Goodwin may be read as an experiment in plot assembly which fails. In the detective genre, as Peter Brooks explains, 'the narrative chain, with each event connected to the next by reasoned causal links, marks the victory of reason over chaos, of society over the aberrancy of crime'.[18] This is exactly what does *not* happen in *Sanctuary*. The danger in allegorising the characters – of seeing Popeye as the 'quintessence of evil', for instance – is that such readings run the risk of making the ending of the novel sound too positive and final.[19] The death of Popeye is a judicial mistake, a hint that a coherent narrative chain has not been formed and a hint too that the legal categories of innocence and guilt will not quite fit the facts.

The trials in *Sanctuary*, and that of Goodwin in particular, do not demonstrate the working-out of justice or the triumph of rationality. Rather they underline the violence within town life. Faulkner has already conditioned the reader to accept a lot of casual verbal violence: a track is a 'scar', a building is 'slashed' with light, and so on. *Sanctuary* may be divided into four sections each of which ends with a death (those of Tommy, Red, Goodwin and Popeye), and the distinction between the first two and the subsequent ones blurs when we remember that both Goodwin and Popeye are convicted in error. The righteous anger of the townsfolk which leads them to set the fire constitutes a hypocritical denial of their own desire to rape Temple, which Faulkner points out clearly in chapter 4. The novel is, in other words, based on concealment, and in this it resembles Faulkner's story 'Dry September', which describes the lynching of a negro suspected of molesting a local spinster. Fire figures in this story too, but only as a metaphor of the rising anger against the negro; and concealment, or rather self-deception, emerges through the elaborate set of euphemisms the men use to gloss over the nature of their action in that story. The other function of Goodwin's trial is to question the nature of the reader's reaction to events. Faulkner has used angles of vision to implicate the reader in voyeurism and a vicariously sadistic interest in Temple's fate. When it is revealed that Popeye himself watched while Temple had sex with Red, the reader is implicitly drawn into the perspective of a murderous psychopath. And, since the angle of vision in the trial is from the spectators towards Temple, essentially recapitulating the images which open chapter 4, the reader is involved in the perspective of the very townsfolk whom Faulkner has been mocking for their hypocrisy.

If Temple and Popeye do represent principles, allegorical figures of sexuality and violence, the death of Popeye does not purge the novel of violence or evil, since Faulkner has repeatedly implied a common desire among the local menfolk to violate Temple. Popeye simply enacts in a grotesque form the longed-for sexual attack. The novel's repeated linkage of sex with violence establishes an inevitability in the meeting between Temple and Popeye which has nothing to do with their 'character' or even with plot plausibility; it is after all an accident which forces Temple and Stevens to stay at the Old Frenchman place. The action of the novel may be seen as a means of making explicit the verbal and physical innuendoes which pack the sexual transactions of the town, and of showing what happens when the restraining decorum imposed by social *mores* and the legal system is temporarily transgressed. The last six chapters thus represent an attempt to reimpose that decorum, however hollow the attempt might seem to the reader, for town society has been shown to be riddled with hypocrisy, and the legal–political system has been shown, through Clarence Snopes, to be full of corruption.

Notes

1. William Faulkner, 'Introduction to Modern Library Edition of *Sanctuary*, 1932', in James B. Meriwether (ed.), *Essays, Speeches and Public Letters* (London: Chatto and Windus, 1967) p. 177.
2. Douglas Tallack, 'William Faulkner and the Tradition of Tough-Guy Fiction', in Larry N. Landrum, Pat Browne, and Ray B. Browne (eds), *Dimensions of Detective Fiction* (Bowling Green, Ohio: Popular Press, 1976) p. 260.
3. William Faulkner, *Novels 1930–1935: As I Lay Dying, Sanctuary, Light in August, Pylon*, ed. Noel Polk (New York: Library of America, 1986) p. 260. This edition contains the only reliable text of the novel. Subsequent page references are given in the text.
4. John Bassett (ed.), *William Faulkner: The Critical Heritage* (London: Routledge and Kegan Paul, 1975) p. 112.
5. Elizabeth M. Kerr, *William Faulkner's Gothic Domain* (Port Washington, NY: Kennikat Press, 1979) p. 93. Other obvious traces of traditional Gothic include the ruined mansion and the villain (Popeye) dressed in black.
6. Eve Kosofsky Sedgwick, *The Coherence of Gothic Conventions* (London: Methuen, 1986) p. 16.
7. William Rossky, 'The Pattern of Nightmare in *Sanctuary*; or, Miss Reba's Dogs', *Modern Fiction Studies*, 15 (1969–70) 505.
8. *Writers at Work: The 'Paris Review' Interviews* (London: Secker and Warburg, 1958) p. 125.
9. Bassett, *Faulkner: The Critical Heritage*, p. 109.
10. *Writers at Work*, p. 123.

11. William Faulkner, *Sanctuary: The Original Text*, ed. Noel Polk (London: Chatto and Windus, 1981) p. 16.
12. Sigmund Freud, *Introductory Lectures on Psychoanalysis* (Harmondsworth: Penguin, 1973) p. 192.
13. In this astonishing passage Benbow appropriates Temple's consciousness to himself in a fantasy incursion as the pronoun shifts into the feminine. The birth/voiding image then reverses from a black figure on a white ground into the opposite as 'Temple' becomes what she sees.
14. Faulkner, *Sanctuary: The Original Text*, p. 300; Noel Polk, 'The Space between *Sanctuary*', in Michel Gresset and Noel Polk (eds), *Intertextuality in Faulkner* (Jackson: University Press of Mississippi, 1985) p. 25.
15. *Selected Letters of William Faulkner*, ed. Joseph Blotner (New York: Random House, 1977) p. 24.
16. Joseph Blotner, *Faulkner: A Biography* (New York: Random House, 1974) I, 610. On Faulkner's use of the Gothic genre see Kerr, *Faulkner's Gothic Domain*, ch. 5; and on his use of the hard-boiled genre see Tallack, 'William Faulkner and the Tradition of Tough-Guy Fiction', in Landrum *et al.*, *Dimensions of Detective Fiction*, pp. 247–64.
17. Bassett, *Faulkner: The Critical Heritage*, p. 122.
18. Peter Brooks, 'Psychoanalytic Constructions and Narrative Meanings', *Paragraph*, 7 (1986) 54.
19. Joanne V. Creighton, 'Self-Destructive Evil in *Sanctuary*', *Twentieth Century Literature*, 18 (1972) 261.

6

Robert Bloch's *Psycho*: Some Pathological Contexts

DAVID PUNTER

Of all the horror myths which have sunk into the Western unconscious during the twentieth century, *Psycho* is one of the most powerful, although principally in its manifestation in Hitchcock's film. Here I want to say a little about Robert Bloch's original story, published in 1959, and to put some specific questions about it. It needs to be noted at the outset that this is an odd and difficult task, because of a peculiarity in the story itself: which is that it contains its own psychological explanation, attached near the end as an authenticated account by a psychiatrist of a series of events which were, in fact, closely based on real incidents.

In Bloch's *Psycho*, Mary Crane, engaged to marry Sam Loomis but compelled to wait because of Sam's financial problems, steals $40,000 and drives off to join him. On the way she stops at a lonely motel, run by Norman Bates and his sick mother. Bates rents her a room which is connected by a peephole to his own office. Observing her undress and go into the shower, he starts to drink while meditating on the dirtiness of women, and briefly passes out.

When he wakes up, he sees that she has been brutally murdered, and concludes that only his mother could have done it. To protect her, he disposes of the body. Meanwhile, Sam is disturbed at his hardware store by the arrival of Lila, Mary's younger sister, who is searching for Mary; and they are simultaneously visited by Arbogast, a private detective hunting for the stolen money, who has tracked Mary this far but has not found her.

Arbogast discovers the motel, the last on his list, and suspects Bates. While Arbogast goes up to the house behind the motel where Bates and his mother live, a worried Bates again starts to drink and passes out; and, when he too heads for the house, he finds Arbogast also killed, and goes through the same procedure to protect his mother from the consequences of her deranged crimes.

When Arbogast does not return to town, Lila persuades Sam to come with her to the motel, where they book into the room Mary had occupied and discover enough to make them suspect Bates of murder. They plan for Sam to keep Bates in conversation while Lila goes off to phone for help. Bates is again drinking, and as he continues he tells Sam something of the truth. However, before Sam can act, Bates knocks him out, after having warned him that, instead of going for the sheriff, Lila has gone up to the house, where she is searching on her own for further clues.

We next switch to Lila, who explores the house, discovering Bates's bedroom (he still sleeps in a cot) and also the mother's bedroom, which is oddly untouched although the bed itself bears traces of recent occupancy. She eventually goes down to the cellar and, while searching it, discovers instruments of the taxidermist's craft (we already know of this hobby of Bates's). She then hears footsteps overhead and, in her panic, accidentally finds herself in an inner room.

Within it, she finds to her horror the decomposed corpse of Bates's mother, and screams, 'Mrs Bates!' An answer comes – not from the corpse but from Bates himself, who is descending the cellar steps wearing his mother's clothes and wielding a knife. Before he can get to Lila, however, he is overpowered by Sam, who has conveniently come round in the nick of time.

In an aftermath, we are told that Bates's mother had in fact died some twenty years before, along with her lover. It was supposed at the time that they had made a suicide pact; Bates had been committed to hospital at the time because of his supposed grief. However, it emerges that Bates had forged the suicide note, had himself killed the couple, and had subsequently, in a fit of remorse, exhumed his mother's body; it is this body that he has been living with ever since, and thus it is he who has killed Mary and the detective.

The psychiatrist's explanation follows, and takes fairly conventional lines, dwelling on Bates's early domination by his mother, who had conceived a morbid hatred of men when Bates's father had walked out on her shortly after the son's birth. Bates, we are told, had developed a triply fragmented personality after murdering his mother: the conventional adult who ran the motel, the child who could not escape from under his mother's thumb, and the mother herself.

In a chilling footnote, we encounter Bates in his psychiatric hospital, the previous gaps in his fragmented personality now closing as adult and son vanish into the psyche of the mother – a mother who, having been, as she says, silent for these twenty years, must now remain silent for the rest of her life, and so motionless that everybody will realise that she 'wouldn't even harm a fly'.[1]

This tale of psychic splitting is told tersely and even conventionally: the characters of the Crane sisters and Sam Loomis step straight from the pages of pulp fiction; Arbogast with his cigarettes and trilby is another avatar of Humphrey Bogart. The power lies in Bloch's ability to manipulate our uncertainties: although quite early on we learn that Bates's version of his mother's life/death does not square with other known facts, the reasons for this discrepancy remain in doubt until the *dénouement*.

There are also blurrings of boundaries: at the beginning, Bates is in conversation with his mother, and one could say that this hardly squares with external reality. But Bloch would have a ready answer for this: the personality with which he is dealing is so far disintegrated that rival accounts proliferate, and the conversation between Bates and his mother may be seen as a spur to his actions as much as anything which happens in a validatable outer world.

Psychoanalytically, though, *Psycho* is less a story of the disintegration of a personality than one of a massive attempt by the psyche to *reseal* itself; and, of course, it could be said that in this sense it depicts a successful strategy of the unconscious.[2] Faced by the strain of maintaining a multiplicity of personalities, Bates has to perform actions which will make this situation unsustainable, and will thus make possible its replacement by a forcible reunification on one side or other of the border of psychosis – which side matters little. And, again, it is no accident that this resealing takes place in a mental hospital, precisely the place where the original splitting occurred as a paradoxical effect of Bates's attempt to heal the gaps in his *outer* world through the double murder – a double murder itself replicated by the double slaying of Mary and the detective. Farther than these 'duplicities', one might say, Bates cannot go, because to encounter triplicity would be to encounter, without insulation, a replication of the pattern on which his own inner life is modelled; therefore the salvation of Lila figures as non-accidental even within the terms of the *deus ex machina* ending.

It is at this point that we may start to think more deeply about what is told in this 'tale of the unexpected', and this will involve looking not only at the 'story' itself, but also at the triple structure – account, diagnosis and aftermath–footnote – into which the book itself falls. I propose to do this by asking some questions which remain unanswered in the text, and by looking at other fictional analogies for the psychic structuring explored in *Psycho*.

THE SPUR TO ACTION

One of these questions is: why does Bates kill Mary Crane? The diagnosis does not offer an answer. It offers, indeed, an account of Bates's psychic structure and of the originating traumatic events which sparked the present shaping. It also makes suggestions as to why Bates might indeed be spurred to murderous thoughts by the sight of a woman's naked body. But we are surely not meant to suppose that, given his apparatus of peephole and adjoining rooms, this is the first opportunity for murder Bates has had in twenty years of running a motel, even if it is somewhat off the beaten track.

I believe the text offers two possible answers, without fully validating either of them. We have already alluded to one of them, which is the conversation between Bates and his 'mother' (that is, the conversation within Bates himself) at the beginning of the novel. It could be said that the tenor of this conversation suggests that Bates has had enough of his mother's dominance, and that this provides him with the impetus for the make-or-break attempt to reintegrate what has been severed within him.

But the texture of the conversation simultaneously undermines this interpretation, for we are told that this kind of interchange has occurred many times before; we are therefore enjoined by the text to see it as part of a continuing process of rememoration, and as such it cannot be considered to constitute a rupture within the traumatic structure. Certainly it illumines the tension between Bates-as-child and Bates-as-mother; but it does nothing to account for the specific slaying of Mary Crane.

The other possibility occurs, significantly, on the final page of the story, when Bates-as-mother is recalling the 'evil' of Bates-the-adult, whom she now holds responsible for the murders, 'the deaths of two innocent people – a young girl with beautiful breasts and a man who wore a gray Stetson hat'.[3] One interesting point

here is that it is a double death which is referred to, the deaths of
a man and a woman; although the deaths do not actually occur
simultaneously, we are reminded of the way in which Bates
continually supposes, once he has murdered Mary, that somebody
will turn up looking for her (although this is to impute a kind of
psychotic prescience for which there is very little other evidence);
yet Arbogast is really too shadowy and conventionalised a presence
to stand in for Joe Considine, the mother's murdered lover. Also,
the link between Arbogast and Mary is non-existent: they have
never even met.

The allusion to Mary's breasts, her physicality, is, I believe, more
interesting. It is the only such allusion in the book, although
Hitchcock, with his masterly use of 'voyeurism', emphasised Janet
Leigh's physique in the film version. Again, we would be hard-
pushed to believe that Bates has not observed a naked woman
through his peephole before; but the issue does take us back again
to the beginning, where Bates-as-mother accuses his childhood
self of being a 'Mamma's Boy', with all that implies of failed
nurturing.[4]

These images can be connected too onto Bates's drinking, his
decision to suckle himself in compensation for the mothering he
has not had. It is precisely the drinking which frees part of his
personality from constraint and, through the medium of the
blackout, allows the murderer to take over in the attempt to find
psychic unity as a sublimation for the failed unity of mother and
child. Within the complexities of Bates's attitudes to women, we
can then trace a double attitude to being nurtured: the image of
peace fatally conjoined to a rechilding and removal of personal
control.

Under these circumstances, Bates's culminating attitude towards
the feminine can only be one of absorption. He murders Mary,
and in fact decapitates her, paving the way for the moment when
his own head/mind can finally and fully become that of a woman,
a female brain to match the female attire and resolve the sexual
split. In his gaze through the peephole, he begins the process of
taking Mary inside himself; but he can only complete this cycle in an
insulated way, by permitting his 'mother' to have the (murderous)
contact which he, as child or as adult, regards as forbidden.

We thus need to see *Psycho* as a drama of the vicissitudes of the
psyche entrapped in a wish to be loved; and, more particularly, of
a male psyche caught between images of the woman-as-mother

and the woman-as-lover. Under the circumstances described, what is experienced is a mismatch between the inner and the outer, between the presumed full splendour of the 'adult' inner self, as an adolescent will often experience it, and the accidentally acne-pitted outer countenance which will render this splendid person invisible.

In Bates's case, the split is vividly displayed in transvestitism, a transvestitism which not only hides the shamed male contour from the outside world but also hides Bates's own actions from himself. The parallel which I would like to mention here is with another psychopathological novel, Patrick Süskind's *Perfume: The Story of a Murderer* (1985).

Here the protagonist, Grenouille, is again, and particularly brutally, starved of mother love: he is born and abandoned on a garbage heap, and shortly afterwards his mother is executed. But Grenouille's story is mainly oriented by Süskind's key device, which is to make him a unique master of scent and perfume, and the central trope of the story has to do with Grenouille's superior olfactory abilities. It is therefore these he uses, for two separate but linked purposes: first, to reproduce the perfume which, of all others, has most attracted him – which is, perhaps unsurprisingly, that of a pure and innocent maiden; and, second, to create a perfume which will make him, Grenouille, loved by everybody, a perfume which will convince the entire world that he is a man of the sincerest and noblest intentions.

Like Bates, then, he is in the business of taking on the outer contours of the feminine to provide him with an 'internalised' source for the love of which he has been starved; and like Bates he assumes, without the necessity of thought, that the destruction of women is the only means by which this can be achieved. What we might say about both Bates and Grenouille is that they have discovered within their own psyches images of themselves which are such frighteningly 'bad objects' that they cannot be contemplated at all, but must be covered in the feminine clothing or perfume which will simultaneously conceal this ugly, horrifying inner man from bystanders and re-create him in a form which will contain within itself the ambiguous, comforting yet destructive form of mother love that he has experienced in all his fantasies and yearnings.[5]

What is obviously confused here is the line between person and object. If the personality is split into fragments, then there may follow a tendency for that individual to perceive others as also in fragments; which on the one hand absolves him of the responsibility for treating them as persons, and on the other makes them appropriable by him as substitute parts for his own missing organs. Some of these parts, the breasts perhaps in particular, will in turn remind him precisely of the deficiencies which are motivating his own forgettings and evasions. They must thus be dealt with in some way, for there are only two possible outcomes to this psychotic splitting: psychotic reunification, as with Bates, or physical obliteration, as with Grenouille, who is finally torn apart by people precisely because he has made them love him to distraction/destruction.[6]

THE THIRD PERSON NORMAL

In the above, I have talked mostly about two of Bates's personality fragments, Bates-as-child and Bates-as-mother. But Bates has a triple personality; and alongside, or within the continuing child–mother conflict there is also Bates-as-adult, the 'normal' person who continues to feed himself, to run the motel, to gather firewood. And this prompts us to recall a third *différance* in the encounter between Bates and Mary; for we are told that she is the first, and thus only, person whom he has ever invited to the house behind the motel.

We may thus hypothesise that this penetration of the inner sanctum is the source both of intense desire and of intense fear: Bates wishes his inner secrets to be probed in at least a single flirtation with the reality principle, but at the unconscious level he also uses this invited penetration as symbolic evidence of the threat which is continually posed to his fragile personality by the outer world. Mary's presence in the house constitutes the only evidence of a 'normal' interest on Bates's part in the opposite sex; but it is precisely this moment of normality which contributes to placing the long-delayed question about stability at the forefront of his warring psyche.

What is important, I think, about this 'normal' adult within the traumatic structure is that it represents routine; and routine is the sign for a reversible mastery, the adult's mastery of outer events through prediction and reliability, and at the same time the domination of the person by events which will continue to flow in predestined ways despite the individual's attempts at control. We may thus see the 'normal' Bates as representing a midpoint of power: where Bates-as-mother and Bates-as-child stand for unresolved problems about omnipotence and domination. Bates the harmless motel-keeper stands on a conventional edge where power is actually limited and clear.

We are thus returned to the underlying symbolism of Bates's drinking, which again takes on the form of a triple sign. First, as we have seen, it forms a substitute gratification for Bates the thwarted child. Second, it forms a moment of escape from the control of the mother, both in its revolt against social convention and also in its loosening of restraint. Third, it represents, to Bates, 'normal' male adult activity, and in this sense it again returns us to the problems of control, because it stands as the sign for a habit which, so Bates thinks, is under the control of the rational mind when in fact it is vividly demonstrated to us that the mind loses its control under precisely this influence.

Bates the adult needs objects to validate his adult status; but in this respect he is a collector. He gathers firewood; he collects stuffed animals; he collects books of various kinds, including pornography, which can be seen as the motif of the collector *par excellence*. In these attempts at collection, we may see Bates as trying to establish a psychic and physical terrain of his own, away from the omniscience of his mother; we may also think metaphorically about his attempts to 'collect' himself – to get himself, as it were, all in one place at the same time.

In this respect, Bloch's portrayal of Bates is startlingly different from the Anthony Perkins portrait in the Hitchcock film. Where Perkins is dark, moody, halting, Bloch's protagonist is fat, balding, gingery, perhaps even benign. He has, in effect, protective colouring; and it is this ability of the psychotic to sink into the texture of everyday life which repeatedly fascinated Bloch as writer and film-maker.

And this reminds us of another question, which is about Mary herself. Why, after all, does it matter that she has committed a criminal act? Bates never discovers the money, which is in fact hidden in the car which he buries in the swamp. I would suggest that at least part of the point here is indeed to underline the structure of 'hiddenness' in the story; for Mary herself is a 'hidden' person. First, we know that she hides her own motives from herself: she believes herself to be in love with Sam, but we are also given strong hints that this is really a mask for her increasing fears about isolation and emotional waning. Second, she makes a self-defeating and ultimately unsuccessful attempt to 'hide' her own tracks: seen from, as it were, a low angle, her device of several times exchanging cars seems likely to succeed, but in fact Arbogast follows her easily.

Third, and most important, we are told that she has, in fact, always been largely 'hidden' from her lover Sam and even from her own sister; they do not know what to make of the accusations that she is a thief, and as they draw closer to solving the mystery of her disappearance they simultaneously draw closer to realising the inexplicability of her personality. In fact, she is dispensed with in a double way in the novel: physically by Bates, but also emotionally by Sam and Lila, who, it is hinted, may 'get over' her absence by getting together themselves.

In fact, when Lila first appears in Sam's store, he initially mistakes her for Mary, and this underlines a general point in the story about the replaceability of women. For Bates, women are no longer real people; his vision of them is wholly a mapping onto the template of his mother which is deeply engraved in his mind. But we may then hypothesise that the very *structure* of the story underlines this replaceability, and we are thus urged to read Bates's plight, and the ease with which it is passed off as normality – the ease, in fact, with which mother and child in Bates have cohabited with Bates-as-adult for twenty years – as symbolic of a general structure in the community, whereby women are objectified and can thus be dealt with as replaceable things rather than as people; because, presumably, their real power is too awesome for men to deal with, because they have come, in a substitutive way, to represent the mystery of personality which is taken as having caused psychic and social fragmentation.

These motifs of collection, objectification and 'normal' ritual find a natural analogy in John Fowles's *The Collector* (1963). Here again we have a psychotic subject who is perfectly able to hold down an ordinary job; who also evinces a strong need to collect living things – in this emblematic case, butterflies and then real girls; and who also kills in an attempt to reincorporate within himself his own absences. Fowles's novel is also a parable about the damming-up of creativity; his protagonist's habit of collecting is counterposed to the 'genuine', if questionable, engagement with art symbolised by his art-student captive, Miranda.[7]

What lies behind this is the damming-up of creative possibilities for the self, the impossibility of escape from patterning; and here we may call to mind Walter Benjamin's resonant account of the habits of the collector in modern society, and the role of collectable objects as substitutes for real relationships.[8] The collector believes himself to be in control of his collection; but at the unconscious level what has happened is that the person has consigned control to a set of routinised paths which serve to deflect and reduce the feared area of freedom.

We therefore find ourselves questioning the 'third person normal' in Bates's psychic construction. After all, it is this personality fragment which in fact stands guard over the others, protecting them, as it were, from the harsh truths of the outer world in a savage parody of the 'male' role in protecting mothers and children. Bates has constructed his semblance of adult masculinity along lines suggested by society, and it works; the sheriff, the representative of law and order, is able to see Bates as a little eccentric, but no more than that, for within this community of role models Bates stands as the symbolic representative of 'family life' reduced to a stark conflation of psychic agony.

THE CONTROL OF DETAIL

One of the characteristics of Bates's condition is a reversal of priority whereby large-scale features of life – love, murder, the rights of other people – slide into the background, and the small details of practical arrangements, whether these are to do with the opening-hours of the motel or with the disposal of corpses and vehicles, assume greater importance. Bates is obviously proud of his command of detail in, for example, the way in which he meticulously covers up for his 'mother''s crimes.

It is as though, in Bates, we are watching somebody in whom the narrator's art has been taken to extraordinary extremes. What he has done is to set up a 'suspension of disbelief' among the various parts of his own psyche; in place of the tales told us by our mothers we have tales told *to* mother to comfort her in her sleep. Once that fiction – that his mother's corpse is alive – has been established, then he is free to concentrate on the embellishments, on the precise evidences of verisimilitude, to etch in the clear details against a massive and looming fictional backdrop.

Again, we may sense here some curious version of gender relations. The overarching fiction is, as we have seen, a protective one: that the mother must be protected from the consequences of her crimes. It is as though it is the male role to set up the framework in which play can take place: simultaneously mother and child are thus protected from knowledge which only the adult male should have, and at the same time the more feminine sides of Bates are allowed to work on detail in the other sense of (transvestite) adornment.

I would like here to mention another of Bloch's novels, *American Gothic* (1974). The central character here is again a murderer of women, G. Gordon Gregg; and again here Bloch is taking the frame of an actual criminal history and searching in it for clues about the kind of psychic structure which might lie behind these crimes.

Gregg's story is replete with Gothic trappings: it is set in a modern castle full of secret passageways, slaughterhouses, hidden doors, and comes to an appropriately melodramatic conclusion. Among other things, Gregg is a pharmacist and a master-hypnotist, a clear descendant of villainous alchemists in the tradition of Frankenstein. But in the end it appears that Bloch is as puzzled about his motivations as we are, and offers two interlocking but disparate accounts.

Below the surface, we are allowed to surmise that this is another pathological account, and that Gregg enjoys his grisly work. But this, of course, is not the way he sees it. He again regards his victims as simply objects; what he wants from them, or so he believes, is simply their money. But he wants this not in any empty spirit of acquisition: 'it wasn't swindling', he explains to Crystal, who is intended to be another of his victims; 'it was a business matter. Building a place like this, carrying out my plans. You've got to find working capital, that's the primary rule of economics.'[9]

As he goes on to explain, he is only doing what everybody else is doing. The whole story is set against the background of the Chicago World's Fair of 1893. 'Look at the Fair', Gregg continues, 'and you'll see. The big exhibits – the steel industry, the railroads, textiles, armaments: don't you think the men behind them had to do their share of what you call swindling? Banking, insurance, real estate, I don't care what it is, you've got to look sharp, cut corners, take whatever steps are necessary.'

'He believes it,' Crystal realises, 'he really believes it! A businessman, dealing in death. A salesman, dedicated to making a killing.' But then she remembers the other aspects of Gregg's 'work' that she has seen, the hearts of all his victims carefully removed and kept in jars, and goes through a vertiginous process of trying to match the two stories, the businessman's detailed accounts with the psychopath's mania for collecting.

We may go in several directions from this point. On the one hand, we may trace the psychic effects of capitalism, the implanted need for success and profit, the apparent need to treat other people as objects in the process of engaging successfully in business. On the other hand, we may think about the psychological need for domination and possession which the castle represents. The concentration on detail connects with the need for secrecy; it is only through an intense absorption in detail that one can escape from the all-seeing eye of mother, and simultaneously prove one's command of the outer world.

But this need to command is itself merely the psychic residue of unaccommodated problems with omnipotence; if anybody were allowed to penetrate the bedroom, all of the child's secrets would be revealed, all that lies behind the accurate and neat accounts, the ledgers of profit and loss. And the term 'loss' perhaps reminds us of what is most important for Bates and Gregg: that there should be no loss to the self, no further erosion or leakage of that which is to be so preciously guarded because it is so fragile, the sense of a maturity precariously achieved and maintained only through an increasingly detailed elaboration of an overarching fiction.

What we have here are examples – Bloch's protagonists, Süskind's Grenouille, Fowles's collector – of men who are engaged in massive efforts to bring back together sundered psyches. The principal means for doing this, however, is not an exploration back into the dark. The house behind the motel, Grenouille's parentage – these are areas too frightening to be contemplated: because they contain the real secrets of birth and death, they represent the live female body which is not to be admitted to the light of day but is to be pushed ever deeper into the swamp.

Instead, the psychic effort is directed to the 'front office' – the motel itself, Gregg's pharmacy, the exterior of the collector's specially purchased cottage – to ensure that these environments are sealed against leakage; which is also, of course, to ensure that they are insulated against the disclosure of truth. Here in these offices and places of business, there is a mass of neatly arranged detail, under steady surveillance because in this way the gaze can be averted from the brutal facts which, meanwhile, are felt to be mysteriously amassing themselves behind one's back.

In this respect, we may also return to *Psycho* and to the originating 'details' of Mary's theft and what lies behind it, which is Sam's insolvency. This is not, Bloch points out, Sam's fault: on the contrary, he has inherited debts, and it is a mark of his rare probity that he is determined to pay them off before marrying his fiancée. But, by a significant twist, were it not for these debts there would have been no robbery; and Mary too, perhaps, is trying to seal her psyche against leakage, against the awesome drift into middle-aged spinsterhood. In a last desperate effort, she attempts to find a substitute gratification in the outer world, instead of looking into the forbidden dark spaces, where one's own real death may be a fact which has to be encountered.

CONTAMINATION AND DEATH

In 'A Girl Like Me', a recent story by a Hong Kong Chinese writer who uses the pen name Xi Xi, we hear the first-person story of a girl who, like Mary Crane, is approaching with fear a time of life when she may be considered, or consider herself, unmarriageable. She is waiting to meet her present lover – her last hope, so we are led to believe, of a decent marriage.[10] She is waiting with a kind of trepidation which also verges on a blank despondency. He has asked to see her place of work. She has told him – as, she tells us, she has told his predecessors – that she is a beautician, and in a sense this is true, but as the story goes on we realise that her actual work is to beautify the dead: she works in a funeral parlour.

She has no friends; they are, she says, too scared of her pallor, of the strange, unplaceable odour which clings to her – her present boyfriend has so far mistaken it for Cologne, but it is the residue of pickling-alcohol. She sees herself as a paradoxical image of contamination; she works too close to death for the living to want to have to do with her, even though she is also aware that the dead have a pure and sterile beauty of their own.

The ending of the story is entirely ambiguous: we are not told whether or not her boyfriend will go the way of the others. But what we are told of is her own prefiguration of failure, her doom-laden awareness that she carries with her the smell of too much reality. I cite 'A Girl Like Me' because I believe it reminds us of something of the fear behind the psychopathologies we have been discussing: a fear of death which is made over into a wish to place death entirely in others, to kill them psychically by reducing them to objects and fragments, and then freely and guiltlessly – because they are *already* no longer persons – to kill them physically, in order, at least in part, to take on their protective colouring.

The fate of Xi Xi's heroine is not to enact this series of substitutive acts but, instead, to represent in her own person precisely the final caring of which the male protagonists are so afraid. It is as though she takes to a deathly extreme the fate of the objectified woman, the object of the collector's pornography. She it is who can admit, has to admit every day, that the dead are dead; but for this clear perception of reality, which is also an act of feminine nurturing, she may never be forgiven.

One thing which is quite remarkable about the four male protagonists we have discussed is their extraordinary busyness (and business). The perversions of gender relations from which these psychic structures stem come partly from masculine respon-ses to the role model of masculinity: these are 'heroes' who have to take care of every eventuality, and who, in the particular case of Norman Bates, claim to be doing so in order to protect their nearest and dearest. It is as though they are each parodies of the man out and about in the world: Grenouille and Gregg are unabashed careerists; Bates and Fowles's collector are driven to further and further controlled paroxysms of activity as they seek endlessly to spin out the webs of practical implication of acts which are themselves deflections from the truths of the outer world.

Against these images Xi Xi places an image of feminine stillness, but this is a stillness of mature acceptance which also knows that, at every turn, it will be objectified and misinterpreted, as societies of achievement which have no use for stillness and which have resigned their hopes for psychological integration reject the ben-eficial wealth of significances in death. In this context, *Psycho* can be seen to pose an important question: what is actually going on behind the façade of busy normality which characterises social life?

But what this attempt to disclose the reality behind the cover story in fact comes up against is a set of intractable splits. A diagnosis can always be offered, but we have also to contend with that further aftermath in which the mother in Bates takes over the controls of the psyche. Clearly there is no world in which these two discourses can be made to interlock or inform each other, because there is no available single subject position from which they could feasibly both originate. The complexity of the disordered psyche evades scrutiny in a parallel yet opposite way to the evasion which occurs when Sam and Lila try to remember Mary and end up admitting at least partly for their own convenience, that they never understood her.

And what lies behind this is not only a fear but also a wish: a wish to multiply those aspects of being-in-the-world which deliberately avoid comprehension, because comprehension model-led on inadequate mothering figures on the psychic landscape as a deadly surveillance, a surveillance which in effect threatens the assumed sovereignty of the omnipotent subject. In this world there is only absolute power or absolute powerlessness: Bates's peephole observation of Mary, or Bates wilting before the grim looks of his fantasised mother.

Notes

1. Robert Bloch, *Psycho* (New York: Hale, 1959) p. 126.
2. Cf. the account of narcissism in Karen Horney, *New Ways in Psycho-analysis* (New York: Kegan Paul, Trench, Trübner, 1939) pp. 88–100.
3. Bloch, *Psycho*, p. 126.
4. See ibid., pp. 11–12.
5. Cf. H. K. Fierz, 'The Clinical Significance of Extraversion and Introversion', trs. C. Rowland, in *Current Trends in Analytical Psychology*, ed. Gerhard Adler (London: Tavistock, 1961) pp. 89–97.
6. See Patrick Süskind, *Perfume: The Story of a Murderer*, trs. J. E. Woods (London: Hamish Hamilton, 1986) pp. 261–3.
7. See John Fowles, *The Collector* (London: Jonathan Cape, 1963) pp. 45, 58, 82.
8. Cf. Ackbar Abbas, 'Walter Benjamin's Collector: The Fate of Modern Experience', *Working Papers of the Centre for Twentieth-Century Studies*, no. 3 (Milwaukee: University of Wisconsin, 1986).
9. Robert Bloch, *American Gothic* (New York: Tor Books, 1974) p. 206.
10. See Xi Xi, *A Girl Like Me, and Other Stories*, Afterword by S. C. Soong (Hong Kong: Renditions Paperbacks, 1986) pp. 1–16.

7

A Feminist Approach to Patricia Highsmith's Fiction

ODETTE L'HENRY EVANS

A critical examination of the work of Patricia Highsmith from a feminist standpoint unavoidably presents a number of challenges, the first being the difficulty of ascertaining precisely to what genre her novels belong. To see her as a 'crime writer' would be inaccurate as well as limitative, since it would mean ignoring certain elements of her stories which are outside the usual crime–detection–arrest pattern. To call her a mystery writer may be more accurate, since she was once awarded the Edgar Allan Poe Scroll by the Mystery Writers of America, yet the nature of mystery in her novels differs greatly from what is usually expected, in so far as it never comes from wondering who the evildoer is; instead it is connected with what kind of person he is, or more accurately it enfolds the reasons which make him progressively deviate from the norm and become a murderer.

Patricia Highsmith herself stated that she was 'interested in the effect of guilt on [her] heroes'[1] and her study of the invisible 'glass cell'[2] which surrounds and isolates the criminal is one of the remarkable features of her work. It may well be that this is the key to understanding the precise nature of her work, and it will need to be examined in relation to feminist critical theories in order to establish accurately the status of the work defined as woman's writing.

It has been said that there are as many forms of feminism as there are women, and, while this can only be seen as a reduction to the absurd, the fact remains that a number of tendencies exist, some mainly concerned with everyday social issues, and others, more particularly among French women writers and critics, essentially involved in debating the intellectual aspects of feminism. One important element of this approach has been the redefinition of what is meant by women's writings, no longer in relation to male literature (for instance, being 'potentially as good as . . .' or 'indistinguishable from . . .'), but in relation to language itself as a means of expressing the inner consciousness of the female writer, proceeding, in other words, according to what Róisîn Battel calls the 'rejection of phallic discourse'.[3]

This concern with language or, more precisely, with the creation of languages (discourse) can operate at the linguistic level of language, involving considerations of form, organisation, vocabulary, syntax which, in the discourse, reflect female identity, or it can explore the deeper layers of the text to search for a novel apprehension of the unconscious as expression of the female psyche – in other words, a writing of self. The corpus of literary analyses which has been produced during the past twenty years or so has amply demonstrated the value of textual deconstructions at linguistic and at psychoanalytical levels in establishing a formula able to define accurately the specificity of woman.

The advantage of this two-pronged investigation is that it not only covers the manner in which a woman writer expresses herself within a literary text, but also encompasses her selection of plots, and her presentation of episodes and characters, thus highlighting in turns the various strands of a complex pattern.

What criteria should then be considered in this quest for an 'authentic' feminine voice?

Traditionally, women writers have been seen as lacking the sense of logic, universality and objectivity which is commonly thought to characterise the production of male authors, so much so that, if a woman succeeded in that field, as, for example, George Eliot did, she was accused of 'committing atrocities with it that beggar description'.[4] Women were, on the other hand, credited with a gift for immediate empathy with the world around them, as well as an appreciation of each of its separate elements. In that connection it may be interesting to hear Jan Morris, who before undergoing a sex-change was a man, explain that, as far as she is concerned, the most thrilling thing about being a woman is that she no longer feels remote and alienated from her urban surroundings, but is deeply conscious of being part of them.[5]

No such empathy, however, is in evidence in the novels of Patricia Highsmith. At best, the surroundings are indifferent, and not infrequently they are hostile. The comfortable home of Vic and Melinda Van Allen, in *Deep Water*, is never described; there is mention of a 'nice' house, a 'good' phonograph and a 'favourite armchair', and also a dented metal vase, since Melinda is prone to throwing things when annoyed, but nothing more.

Similarly, in *The Glass Cell*, when Carter is released from the penitentiary, it is obvious that his wife has taken particular care to make their flat attractive for his return, yet there is only a brief reference to a rubber plant and to some 'gladioli in a large vase', without even, as one would have expected, a notation of colour. The only colour mentioned, in fact, is that of the 'two thick red books'[6] on the chest of drawers, right in the bedroom. These crimson-coloured law books belong to Sullivan, the lawyer initially commissioned to establish Carter's innocence, who is now Hazel's lover and will eventually be killed by Carter.

Julia Kristeva, a radical feminist as well as a rigorous theorist, realised that there was no single feature that could identify or characterise all feminine texts, and that most texts can dissolve identities, as she illustrates with reference to avant-garde authors such as Joyce and Artaud. Indeed, while postulating a distinction between man's and woman's writing, she asserts that, to the extent that it is not a natural construct, the term 'woman' itself can not be defined: 'La femme ce n'est jamais ça' ('Woman is never what one supposes').[7] Criteria are therefore to be sought in the social rather than the individual context. Following this line, Kristeva argues that women, because of their social roles, tend to be more mindful of ethics and to create a 'maternal' climate of calm and tenderness, so that, when a woman novelist writes, she either reproduces a real family or, at least, creates a similar imaginary one.[8]

This is rather less easy to identify, but, for all that, there is no evidence that Patricia Highsmith's own affective or moral values play a part in her novels. She does not write in the way, for instance, that Claudine Herrmann suggests: 'As soon as a woman speaks up, it is usually to reclaim the right to the present moment, to affirm the refusal of a life alienated in social time which is so hostile to interior time.'[9] Little of what apears in the novels relates exclusively to the present, the general tendency being to anticipate future events. This is even more apparent in the short stories, where the first words prefigure the tragedies to come. The opening sentence of 'The Birds Poised to Fly'[10] – 'Every morning, Don looked into his mailbox, but there was never a letter for him' – takes the reader to the very centre of the drama, the awaited letter that his girlfriend Rosalind does not write. His frustration tempts him to look into the mailbox next to his own, where a fickle boy friend has left uncollected a love letter from another girl.

Similarly, the words 'Stanley Hubbell painted on Sundays', which open 'The Barbarians', identify the relaxing occupation so dreadfully spoilt by the raucous exclamations and shouts of the ball-players under Hubbell's window. He drops a stone from his window onto a player's head, nearly killing him.

By such means, time is made into a continuum. This contradicts also Virginia Woolf's contention that feminine writing explodes time into a series of 'moments', each complete in itself, in an effort to distance the text from the masculine tenets of logic and of strict temporal and causal perspective.

Undoubtedly Virginia Woolf insisted on using that disjointed form herself – in *Mrs Dalloway* for instance, where only one ordinary day in the life of a married woman is depicted. This proved a fitting demonstration of her belief that 'how one writes is more important than what one writes', but the fact remains that many women writers, past and present, have chosen to work within a logical context.

This, at least to some extent, is probably what led to a reappraisal of the question and prompted some radical feminists to wonder whether it made sense, intellectually as well as politically, for women to attempt to write in a 'new' language which, in order to be their own, would reject logic. Such a 'discourse that surpasses the regulated phallocentric system', as Hélène Cixous defines it,[11] may distinguish a feminine text from a masculine one, but at the same time it may prove self-destructive.

It may be more fruitful to accept, as John Stuart Mill,[12] Mary Wollstonecraft[13] and more recently Simone de Beauvoir have maintained that women, like men, are part of the human race and therefore that their writing – meaning the terms they use, their style or the structure of their discourse – is not gender-oriented.[14] The way would then be open to consider Patricia Highsmith's work as part of a feminine corpus of production, and to see whether a psychoanalytical investigation of her plot and character presentation yields elements which can be related to another aspect of feminine writing: that which consists in liberating and expressing the unconscious, as specifically shaped by a woman's perception of it.

A brief survey of Patricia Highsmith's novels shows that the great majority of her central characters – often psychopathic killers –

are male. As statistics demonstrate that most violent criminals are men, here selection can legitimately be seen as representative rather than sexually biased, although, to be fair, some of her killers, such as the snails which appear in two of her stories, can hardly be fitted into statistical realism.

In the novels dealing with male criminals, the distinctive function of women can, however, be observed either in gender-oriented social relations or in the woman's distinctive nature. The feminist standpoint, which here can be termed as 'feminine epistemology',[15] goes beyond the appearance of women's function – love, mother-hood, care of the home and of the outside world – in order to explore the systemic relations of a sex–gender universe.[16] The Marxist view of gender-related functions sees these as derived from forms of labour, with men, traditionally, dominant in the fields of science and technology, and endowed with cognitive and objective rationality, while women are closer to nature and more subjective and emotional, so that for them labour and love become inextricably mixed.[17]

Women's traditional work primarily involves the bearing and bringing-up of children, and in that connection it can be noted that in Patricia Highsmith's novels children often appear as part of the family unit. The 'care' they receive from their mothers varies greatly, although it never appears as loving and tender. It seems to range from bland duty or indifference to sheer brutality.

In *The Glass Cell*, there is no doubt that the little boy Timmie is reasonably well looked after by his mother, but, for instance, despite the boy's obvious distress at having a father in prison (Carter has been imprisoned for embezzlement, although he is in fact innocent), she writes calmly to her husband that 'Timmie is bearing up pretty well. I lecture him daily, though I try not to make it sound like a lecture. The kids are picking on him at school of course . . . .'[18] When Carter has been released, she does not bother to come home from work on her birthday, but goes straight on to a party, despite the fact that Timmie is waiting expectantly to give her his present: 'Timmie had bought a white slip with brown embroidery . . . quite an expensive item.'[19] By contrast, he is shown real affection by his father, who makes various gifts for him while he is in prison, including 'a good sized chest of oak with [his] initials carved in its lid'.

When the boy accidentally cuts his hand, it is again his father who shows concern, while, on another occasion, he is shown

companionably washing the dishes with Timmie drying and
putting them away. Obviously, when we compare Carter's attitude
towards the boy to that of his wife, who is secretely conducting
her longstanding love affair, we have to conclude that Patricia
Highsmith depicts the behaviour of the couple towards their child
in a non-stereotyped way.

It could be argued, of course, that Carter's caring attitude is
meant to stress how fundamentally honest and decent he is, since
his arrest has been due to a false testimony. However, if we
consider another novel, *Deep Water*, we find a similar contrast
between mother and father. The mother, Melinda Van Allen, is
indifferent to her daughter Beatrice, known as Trixie: 'She had not
wanted to have a child, then she had, then she hadn't, and finally,
after four years, she had wanted one again, and finally produced
one.'[20] It is left to her father to care for her: 'Just then Trixie's
pyjama clad form appeared in the doorway. "Mommie!" Trixie
screamed, but Mommie neither heard nor saw her. Vic got up and
went to her. "S'matter, Trix?" he asked, stooping by her. "I can't
sleep."'[21] The tragedy here is, of course, that the father is a
psychopath, and that the story as it develops takes him from the
faintest stirring of an unbalanced mind to the full-blown horrors
of successive murders, culminating in the strangling of his wife.

Through all this, Trixie is ignored by her mother, but an object
of concern for her father. He is sorry for what will happen to her,
and at the very end, when he walks out of the house with the
police officer who has just arrested him, his befuddled mind
conjures a vision of the child: 'He saw Trixie romping up the lawn
and stopping in surprise as she saw him with the policeman, but
frowning at the lawn, Vic could see that she wasn't really there.
The sun was shining and Trixie was alive somewhere.'[22]

We should certainly search in vain for an expression of 'woman's
writing' in this novel, if we mean by that writing expressive, even
if only subconsciously, of women's feelings of love and tenderness,
of role-playing. What is more, in 'The Terrapin' there is a little
boy, Victor, whose mother is even more devoid of understanding
and affection. She never pays attention to anything he may have
to say, never even listens to him, and, despite the fact that she is
a professional illustrator of children's books, she has no understanding of his longing to look 'grown up', to wear long trousers
and sturdy manly shoes. All she can say, in her stiff foreign accent,
is 'Veector, you are seeck. And retarded. You know that?'[23] She

makes fun of him, slaps him, and when, one day, she brings a terrapin to cook for the 'ragoût', the boy's show of affection for the poor animal only seems 'seeck' to her and she refuses even to let him take it downstairs to show to his friend. When she cuts up the creature to cook it, his latent hatred for her crystallises:

> He thought of the terrapin, in little pieces now, all mixed up in the sauce of cream and egg yolks and sherry in the pot in the refrigerator. His mother's cry was not silent [like the terrapin's had been], it seemed to tear his ears off. His second blow was in her body, and then he stabbed her throat again. Only tiredness made him stop.[24]

Giving up the search for maternal care, we might look instead for qualifiers of sexual difference, taking as our point of departure the traditional association of female sexuality with passivity, the opposite of masculine thrusting aggressiveness. Freud, in *The Disappearance of the Oedipus Complex* (1933), equates 'feminine' with vagina and 'virile' with penis, concluding that 'anatomy is destiny'. Feminist theorists usually contradict him by insisting upon a valorisation of individuality, perhaps through refusing marriage: Simone de Beauvoir, for example, remarked that she could have married Sartre, but would thereby have ceased to be herself.[25] Other feminists have sought to assert control of their lives by selecting a variety of lovers and partners, or by aggressively preserving their virginity, or by becoming part of a familial community, as Germaine Greer suggested,[26] or an all-female group, like the women of Greenham Common[27] – in other words, as Dale Spender expressed it, by altering the pattern of relations with men, making the woman an autonomous subject revelling in her regained freedom from sexual bondage; 'Men is an issue over which feminists agonise.'[28]

In Patricia Highsmith's novels, relationship patterns involving women mostly involve married women who indulge in extra-marital affairs. One such woman is Hazel in *The Glass Cell*, who, however, writes to her imprisoned husband every day, being supporting, cheering him up through his various unsuccessful appeals and eventually welcoming him home: 'Hazel kissed him on the cheeks, then on the lips. She was crying. She was also laughing. Carter blinked awkwardly at the lights that seemed so bright, at the dazzling colour everywhere.'[29] She retains this fondness to the end, even to the extent of forgiving him for having killed her lover.

Her lover is the lawyer, Sullivan, who seems to hover in the background from the start, offering assistance and organising holiday outings; but, when asked by her husband, she repeatedly denies that they have an adulterous relationship: '"I hear you are seeing Sullivan a lot," he said, and saw in her face that he had hurt her. "I see him as often as I tell you I see him . . . ."'[30] She goes on denying it until caught, when she has recourse to the old traditional formula: 'You don't understand women.' Whether this affair was deliberately initiated by her, or whether she drifted into it because she enjoyed the lawyer's protective presence, felt attracted to him, or could not resist his advances is certainly never made clear; all she will say is 'it happened while you were in prison'.

Initially, one may feel that she was fond of her lover, since she appears 'ravaged with grief' when she hears that he has been killed; she wants his murderer found and punished, and yet, when she realises that her husband is the killer, she only tells him, 'Everything is going to be all right!'[31] The level of natural determinism in her attitude must be seen as rather limited.

Melinda, in *High Water*, is unfaithful on a grander scale and makes clear her evident desire to attract men. She smiles 'a gay catch-me-if-you-can smile' over her shoulder whenever someone she fancies comes near, and, as a result, jealousy will be the motive for a whole series of murders, although the first lover is disposed of simply by a threat. Melinda does not miss him, as she is already having an affair with a not-too-bright instructor at a riding-academy, who is succeeded by a very young record salesman, and others. So, on the surface, there seems to be evidence of feminist self-assertion, in the form of a determination to live to the full. Life for Melinda is 'the pursuit of a good time'.[32]

Her husband's jealousy would then present a dreadful, murderous but totally logical reaction. This is, however, not the case, and again the opacity of the character's mind makes a definite judgement impossible. Melinda's husband is unbalanced from the outset, as his passion for bedbugs and snails shows; his soft even voice and his fixed smile ought to give him away, and so should some of his odd statements, such as 'I have an evil side too, but I keep it well hidden', which cause further distortion to the portrait.

There remains, however, the possible argument that, by

destroying the masculine image and altering the powerful emotion of jealousy to make it into the pathetic blubberings of a monster, another form of feminist writing is realised, akin to that suggested by a radical French feminist, Annie Leclerc: 'One must not wage war on man. That is his way of attaining value. . . . One must simply deflate his values with the needle of ridicule.'[33] This might also account for the presentation of other male 'heroes' in what seems the same 'destructional' perspective, where apparent logic turns to aberration. Could it be that Patricia Highsmith, as an *Observer* critic once suggested, 'writes about men like a spider writing about flies'?[34]

This is a tempting approach; indeed Peter Knoppert, in the story 'The Snail Watcher', shares Vic Van Allen's sick fascination for snails. He watches and breeds them until they fill the living-room, cover the walls and eventually suffocate him: 'There were snails crawling over his eyes. Then just as he staggered to his feet, something else hit him. . . . He was fainting. His arms felt like leaden weights as he tried to reach his nostrils, his eyes, to free them from the sealing, murderous snail bodies.'[35] Snails in fact appear again as deadly animals, this time in giant form, in the story titled 'The Quest for Blank Claveringi',[36] where they deliberately set out to kill the distinguished, but far too arrogant, professor of zoology.

What makes it difficult, nevertheless, to see such effects as a 'destructional' feminist expression is the presence in the novels of female criminals, some of them just as subject to psychopathic disorders as Highsmith's males. Perhaps the most haunting example is that pretty young woman Lucille Smith in 'The Heroine',[37] so determined to make good and to lead a happy life, to forget her own mad, wild-eyed mother. Having secured an ideal job as a nursemaid in a beautiful and happy household with two lovely children, she none the less eventually turns pyromaniac and sets fire to the house.

There is also, in 'When the Fleet Was in in Mobile',[38] which Graham Greene called his favourite story, the haunting portrait of Geraldine, who reveals in the disconnected form of an interior monologue what seems to be the cruel and obsessive character of her husband, so that her action in killing him seems fully justified. Slowly, however, her own underlying irrationality emerges, together with the echoes of some past nymphomania which drove her to meet the sailors 'when the fleet was in'. In the end, as

Graham Greene so pithily put it, 'what seemed at first a simple little case of murder' becomes an unbearably claustrophobic experience.[39]

The fascination of Patricia Highsmith's characters lies precisely in the way their twilight world is painted, in small impressionistic touches. They see themselves as normal and may appear so to casual onlookers, yet, when details of their speech or behaviour are sifted carefully, the flaws in their make-up come to light, and one can foresee the horrors to come.

Similarly, in *Those Who Walk Away*, what begins as the natural grief of a father whose daughter had committed suicide, and his unjustified but understandable anger against his son-in-law, develops progressively into an obsessive stalking of the tragic young husband through the narrow passages and the piazzas of Venice:

> Ray [the young man] had started suddenly, but he had stopped walking. In the shadows ahead emerging from a triangular shadow that clung to a small church like a dark pyramid, he saw Coleman [his father-in-law] looking over both shoulders, obviously looking for something, someone.
> 'What is it?' Antonio asked.
> 'Nothing. I thought I saw someone.'
> 'Who?'
> Coleman was still in sight. Then in another second he wasn't. He had vanished in the slit on an alley on the left of the church square.[40]

And it may well be that it is at that level, when the extraordinary accuracy of Highsmith's observation is realised, and when her gift for psychoanalysis is recognised, that one can legitimately re-examine the possibility of a feminine form of writing. It has been said that it is an oppression to force women to adhere to 'the stereotype of a passive powerless and sexually masochistic femininity', yet, as Deborah Cameron states,

> It seems to offer us through its account of the construction of the self in family relations and the unconscious mind, an understanding of how subordination can be internalised deep in our personalities. Moreover it is centrally concerned with the

forging of sexual identity and with the extreme importance of the sexual in all aspects of mental life.[41]

In that light, the stories of Geraldine and of Ray's father-in-law, for instance, have all the concepts posited first by Freud and renewed by Lacan in a purely masculine context, and eventually enlarged and 'feminised' by women such as Hélène Cixous, a lecturer in psychology, in *The Laugh of the Medusa*,[42] and Luce Irigaray, initially a member of the Lacanian school. Irigaray, realising how Lacan's theories were limited by their exclusion of women, attempted a reappraisal of women's relation to their unconscious, which she sees as radically different from men's – a belief which leads her to wonder whether women are not in fact *the* unconscious which their writing reveals.[43]

It is certainly true that in Patricia Highsmith's novels the unconscious is reconstructed through language, to the extent that Coleman, for example, in *Those Who Walk Away*, 'recognises' his dead daughter's scarf in the different, newly bought scarf that he pulls out of his hated son-in-law's pocket,[44] and that Geraldine, in 'When the Fleet Was in in Mobile', can 'hear' the words spoken by her father when she was a child, by her friend Marianne when she was young, or, more recently, by her now supposedly dead husband, just as clearly as she hears the woman speaking to her on the bus, or the man that she meets during the ride on the merry-go-round. Past and present are fused in her mind in such a way that submerged memories partly resurface and she 'recognises' an old boyfriend, far more real to her, in the unknown state policeman who comes to take her back. At the end, her madness taking over, she screams while holding her fists in front of her eyes to blot out reality: 'Then his face [the policeman's] and the lights and the park went out, though she knew as well as she knew she still screamed that her eyes were open under her hands.'[45]

It would seem fair to accept that the wealth of details given to express in terms of language a range of emotions which escape the mould of logical reality, and the empathy which emerges from Patricia Highsmith's pages for the characters who, despite their desire or their illusion, cannot come to terms with others or cope with the outside world, bring her work within the scope of feminine writing – not at the superficial level that some feminist propagandists have surmised, but in the deeper realm of psychoanalysis where the act of writing is an exploration of the unconscious and where women have excelled from time immemorial, in a way which makes them enthralling tellers of tales.

Notes

1. Patricia Highsmith, Foreword to *Deep Water* (Harmondsworth: Penguin, 1957).
2. This is, in fact, the title of one of her novels.
3. Ròisìn Battel, *The Feminist Anti-text*, Women Studies Occasional Papers no. 2 (Canterbury: University of Kent, 1983) p. 14.
4. Virginia Woolf, *A Room of One's Own* (London: Hogarth Press, 1928) p. 73.
5. Jan Morris, *Conundrum* (New York: Harcourt Brace, 1974] pp. 156–8.
6. Patricia Highsmith, *The Glass Cell* (London: Heinemann, 1965) pp. 110–11.
7. Julia Kristeva, interview in *Tel quel*, no. 59 (1974), repr. in *Polygone*, a collection of Kristeva's writings (Paris: Seuil, 1977).
8. Ibid.
9. Tr. Marylin R. Schuster in Elaine Marks and Isabelle de Courtivron (eds), *New French Feminisms* (Brighton: Harvester, 1981) p. 172.
10. One of the short stories collected in Patricia Highsmith, *Eleven* (1945; London: Heinemann, 1970).
11. Hélène Cixous, *Le Rire de la Méduse*, trs. K. and P. Cohen as *The Laugh of the Medusa*, in *Signs*, i, no. 4 (Summer 1976). Cf. also Xavière Gauthier, 'Existe-t-il une écriture de femme?', in *Tel quel*, no. 58 (1974).
12. Helen Taylor (his stepdaughter), 'The Ladies Petition', in *Westminster Review*, Jan. 1867; quoted in J. Mitchell and A. Oakley (eds), *What is Feminism?* (Oxford: Basil Blackwell, 1986).
13. Mary Wollstonecraft, *A Vindication of the Rights of Women* (1792; New York: Norton, 1967) p. 220.
14. Simone de Beauvoir, Introduction to *Le Deuxième Sexe* (Paris: Gallimard, 1949), tr. H. M. Parshley as *The Second Sex* (New York: Knopf, 1952).
15. Cf. Nancy Hartsock, 'The Feminist Standpoint', in S. Harding and M. B. Hintikka (eds), *Discovering Reality: Feminist Perspectives in Epistemology, Metaphysics, Methodology and Philosophy of Science* (Dordrecht: Reidel, 1983).
16. Hilary Rose, 'Women's Work; Women's Knowledge', in Mitchell and Oakley, *What is Feminism?*
17. See J. Finch and D. Groves (eds), *A Labour of Love: Women, Work and Caring* (London: Routledge and Kegan Paul, 1983).
18. Highsmith, *The Glass Cell*, p. 12.
19. Ibid., p. 123.
20. Highsmith, *Deep Water*, p. 22.
21. Ibid., p. 28.
22. Ibid., p. 259.

23. Highsmith, *Eleven*, p. 33.
24. Ibid., p. 44.
25. Simone de Beauvoir, interview with Alice Schwartzer, July 1972, quoted in Marks and Courtivron, *New French Feminisms*, p. 143.
26. Germaine Greer, *Sex and Destiny* (New York: Harper and Row, 1984) p. 268.
27. See Lynne Jones (ed.), *Keeping the Peace* (London: Women's Press, 1983).
28. Dale Spender, 'Common Themes', in Mitchell and Oakley, *What is Feminism?*, p. 217.
29. Highsmith, *The Glass Cell*, p. 107.
30. Ibid., p. 164.
31. Ibid., p. 248.
32. Highsmith, *Deep Water*, p. 22.
33. From Annie Leclerc, *Parole de femmes* (Paris: Grasset, 1974), tr. G. C. Gill in Marks and Courtivron, *New French Feminisms*, pp. 80–6.
34. Quoted on back cover of *Deep Water*.
35. Highsmith, *Eleven*, p. 10.
36. In Highsmith, *Eleven*.
37. Ibid.
38. Ibid.
39. Graham Greene, Foreword to *Eleven*, p. xi.
40. Patricia Highsmith, *Those Who Walk Away* (London: Heinemann, 1967).
41. Deborah Cameron, *Feminisms and Linguistic Theory* (London : Macmillan, 1985) p. 117.
42. Cixous, *The Laugh of the Medusa*, in *Signs*, i, no. 4, pp. 875–93.
43. See for example, Luce Irigaray, *Ce sexe que n'en est pas un* (Paris: Minuit, 1977).
44. Highsmith, *Those Who Walk Away*, p. 241.
45. Highsmith, *Eleven*, p. 67.

8

Shirley Jackson and the Reproduction of Mothering: *The Haunting of Hill House*

JUDIE NEWMAN

One of the most enduring mysteries of horror fiction consists in its exploitation of the attractions of fear. Why, one may ask, should a reader seek out the experience of being terrified, particularly by horror fiction, which adds abhorrence, loathing and physical repulsion to the purer emotions of terror evoked by the supernatural tale? For H. P. Lovecraft[1] the answer lay in the human fear of the unknown. Freud,[2] however, developed a different hypothesis, describing the experience of the 'uncanny' (*unheimlich*) as that class of the frightening which leads back to what is known of old and long-familiar. Observing that *heimlich* (familiar, homely) is the opposite of *unheimlich*, Freud recognises the temptation to equate the uncanny with fear of the unknown. Yet he noted that *heimlich* also means 'concealed', 'private', 'secret', as the home is an area withdrawn from the eyes of strangers. In Freud's argument, therefore, the experience of the uncanny arises either when primitive animistic beliefs, previously surmounted, seem once more to be confirmed (Shirley Jackson's 'The Lottery' is a case in point) or when infantile complexes, formerly repressed, are revived (a theory which brings *The Haunting of Hill House* into sharp focus). For Freud, various forms of ego disturbance involve regression to a period when the ego had not marked itself off sharply from the external world and from other people. In the context of a discussion of ghosts and doubles, Freud cites Otto Rank's description of the double as originally an insurance against the destruction of the ego, an energetic denial of the power of death. (In this sense the 'immortal soul' may be considered as the first double of the body.) The idea of doubling as preservation against extinction therefore springs from the unbounded self-love of the child. When this stage of primitive narcissism is surmounted, however, the double reverses its aspect, and, from being an assurance of immortality,

120

becomes the uncanny harbinger of death and a thing of terror. Since Freud considered art as an organised activity of sublimation, providing the reader with pleasures 'under wraps', it is tempting to argue that the horror tale actively eliminates and exorcises our fears by allowing them to be relegated to the imaginary realm of fiction.[3] Rosemary Jackson, however, has indicated the case for the fantastic as a potentially subversive reversal of cultural formation, disruptive of conventional distinctions between the real and the unreal.[4] Arguably, although Shirley Jackson builds her horrors on the basis of the *heimlich* and of repressed infantile complexes, in the process she subverts the Freudian paradigm, both of art as sublimation, and in broader psychoanalytic terms. In this connection, new developments in psychoanalytic theory offer fresh insights into Jackson's work.

Recent feminist psychoanalytic theorists[5] have set out to revise the Freudian account of psychosexual differences, which bases gender, anatomically, on possession or lack of the phallus. In the Freudian paradigm, the male achieves adulthood by passing through the Oedipus complex, which fear of castration by the father induces him to overcome. Fear facilitates acceptance of the incest prohibition, promoting the formation of the superego, which thereafter polices desire in accordance with adult social norms. In a parallel development, the female discovers the lack of the phallus, sees herself as castrated, recognises her mother as similarly inferior, and therefore abandons her attachment to the mother to form the Oedipal relation with the father, which is the necessary precursor of adult heterosexual relationships – always the Freudian goal. Feminist analysts, however, have shifted the focus from the Oedipal to the pre-Oedipal stage, tracing the influence of gender on identity to the dynamics of the mother–infant bond. Nancy Chodorow in *The Reproduction of Mothering* offers a persuasive analysis of early infant development in these terms. Because children first experience the social and cognitive world as continuous with themselves, the mother is not seen as a separate person with separate interests. In this brief period of immunity from individuality, the experience of fusion with the mother, of mother as world, is both seductive and terrifying. Unity is bliss; yet it entails total dependence and loss of self. In contrast the father does not pose the original threat to basic ego integrity, and is perceived from the beginning as separate. Thus, the male fear of women may originate as terror of maternal omnipotence in consequence of the early dependence on the mother, and may be generalised to all women (in images such as the witch, the vampire and the Terrible Mother[6]) since it is tied up with the assertion of gender. Boys define themselves as masculine by difference from, not by relation to, their mothers. Girls, however, in defining themselves as female, experience themselves as resembling their mothers, so that the experience of attachment fuses with the process of identity formation. Girls therefore learn to see themselves as partially continuous with their mothers, whereas boys learn very early about difference and separateness. Male development therefore entails more emphatic individuation, and more defensive firming of experienced ego boundaries, whereas women persist in defining themselves relationally, creating fluid, permeable ego boundaries, and locating their sense of self in the ability to make and maintain affiliations. Female gender identity is therefore threatened by separation, and shaped throughout life by the fluctuations of symbiosis and detachment from the mother. Girls may also fear material omnipotence and struggle to free themselves, idealising the father as their most available ally. Daughterly individuation may be inhibited by paternal absence and by over-closeness to mothers, who tend to view their daughters as extensions of themselves. Conversely, coldness on the mother's part may prevent the loosening of the emotional bond because of the unappeased nature of the child's love. In maturity women may form close personal relationships with other women to recapture some aspects of the fractured mother–daughter bond. Alternatively they may reproduce the primary attachment, by themselves bearing children, thus initiating the cycle once more, as the exclusive symbiotic relation of the mother's own infancy is re-created. Mothering therefore involves a double identification for women in which they take both parts of the pre-Oedipal relation, as mother and as child. Fictions of development reflect this psychological structure. Recent reformulations of the female *Bildungsroman*[7] have drawn attention to the frequency with which such fictions end in deaths (Maggie Tulliver, Rachel Vinrace, Edna Pontellier) understandable less as developmental failures than as refusals to accept an adulthood which denies female desires and values. In addition, a persistent, if recessive, narrative concern with the story of mothers and daughters often exists in the background to a dominant romance or courtship plot.

An exploration of *The Haunting of Hill House* in the light of feminist psychoanalytic theory reveals that the source of both the pleasures and the terrors of the text springs from the dynamics of the mother–daughter relation with its attendant motifs of psychic annihilation, reabsorption by the mother, vexed individuation, dissolution of individual ego boundaries, terror of separation and the attempted reproduction of the symbiotic bond through close female friendship. Eleanor Vance, the central protagonist, is mother-dominated. On her father's death the adolescent Eleanor was associated with an outbreak of poltergeist activity, in which her family home was repeatedly showered with stones. The event invites comparison with 'The Lottery', in which the victim of the stoning, Tessie Hutchinson, is not only a mother, but a mother who sees her daughter as so much an extension of herself that she attempts to improve her own chances of survival by involving Eva in the fatal draw. Eleanor clearly resented her recently dead mother, whom she nursed for eleven years: 'the only person in the world she genuinely hated, now that her mother was dead, was her sister' (p. 9).[8] Initially her excursion to Hill House to participate in Dr Montague's study of psychic phenomena appears as an opportunity for psychological liberation, the first steps towards autonomy. The trip begins with a small act of assertion against the mother-image. When Eleanor's sister refuses to allow her to use their shared car ('I am sure Mother would have agreed with me, Eleanor' – p. 14), Eleanor reacts by simply stealing it, in the process knocking over an angry old woman who is clearly associated with the 'cross old lady' (p. 10) whom she had nursed for so long. Once *en route* Eleanor is haunted by the refrain 'Journeys end in lovers meeting', suggesting (as the *carpe diem* theme of the song confirms) that Eleanor's goal is the realisation of heterosexual desires.

Eleanor's fantasies on the journey, however, imply that her primary emotional relation remains with her mother. In imagination she dreams up several 'homes', based on houses on her route. In the first, 'a little dainty old lady took care of me' (p. 19), bringing trays of tea and wine 'for my health's sake'. The fantasy reveals just how much Eleanor herself wishes to be mothered. In the preceding period, as nurse to a sick mother, Eleanor may be said to have 'mothered' her own mother, losing her youth in the process. A second fantasy centres upon a hollow square of poisonous oleanders, which seem to Eleanor to be 'guarding something' (p. 20). Since the oleanders enclose only an empty centre, Eleanor promptly supplies a mother to occupy it, constructing an enthralling fairy world in which 'the queen waits, weeping, for the princess to return' (p. 21). Though she swiftly revises this daydream of mother–daughter reunion, into a more conventional fantasy of courtship by a handsome prince, she remains much preoccupied with images of protected spaces and magic enclosures, of a home in which *she* could be mothered and greeted as a long-lost child. A subsequent incident reinforces this impression. Pausing for lunch, Eleanor observes a little girl who refuses to drink her milk because it is not in the familiar cup, patterned with stars, which she uses at home. Despite material persuasion, the child resists, forcing her mother to yield. The small tableau emphasises both the child's potential independence and resistance to the mother, and the attractions of the familiar home world, here associated with mother's milk and starry containment. Eleanor empathises with the little girl's narcissistic desires: 'insist on your cup of stars; once they have trapped you into being like everyone else you will never see your cup of stars again' (p. 22). Eleanor's final fantasy home, a cottage hidden behind oleanders, 'buried in a garden' (p. 23), is entirely secluded from the world. Taken together, her fantasies suggest her ambivalent individuation and the lure of a magic mother-world. They form a striking contrast to the reality of Hillsdale, a tangled mess of dirty houses and crooked streets. For all its ugliness, however, Eleanor deliberately delays there over coffee. Despite her reiterated refrain 'In delay there lies no plenty', Eleanor is not quite so eager to reach her goal and realise her desires as she thinks. Another scene of enforced delay, negotiating with a surly caretaker at the gates of Hill House, further retards her progress. The emphasis here on locked gates, guards against entry, a tortuous access road, and the general difficulty in locating the house reinforces the impression of its desirability as *heimlich*, secret, a home kept away from the eyes of others.

Entry to this protected enclave provokes, however, a response which underlines the consonance of the familiar and the uncanny: childish terror. Afraid that she will cry 'like a child sobbing and wailing' (p. 34), tiptoeing around apprehensively, Eleanor feels like 'a small creature swallowed whole by a monster' which 'feels my tiny little movements inside' (p. 38). The intra-uterine fantasy immediately associates Hill House with an engulfing mother. Eleanor's fellow guest, Theo, reacts in opposite terms, characterising the two women as Babes in the Woods (abandoned by parents) and comparing the experience to the first day at boarding-school or camp. The vulnerable continuity between fear of engulfment and fear of separation is indicated in the women's response to the threat. Reminiscing about their childhoods, they eagerly associate themselves through fancied family resemblances, until Theo announces that theirs is an indissoluble relationship: 'Would you let them separate us now? Now that we've found out we're cousins?' (p. 49). Yet on the arrival of the remaining guests, Luke and Dr Montague, Theo's assertion of female strength through attachment is swiftly replaced as the four establish their identities, in playfully exaggerated form, through separation and differentiation: 'You are Theodora because *I* am Eleanor'; 'I have no beard so *he* must be Dr Montague' (pp. 53–4). Fantasy selves are then elaborated. Luke introduces himself as a bullfighter; Eleanor poses as an artist's model, living an 'abandoned' life while moving from garret to garret; Theo describes herself as a lord's daughter, masquerading as an ordinary mortal in the clothes of her maid, in order to escape a parental plot of forced marriage. Interestingly, though both women characterise themselves as homeless, Eleanor converts homelessness into an image of abandonment, Theo into active escape from an oppressive parent by asserting a different identity. For Eleanor, however, identity remains elusive. In envisaging herself as an artist's model she acquiesces in a self-image created by a controlling other.

Introductions over, the foursome make a preliminary exploration of Hill House which confirms its character as an ambivalent maternal enclave. Comfortable, its menu excellent, the house has 'a reputation for insistent hospitality' (p. 59), and is distinguished by inwardness and enclosure. Labyrinthine in layout, its concentric circles of rooms, some entirely internal and windowless, make access to the outside world problematic. Doors close automatically on its occupants, who are further confused by its architectural peculiarities. In Hill House every apparent right-angle is a fraction off, all these tiny aberrations of measurement adding up to a large overall distortion, which upsets the inhabitants' sense of balance. An encircling verandah obscures awareness of the distortion. While this structure mirrors the conventional twisted line of Gothic (in plot as in architecture), baffling the reader's sense of direction and threatening to lead at any point out of one world and into another, it also emphasises an internalised entrapment which threatens reason and balance. Luke is in no doubt as to the house's identity: 'It's all so motherly. Everything so soft. Everything so padded.

Great embracing chairs and sofas which turn out to be hard and unwelcoming when you sit down, and reject you at once –' (p. 174). The ambivalent suggestions here of maternal comfort and maternal rejection invite comparison with *The Sundial*, in which the labyrinthine connection between mother as security and mother as trap is foregrounded in a physical maze, to which only Aunt Fanny knows the key. The pattern of the maze is built upon her mother's name, Anna, so that, by turning right, left, left, right, then left, right, right, left, the centre is reached. As long as the mother's name is remembered, Fanny is secure in 'the maze I grew up in',[9] despite the activities of the matriarch, Orianna, the murderess of her own child.

Paradoxically, the doctor's history reveals that Hill House is actually notable for an absence of mothers. The first Mrs Crain died in a carriage accident in the drive, the second in a fall, the third in Europe of consumption. Since Hugh Crain's two daughters were therefore brought up without a mother, the house is simultaneously associated with mothering and with motherlessness. Later the older of the two daughters took possession of the house, dying there amidst accusations that her young companion had neglected her. The latter, persecuted by the younger sister's attempts to regain the house, eventually hanged herself. The history of the house therefore provides a psychic configuration not unlike Eleanor's own, which also involves a dead mother, two warring sisters, and a neglected old lady. Eleanor later accuses herself: 'It was my fault my mother died. She knocked on the wall and called me and called me and I never woke up' (p. 177). On learning the history of the house, however, Eleanor empathises with the unmothered girls and the companion. Eleanor has been both mother and child. On the one hand she detests the mother's dominance, resenting the loss of her own youth in the forced assumption of the 'mothering' role. On the other, she feels guilt at not having mothered adequately. Both images are internalised so that Eleanor is haunted by guilt as a mother over the neglected child within herself.

As a result two rooms in Hill House are of special significance to her – the library and the nursery, the one associated with the mother, the other with the unmothered child. Eleanor is quite incapable of entering the library: '"I can't go in there." . . . She backed away, overwhelmed with the cold air of mould and earth which rushed at her. "My mother –"' (p. 88). Eleanor's mother had forced her to read love stories aloud to her each afternoon, hence the library's supulchral associations. The library is also the point of access to the tower, where the companion hanged herself. Theo jokes, 'I suppose she had some sentimental attachment to the tower; what a nice word "attachment" is in that context' (p. 88). If attachments can be linked with annihilation and wilful surrender of the self, their absence can be equally damaging. The nursery of the unmothered girls is marked by a cold spot at its entrance 'like the doorway of a tomb' (p. 101). On its wall is painted a frieze of animals which appear as if trapped or dying. Ironically Dr Montague describes this area of cold nurturance as 'the heart of the house' (p. 101).

The stage is now set for the first appearance of the 'ghost', which occurs at the heart of Jackson's novel, almost exactly at its centre. Eleanor's internalisation of both the 'unmothered child' and the 'neglected mother' images is reflected in the double mother–child nature of the haunting. Awakening, Eleanor at first thinks that her mother is calling and knocking on the wall. In fact a tremendous pounding noise, beginning close to the nursery door, accompanied by a wave of cold, has disturbed her. The violence of the phenomenon suggests a force strong enough to threaten the boundaries of the ego; amidst deafening crashes it very nearly smashes in the door. Nevertheless, Eleanor's first reaction is relief that it is *not* her mother, but 'only a noise' (p. 108). Indeed, she sees it as 'like something children do, not mothers knocking against the wall for help' (p. 108). The ghost now undergoes a metamorphosis, its vehement demands yielding to an insidious seductive appeal. The doorknob is 'fondled', amidst 'little pattings' 'small seeking sounds', 'little sticky sounds' (p. 111). The relentless emphasis on smallness and the affectionate pattings suggest a child. Eleanor and Theo, huddled together in fear, have also been reduced to 'a couple of lost children' (p. 111). Importantly, the haunting is limited to the women. (The men, outside chasing a mysterious dog, hear nothing.) Alarmed, Dr Montague draws the conclusion that 'the intention is, somehow, to separate us' (p. 114). Eleanor, however, argues that 'it wanted to consume us, take us into itself, make us a part of the house' (p. 117). The threat which the men perceive in terms of separation is understood by both women in terms of fusion and engulfment. In the light of this identification of the haunting with the reassertion of the ambivalent mother–daughter bond, it is unsurprising that Eleanor awakens next day with a renewed feeling of happiness, a fresh appetite and the urge to sing and dance. When Dr Montague argues for the reality of the haunting, given the presence of independent witnesses, Eleanor cheerfully suggests the possibility that 'all three of you are in my imagination' (p. 118). The doctor's warning that this way madness lies – a state which would welcome Hill House in a 'sisterly embrace' (p. 118) – points to an incipient narcissism in Eleanor which would make self and world conterminous once more, assimilating all to the subjective imagination.

Initially Eleanor responds to the threat of ego dissolution by a strategic attachment to Theo, quickly forming a close friendship in which more than one reader has detected lesbian content (as the film version also implied). A similar uncertainty besets the reader of *Hangsaman*: is Natalie's mysterious friend Tony real, imaginary, supernatural, a double or a lesbian lover? Since Natalie is always terrified of being alone with *her* mother, the attachment may be read as the result of the projection of the symbiotic bond onto an alter ego. Similarly Eleanor fosters autonomy by division, creating in Theo a double as insurance against the destruction of her own self, and as simultaneous confirmation of relational identity. Several incidents in the novel make sense only in these terms. On her first evening at Hill House, Eleanor revels in her own individuality, contemplating her feet in new red shoes: 'What a complete and separate thing I am . . . individually an I, possessed of attributes belonging only to me' (p. 72). In contrast she regards her hands as ugly and dirty, misshapen by years of laundering her mother's soiled linen. Theo, telling Eleanor teasingly that she disliked 'women of no colour' (p. 99), paints Eleanor's toenails red in celebration of her emergent independence. Unlike the highly individuated Theo, Eleanor is drab, mousy, with a tendency to merge into her surroundings. Theo's subsequent casual comment that Eleanor's feet are dirty provokes a violent emotional reaction, for Eleanor cannot cope with the clash between colour and grime, between individuation and association with the mother. The sight of her feet now fills her with an immediate sense of helpless dependence: 'I don't like to feel helpless. My mother –' (p. 99). In what follows Eleanor fluctuates ambivalently between an antagonistic and an associative relation to Theo.

When a second apparent manifestation occurs (the message 'HELP ELEANOR COME HOME' chalked in the hall) Eleanor both revels and recoils. On the one hand the message expresses her own desire for home. On the other, she is anxious at being identified by name. *Her* identity is targeted; she has been 'singled out' (p. 124) and separated from the group. Indeed, the message also effectively divides Eleanor and Theo, sparking a quarrel when each accuses the other of writing it. Eleanor's outburst reveals both her own suppressed need for attention, and her projection of the childish identity onto Theo: 'You think *I* like the idea that I'm the centre of attention? *I'm* not the spoiled baby after all' (p. 124). Separate identity is thus both desired and rejected. When the message is reinscribed on Theo's walls, and her clothes smeared with a substance which may be paint or blood, Theo immediately accuses Eleanor, who views the 'bloody chamber' with smiling satisfaction, admitting that it reminds her of Theo applying red polish (p. 131). The reader puzzles as to whether the hauntings are supernatural or caused by Eleanor, thus drawing attention to the central question of the novel – the degree of Eleanor's independent agency. Eleanor's apparent hostility is double-edged. Scrubbing the colour off Theo, she feels uncontrollable loathing for her polluted alter ego, who is 'filthy with the stuff', 'beastly and soiled and dirty' (p. 132). Watching her, Eleanor thinks, 'I would like to batter her with rocks' (p. 133). The conjunction of the two images of enforced laundering and of stoning indicates Eleanor's hostility to the mother, and to the mother within herself. The destruction of Theo's clothes, however, suggests an attempt to destroy an independent identity (the reader recalls Theo's previous fantasy of disguise), rendering Theo colourless and bringing the women into close association. Theo now has to share Eleanor's clothes and bedroom. As she comments, 'We're going to be practically twins' (p. 133). The entire sequence culminates in an admission from Eleanor of her own fear of disintegration. Contemplating Theo, dressed in Eleanor's sweater and therefore presenting an alternative self-image in which narcissism and self-hate are almost equally involved, Eleanor expresses her desire to return to a state of primal unity:

There's only one of me, and it's all I've got. I hate seeing myself dissolve and slip and separate so that I'm living in one half, my mind, and I see the other half of me helpless . . . and I could stand any of it if I could only surrender.   (p. 134)

Forming a close relation with Theo, constituting Theo as 'other half', are strategies which culminate disastrously in the replication rather than the repudiation of the symbiotic bond, and a desire to surrender autonomy altogether.

In consequence, the subsequent 'haunting' is quite different in character, and limited to Eleanor. In the night Eleanor appears to hear a voice in Theo's empty room: 'It is a child', 'I won't let anyone hurt a child' (p. 136). While the voice babbles, Eleanor tries but fails to speak; only when it pauses is she able to cry out. It thus appears to emanate from her. Indeed, Eleanor recognises its screams from her own nightmares. Throughout the scene Eleanor has been holding Theo's hand for reassurance, clutching it so hard that she can feel the 'fine bones' (p. 137) of the fingers. On coming to consciousness (it has all been a dream) she discovers Theo sitting apart in her own bed, and shrieks, 'Whose hand was I holding?' (p. 137). The juxtaposition of a skeletal dead hand, first as reassurance then as terror, with a child's voice screaming is consonant with Eleanor's deepening neurosis. Although she adopts a mothering role ('I won't let anyone hurt a child') the penalty is to be associated with a form of security which is also a horror, with the mother as death to the self.

In desperation Eleanor makes a last attempt to establish identity outwith the mother–daughter bond. But when she solicits a confidence from Luke, in a bid for a special token of affection, his response horrifies her: '"I never had a mother." The shock was enormous. Is *that* all he thinks of me' (p. 139). Luke's subsequent comment, that he had always wanted a mother to make him grow up, prompts Eleanor's acid reply, 'Why don't you grow up by yourself?' (p. 140), indicating her impatience with a courtship model which provides no escape from the dynamics of the original relationship. That night, when Theo teases Eleanor about Luke, the women are the victims of another haunting while they are following a path through the grounds. Ostensibly squabbling over Luke, they are described in terms which suggest the persistence of a more primary bond. Each is 'achingly aware of the other' (p. 145) as they skirt around an 'open question'. The language suggests that they are trembling on the brink, *not* of an open quarrel, but of mutual seduction: 'walking side by side in the most extreme intimacy of expectation; their feinting and hesitation done with, they could only wait passively for resolution. Each knew, almost within a breath, what the other was thinking, (p. 146).

As they draw closer, arm in arm again, the path unrolls before them through a suddenly 'colourless' (p. 147) landscape, in an 'annihilation of whiteness'. Ahead there appears a ghostly tableau of a family picnic, in a garden full of rich colour, 'thickly green' grass (p. 148), red, orange and yellow flowers, beneath a bright blue sky. Theo's immediate response is to run ahead, screaming, 'Don't look back', placing colourlessness behind her, along with the risk of annihilation in a symbiotic relationship. Eleanor, however, her development definitively arrested, collapses, feeling 'time, as she had always known time, stop' (p. 149). The haunting foreshadows the outcome of their relationship. When Eleanor announces her intention of accompanying Theo to her home, Theo rejects her once and for all, impatient with what she perceives as a schoolgirl crush, 'as though I were the games mistress' (p. 177). As Eleanor's identity founders, Theo's is secured: her clothes are now restored to their original condition.

The image of the two women trampling the 'happy family' vignette under foot also foregrounds the insufficiencies of the Oedipal model, a point which is generalised by Luke's discovery of a book, composed by Hugh Crain for his daughter. Ostensibly a series of moral lessons, with illustrations of Heaven, Hell, the seven deadly sins, the book purports to guide the child in the paths of righteousness, threatening her with various terrible fates, and offering the reward of reunion in her Father's arms in Heaven 'joined together hereafter in unending bliss' (p. 143). The erotic content of the offer is fully revealed in the obscenity of Crain's accompanying illustration to 'Lust'. The pretence of guiding the child's moral development is actually an excuse to indulge in sensation, transgressing in the guise of moral admonition. Jackson thus explodes both the Freudian view of the father as former of the superego, and of art as an activity of sublimation, replacing instinctual gratifications. Here, far from being the basis of psychic ascension, the Oedipal model is an alibi for male self-indulgence, and a legitimation of patriarchal tyranny. Importantly, Crain has cut up several other books to form his own, so that his individual text draws upon all the resources available in the cultural formation of the female subject.

The arrival of Dr Montague's wife, a conventional spiritualist, measures the distance between fashionable psychic explanations and more radical theories of the psyche. The parodic Mrs Montague is primarily notable for the bookishness of her images of psychic phenomena, most of which are drawn from obvious sources.[10]

Thus, receiving a spirit message via 'planchette' from a mysterious nun, she promptly conjures up a monk and extrapolates to a heterosexual courtship model, broken vows and the nun walled up alive. Although a long correspondence in *The Times* in 1939 failed to establish evidence of any such immurement, nuns remain the most common of reported apparitions,[11] their popularity possibly the result of the recognition that the repression of female desires is a source of psychic disturbance (as in *Villette*). 'Planchette' also produces the words 'Elena', 'Mother', 'Child', 'Lost', 'Home', endlessly repeated. As a result of botched introductions Mrs Montague takes Theo for Eleanor, and passes the message to the former. The suggestion lingers that Eleanor's bid for independent identity has failed, and that she is locked into psychic repetition.

It is therefore appropriate that the next haunting repeats the features of the others (Theo remarks on the ghost's exhausted repertoire – p. 166). Noisy knockings are followed by a 'caressing touch' (p. 168) 'feeling intimately and softly', 'fondling' and 'wheedling' at the door, and by a babbling both inside and outside Eleanor's head. For Eleanor, the distinction between self and world is collapsing: 'I am disappearing inch by inch into this house, I am going apart a little bit at a time' (p. 168). As Eleanor resists dissolution, so the house shakes and threatens to fall, until she surrenders: 'I will relinquish my possession of this self of mine, abdicate. . . . "I'll come," she said' (p. 170). Instantly all is quiet, and the chapter ends with Theo's joke 'Come along, baby. Theo will wash your face for you and make you all neat for breakfast' (p. 171). Eleanor has thus given up all hope of mature individuation, welcoming the role of child.

From this point on, only Eleanor is haunted, by ghostly footsteps and a welcoming embrace (p. 178), and by a child's voice at the empty centre of the parlour singing, 'Go in and out the windows' (p. 189) – a singing-game which replaces the earlier refrain. In surrendering to the child within, Eleanor finally becomes herself the haunter, assuming the attenuated identity of the ghost. Rising by night, she thinks 'Mother', and when a voice replies 'Come along' (p. 190) she runs to the nursery, to find the cold spot gone, darts in and out of the encircling verandah, and continues the childish game by pounding on the others' doors. Around her the house is 'protected and warm' (p. 193), its layout entirely familiar. Ego dissolution has become primal bliss. Hearing Luke's voice, she recognises that of all those present she would least like *him* to catch her, and flees from male pursuit into the library, now 'deliciously fondly warm' (p. 193), its rotten spiral staircase perceived not as a danger but as a means of escape. Though in fact Eleanor is caught in a spiral of fatal repetition, moving towards complete annihilation, she is exultant: 'I have broken the spell of Hill House and somehow come inside. I am home' (p. 194). Eleanor has transferred her 'crush' to the house, described by Luke as 'a mother house, a housemother, a headmistress, a housemistress' (p. 176), and now becomes entirely conterminous with her chosen world, alive to sounds and movements in all its many rooms. Unsurprisingly, when Dr Montague excludes her from his experiment, Eleanor finds separation unthinkable and accelerates her car into a tree in the driveway. Her last thoughts reveal a fatal connection between female self-assertion and annihilation: 'I am really doing it, I am doing this all by myself, now, at last; this is me, I am really really really doing it by myself' (p. 205). In the second before collision her last lucid thought is '*Why* am I doing this?' Feminist psychoanalytics offers an answer which is oddly confirmed in the conclusion. The novel closes with a repetition, almost without alteration, of its own original paragraph, as the cycle of creation closes only to begin once more.

If, by repressing desire, human beings condemn themselves to repeat it, the appeal of Jackson's work to both male and female readers is secure. Just as each individual 'haunting' derives its horrors from the fear of regression to infantile complexes, specifically of fusion with the mother, so the general features of Jackson's fiction are comprehensible in terms of the reproduction of mothering. The anticipation of revisionist psychoanalytics in the reformulation of the sources of horror may also be traced in *The Bird's Nest*, which attributes Elizabeth Richmond's breakdown to her motherlessness; in the murdered child of *The Road through the Wall*; in the murderous and eventually murdered mother of *The Sundial*, and in Jackson's own fascination with the Lizzie Borden case, which looms behind the acquitted murderess, Harriet Stuart, of *The Sundial* and the unconvicted Merricat (*We Have Always Lived in the Castle*), who poisons the rest of her family in order to establish the symbiotic bond with her sister. It would be impertinent, not to say impossible, to speculate on the influence of Jackson's own experience of mothering on her fiction. She was herself a devoted mother of four children, as her two humorous chronicles of family life reveal. Interestingly, the titles of these celebrations of maternal experience, *Raising Demons* and *Life among the Savages*, immediately suggest works of horror fiction.

Notes

1. H. P. Lovecraft, *Supernatural Horror in Literature* (New York: Dover, 1973).
2. 'The Uncanny', in *The Standard Edition of the Complete Psychological Works of Sigmund Freud*, ed. James Strachey, vol. xvii (London: Hogarth Press, 1955).
3. See Peter Penzoldt, *The Supernatural in Fiction* (London: Peter Nevill, 1952).
4. Rosemary Jackson, *Fantasy: The Literature of Subversion* (London: Methuen, 1981).
5. See Nancy Chodorow, *The Reproduction of Mothering* (Berkeley, Calif.: University of California Press, 1978); Carol Gilligan, *In a Different Voice: Psychological Theory and Women's Development* (Cambridge, Mass.: Harvard University Press, 1982); Jean Baker Miller, *Towards a New Psychology of Women* (London: Allen Lane, 1978).
6. A motif traced, in Jungian terms, in Jackson's work by Steven K. Hoffman, in 'Individuation and Character Development in the Fiction of Shirley Jackson', *Hartford Studies in Literature*, 8 (1976) 190–208.
7. Elizabeth Abel, Marianne Hirsch and Elizabeth Langland (eds), *The Voyage In: Fictions of Female Development* (Hanover, NH: University Press of New England, 1983).
8. Page references in parentheses relate to Shirley Jackson, *The Haunting of Hill House* (London: Michael Joseph, 1960).
9. Shirley Jackson, *The Sundial* (New York: Penguin, 1986) p. 109.
10. Mrs Montague's discoveries recall the worst excesses of the ghost hunter, at Borley Rectory in Essex. See Harry Price, *The Most Haunted House in England: Ten Years Investigation of Borley Rectory* (London: Longmans, Green, 1940) and *The End of Borley Rectory* (London: George G. Harrap, 1946). Jackson refers to Borley in the text (p. 101). Though an examination of Jackson's sources would run to another essay, it is worth noting that almost all the psychic phenomena are drawn from the above work, including a haunted Blue Room, a cold spot, the girl in the tower, the nun and monk, immurement, the digging-up of an old well (proposed by Mrs Montague), messages on walls and from planchette, nightly crashings and patterings at doors, and investigation by a team of psychic researchers. Jackson described her book as originating in an account of nineteenth-century psychic researchers, almost certainly those of Ballechin House, also referred to in the text (p. 8). See A. Goodrich Freer and John, Marquess of Bute, *The Alleged Haunting of Ballechin House* (London: George Redway, 1899).
11. See Peter Underwood, *Dictionary of the Occult and Supernatural* (London: George G. Harrap, 1978) p. 147.

9

Stephen King: Powers of Horror

CLARE HANSON

PREFATORY MATTERS

In order to approach the power of horror in Stephen King's work we must move circuitously, towards the glimpsed abyss via accounts of the origins of personality offered by psychoanalytic theory, specifically by Freud, Lacan and Julia Kristeva. King's fiction is concerned above all with origins, with the grounds of being. His work betrays a fascination with those primary/primal movements and experiences which impel or force the construction of the self as a gendered social being. I shall argue that his work itself displays or follows an exemplarily 'masculine' trajectory, moving as it were from 'mother' to 'text': in order to show this I must reverse this experiental order to follow the epistemological order of psychoanalytic theory, which developed from a concentration on 'text' to a concentration on 'mother' in its movement from Freud to Kristeva.

I begin with Freud, and his account of the development of the self. According to Freud, one of the most striking and distinguishing features of the human animal is its extreme and extended dependence on its parents after birth. The human being is born, so to speak, prematurely, and requires unceasing vigilance and care before it is able to function independently of its parents. The 'family situation' is thus more or less 'given' in the construction of human personality, although the nature of the family will vary from society to society. Freud also suggests that, while we are born with certain fixed biological needs, such as our need for food, these needs soon become 'perverted' as they become associated/confused with sensations of pleasure (for instance, the pleasure which the infant derives from sucking at the breast). A drive to pleasure is thus established existing independently of need: the object of desire in this sense is by no means fixed (unlike the object of biological need – the breast, for instance). Displacement is thus an

135

inherent part of desire from its inception as part of human experience.

The child in this early stage of development is asocial. She or he cannot be a social animal without a preliminary sense of the self as distinct from others. The movement into social life occurs, according to Freud, via the Oedipus complex, or Oedipal moment. In the early months of life the child exists in a dyadic relationship with the mother, unable to distinguish between self and (m)other. The child is forced out of this blissful state through the 'intervention' of the father. The shadow of the father falls between the child and the mother as the father acts to prohibit the child's incestuous desire for its mother. At this point, the child is initiated into selfhood, perceiving itself for the first time as a being separate from the mother, who is now consciously desired because absent, forbidden. The origin of self thus lies for Freud in this absence and sense of loss. It is too at the point of repression of desire for the mother that the unconscious is formed, as a place to receive that lost desire, and it is at this point of repression that the child's early *transgressive* drives become organised and forced towards genital (and gendered) sexuality.

It is now generally agreed that Freud's account of the little boy's passage through the Oedipus is much more satisfactory than his account of the little girl's: it is hard to escape the conclusion that this was because the theory was originally *founded* on the case of the boy, the theory for the girl being something of a lame extrapolation from an already gendered theory. Yet we must look briefly at Freud's account of both the male and female passage through the Oedipus, as it provides the basis for almost all subsequent theories of the origins of sexual identity. For the male child at the Oedipal moment, it is the father's threat of castration which forces him to abandon his incestuous desire for the mother. As the desire is repressed the child has to move away from the mother, but, in giving up the hope of possessing the mother now, the male child does not give up the hope of *at some time* occupying the place of the father. He is able from this moment to aspire to fatherhood himself, to train himself to occupy the position of father/patriarch. For the little girl the case is far different. The first effect of the intervention of the father is that she will perceive herself as different/castrated, and will thus turn from her mother, perceived as similarly castrated and inadequate, to her father. When she finds that her attempts to 'seduce' her father are unsuccessful, the girl will turn back to the mother, to identify, albeit unhappily, with the mother's feminine role. In place of the penis which she can never possess, suggests Freud, she then posits as an object of desire a baby which will, she hopes, come from the father. Freud does not explain how the girl will ever progress from this incestuous position: the implication is that female sexual desire remains 'blocked', compromised by an ineradicable desire for a father-figure.

The importance of the work of Jacques Lacan lies for us in the further connections which he establishes between the Oedipal moment and the child's entry into language, which he terms the 'symbolic order'. For Lacan, the moment in which the unconscious is created, via the repression of desire for the mother, is one and the same as the moment in which language is acquired, for it is only on perceiving the mother as absent/different from her- or himself that the child will need to name her . Language, like the unconscious, is thus founded upon loss and absence, upon a lack for which it will try endlessly to compensate. This brings us to a further important insight. Lacan sees a fundamental opposition between the languageless pre-Oedipal state which he terms the 'imaginary', and the post-Oedipal world constituted by the entry into a network of social relations and into language. This opposition will be central to our understanding of Stephen King's fiction.

The symbolic is that whole network of family and social relations which the child must 'master' in order to be adequately socialised, and it is a network which leads the child away from the mother to the father. The father represents for the child the 'first term' in the social network, for it is his prohibition of desire for the mother which is the first social force or coercion which the child experiences. The father's role is also crucial in the child's entry into language, which Lacan sees as particularly important in facilitating the child's passage through the Oedipus complex. Lacan suggests that the phallus, the emblem of male sexuality and power, constitutes the 'transcendental signifier'. While the child may already have experienced lack and absence before her/his first perception of sexual difference, sexual difference 'takes up' all previous differences. The primary marker of difference becomes sexual difference, perceived in terms of fullness in the father (possession of the phallus) and lack in the mother (absence of the phallus).

Lacan stresses the importance of language as a means of controlling and marking one's social and sexual identity: in his view, in order successfully to negotiate the Oedipus complex the child must not only order and repress libidinal drives, but also, as it were, fasten onto language as the only means by which we humans may console ourselves for the absence of 'the real'. Language offers our only source of power over all that (such as the mother) which we cannot have, all that which must be consigned in its 'real' excess and radical energy to the unconscious.

This swift summary of the work of Freud and Lacan will serve to highlight the importance of certain fundamenal elements in the construction of the social being: the parents, the unconscious, the symbolic order. The 'narrative' of Freudian and Lacanian theory is of a journey from the chaotic 'other' of the unconscious to the symbolic *order* of language, which is clearly characterised as male-dominated. The work of Julia Kristeva leads us back, however, from a male-dominated symbolic to the mother, and to areas of her dominion and influence which have, Kristeva argues, been underestimated in (male) accounts of the construction and maintenance of human personality. Kristeva is best known for her concept of the semiotic, which she mobilises as a means of locating and inserting 'the feminine' back into the exclusively masculine post-Oedipal world described by Lacan. Kristeva fully accepts Lacan's account of the symbolic order by means of which social, sexual and linguistic relations are regulated by/in the name of the father. She suggests, however, that the symbolic is oppressive because it is exclusively masculine – that is, *because* it is limited, not just because it is limiting (in terms of the actual social and sexual practices which the symbolic order licences). Against the symbolic Kristeva thus sets the semiotic, a play of rhythmic patterns and 'pulsions' which are pre-linguistic. In the pre-Oedipal phase the child babbles, rhythmically: the sounds are representative (though not by the rules of language) of some of the experiences which the child is undergoing in a period when she or he is still dominated by the mother. This semiotic 'babble' thus represents/is connected with 'feminised' experience, which is of course available at this stage to both male and female children. Kristeva argues that this feminised experience is not completely repressed either by male or by female children, but that it resurfaces in adult life as a kind of disruptive influence moving over ordered language/texts. It is in the breaks and 'pulsions' of language and text that we can identify the 'feminine' in all of us breaking up and challenging the symbolic order.

But it is Kristeva's concept of 'abjection' which will be of greatest concern to us in our consideration of horror in Stephen King: indeed, the concept was first formulated in the book called *Pouvoirs de l'horreur* (*Powers of Horror*).[1] Here Kristeva reaches 'back' before the Oedipus complex and the constitution of the self as a subject defined by an object, the (m)other. She posits an earlier 'splitting-off' from the mother which takes place in early infancy: this splitting-off may be defined as the merest preliminary *turning-away* from the mother. The child is not yet a subject nor the mother an object, but the moment of abjection is that in which a space first appears between the two, a space created, necessarily, by a slight movement of rejection or withdrawal. The abject is described in this way by Kristeva:

The abject is not an ob-ject in front of me that I name or imagine. Neither is it this *'ob-jeu'*, *petit 'a'* indefinitely fleeing in the systematic quest of desire. The abject is not my correlate which, by offering me a support on someone or something other, would allow me to be more or less detached and autonomous. The abject shares only one quality with the object – that of being opposed to *I*. But if, in being opposed, the object offers me equilibrium within the fragile web of a desire for meaning which in fact makes me indefinitely and infinitely homologous to it, the *abject*, on the contrary, as fallen object, is what is radically excluded, drawing me towards the point where meaning collapses.

She speaks of

This massive and abrupt irruption of a strangeness which, if it was familiar to me in an opaque and forgotten life, now importunes me as radically separated and repugnant. Not me. Not that. But not nothing either. A 'something' that I do not recognise as a thing. A whole lot of nonsense which has nothing insignificant and which crushes me. At the border of inexistence and hallucination, of a reality which, if I recognise it, annihilates me.[2]

Here Kristeva is suggesting that the abject, representing the primary 'turning-away', can return and rise up through the surface of adult life, welling up to announce its own meaning – which is meaninglessness or fear. Because it is outside (or before) the symbolic order, the abject has no apprehensible meaning, and leads us 'towards the point where meaning collapses'. It is relatively easy to relate this 'whole lot of nonsense which has nothing insignificant and which crushes me' to horror as we associate it with the traditional iconography of horror fiction or horror films. As Kristeva explains, the abject in this sense can be represented by any kind of transgressive state, or any condition which challenges the limits and boundaries of being. She focuses on filth, refuse, cloaca: these 'entities' challenge the limits of being because they are ever on the border of living existence, verging on death or decay. The corpse is the ultimate example of refuse which works in this way to destroy limits; as Kristeva writes,

> The corpse – seen without God and outside science – is the height of abjection. It is death infesting life. Abject. It is something rejected from which one is not separated, from which one is not protected as is the case with an object. An imaginary strangeness and a menace that is real, it calls to us and finishes by devouring us.[3]

However, it is important to note that Kristeva's theory of abjection is founded on a specific turning-away, *from the mother*. The images of abjection which she mentions (blood, faeces, and so on) suggest a preoccupation with the body splitting from itself, but this is a later 'version' or image of the original source of anxiety, the split with the mother, which inspires, both fascination and horror, for the abjected mother both is, and is not, 'me'. In the moment of abjection, 'I expel *myself*, I spit *myself* out, I abject *myself* in the same movement by which "I" claims to be me.' 'I' oscillates between a 'pole of attraction and repulsion'. Hence the compulsive *fascination* of horror: what I am concerned particularly to explore in this essay is the corresponding sense of *repulsion* or distaste for the mother and the maternal body, as this is expressed in a variety of texts.

CARRIE: ABJECTION

Carrie is concerned with an apparently trivial incident – the onset of menstruation in a sixteen-year-old girl – and with its monstrous, far-reaching consequences. The onset of menstruation in Carrie

White is traumatic: this trauma releases her latent 'telekinetic' powers and results in the virtual destruction of the small town in Maine where she has lived all her life. After the disaster we are told that the town is 'waiting to die'. Why should such a trivial-seeming incident have such consequences? Any why should Carrie White be endowed by her creator with 'telekinetic' powers? To answer such questions we have only to turn to Kristeva's developing account of the abject in *Powers of Horror*. As we have seen, Kristeva associates images of *waste* with abjection. She suggests further than this waste falls into two categories: the excremental, which threatens identity from the outside, and the menstrual, which threatens from within. Menstrual waste is for obvious reasons also connected particularly closely with the body of the mother and with 'memories' of the primary abjection of that body.

In *Carrie* we as readers are placed as voyeurs, forced(?) to witness an extreme distaste/horror inspired by the menstrual blood of others. The novel thus functions for its readers as what Kristeva would call a 'defilement ritual', but on a massive scale. The whole novel acts as a purifying rite of passage, exorcising the power of the abject and of the loved/hated maternal body. In *Carrie* the exorcism sets a whole town ablaze, with a fire the fierceness of which mirrors the force of feeling stirred by the menstrual/maternal.

Revulsion from the menstrual 'fires' two of the strongest scenes in the novel. The first is a scene among schoolgirls showering after volleyball. Carrie, showering with the others, sees blood trickling down her leg: she does not yet know what menstruation is and screams, significantly, 'I'm bleeding to death.' The other girls crowd round her with a true herd instinct, chanting 'period, period', 'you're bleeding, you're bleeding':

> Then the laughter, disgusted, contemptuous, horrified, seemed to rise and bloom into something jagged and ugly, and the girls were bombarding her with tampons and sanitary napkins. . . . They flew like snow and the chant became; 'Plug it *up*, plug it *up*, plug it –'[4]

We are told that the girls felt first a 'mixture of hate, revulsion, exasperation and pity', then 'welling disgust': the meaning and force of the group reaction is deepened when this scene is linked metaphorically with a second 'shower' scene. We see this second scene from various points of view, but the full force of the horror is this time felt by Carrie alone as she is once again horribly exposed in front of her peers. As they sit (incongruously) on the 'thrones' set up for the 'King and Queen' of the May Ball, Carrie and her escort Tommy are suddenly drenched in pig's blood. We are shown the childish vindictiveness of the teenage conspirators who have set this ritual scene of defilement up, but there is something deeper than childishness in the boy Billy's chant 'Pig's blood for a pig', and, especially, in Carrie's apprehension of the horror of the scene:

> Someone began to laugh, a solitary, affrighted hyena sound, and she *did* open her eyes, opened them to see who it was and it *was* true, the final nightmare, she was red and dripping with it, they had drenched her in the very secretness of blood, in front of all of them and her thought
> (oh . . . i . . . COVERED . . . with it)
> was covered a ghastly purple with her revulsion and her shame. She could smell herself and it was the *stink* of blood, the awful wet, coppery smell . . . she . . . felt the soft pattern of tampons and napkins against her skin as voices exhorted her to plug it UP, tasted the plump, fulsome bitterness of horror. They had finally given her the shower they wanted.   (p. 167)

The surface of life is peeled back in such a scene to show the abject which lies 'behind' it, that which is 'secret' (blood should remain *within*). Carrie feels 'revulsion' and 'shame', but more significant is the phrase 'the plump, fulsome bitterness of horror'. King suggests through this the primary and affective nature of abjection through its connection with primary sense impressions (here taste) and suggests too the mingled fascination and horror with which we view the abject which is so nearly a part of ourselves. So his almost oxymoronic phrase 'fulsome bitterness' gives us the particular feeling of this kind of horror, the abject as a source of horror. This quality makes us experience an almost vertiginous sense of existing on a borderline between sense and non-sense, meaning and non-meaning.

Carrie thus pivots on the reader's horror of the abject as it resurfaces in adult life, but also exploits the reader's potential pleasure in contemplation of the abject. As one is drawn back to a point before entry into the symbolic order, one may experience pleasure on two grounds. First, one may experience pleasure in breaking the taboos which surround and constitute the symbolic;

one may experience the pleasure of transgression as one reaches back to experience and to a mode of being which is forbidden. Secondly, one may be placed back in touch with the pleasure which one originally felt in the pre-symbolic state, pleasure derived from unmediated experience of the maternal body and of one's own bodily functions.

If *Carrie* as text puts us back in touch with the pre-symbolic it does so despite (or because of?) the fact that for the character Carrie herself there can be no *proper* connection either with the maternal semiotic or with the paternal symbolic. Carrie, like her mother, is doomed to exist as what Kristeva would call a 'borderline case',[5] tied to the ambiguity of abjection, blocked or thwarted in her development. It is significant that both Carrie *and her mother* have an absent father. Mrs White's father was killed in a 'barroom shooting incident' and immediately after this she began to attend 'fundamentalist prayer meetings': the connection between the loss of the father and the turn to extreme religious fundamentalism is made clear. Mrs White's marriage was brief, for Carrie's father was killed, in another accident, before she was born. Mrs White, unstable herself, takes over the role of the father in Carrie's upbringing, acting as a kind of crazed, overstated representative of the symbolic. Uncertain of her own identity, she finds relief in a 'false' identification with the masculine role, and this has the effect – vital of course to the power of the novel – of intensifying Carrie's feelings of disgust and shame towards the feminine and the maternal. Carrie is brought up to fear and distrust the generative sexual powers of the female body: it is impressed on her not only that sex is sinful, but that sex has its origins in the sinfulness of the mother, in her lust and desire. Her mother tells of her own pleasure in the sexual act in a kind of retrospective frenzy of repudiation, and then moves into a ritualistic chant, the main theme of which is again the sinfulness of Eve, who 'loosed the raven on the world' and who was visited by 'the Curse of Blood'.

In the absence of a real father, the image of a 'kind, vengeful' God, to use her mother's happy phrase, takes the place of the father in Carrie's childhood. Godfather, God-the-father instils revulsion from the feminine semiotic but offers no way into the masculine symbolic. Carrie is haunted through childhood by dreams in which she is pursued by a 'mutilated Christ', 'holding a mallet and nails, begging her to take up her cross and follow Him'. Towards the end of the novel, having destroyed an entire town through the force of her telekinetic powers, Carrie makes a last, desperate appeal to God / the masculine / the symbolic, confronting what she sees as 'the abyss'. Her appeal falls into nothingness and she takes the only option left to her if she is going to come to terms with the abjected mother-figure. Carrie and her mother must destroy each other in order to put an end to an intolerable relationship in which each perceives the other as an aspect of herself. Carrie and Margaret White perceive each other as aspects of the self which they reject but from which they can never be freed. Margaret casts her daughter as her own mother, projecting onto the child Carrie the disgust/need which she felt for her own mother, and Carrie returns these ambiguous feelings with interest. Margaret White has, however, moved beyond both a sense of need and the possibility of help by the time we reach the climactic scene of the novel, in which she murders Carrie with the same knife with which she had cut the umbilical cord at the time of Carrie's birth. The weakening Carrie has time only to 'will' the death of her mother before she drags herself off to die in an anonymous parking-lot. Carrie's is a death in which we participate, via the consciousness of a witness, Sue Snell, who finds herself being drawn unwillingly into Carrie's mind at the point of death. What is most striking about this 'horrid' death scene, with its 'orthodox', so to speak, vision of the abject corpse, is the way in which the mother, not the father, is presented as the ground of *all* meaning and being. Sue Snell is overcome by her sense of Carrie's need for her mother, and feels a terror *which she cannot name* as she feels that without the mother she/Carrie cannot *complete her thought*. The mother seems to be at least as important as the father in the mastery of the symbolic as well as immersion in the semiotic:

> (momma would be alive i killed my momma i want her o it hurts my chest my shoulder o o o i want my momma)
> (carrie i)
> And there was no way to finish that thought, nothing there to complete it with. Sue was suddenly ovewhelmed with terror, the worse because she could put no name to it. The bleeding freak on this oil-stained asphalt suddenly seemed meaningless and awful in its pain and dying.
> (o momma i'm scared momma MOMMA)
> Sue tried to pull away . . . . (p. 211)

THE SHINING: THE OEDIPAL

The Shining is one of King's most powerful and haunting novels, bearing comparison with Poe's 'The Masque of the Red Death', the story which provides an epigraph and a central image for King's text. In *The Shining* King is concerned again with the origins of being, with the construction of the subject in the unconscious and conscious mind, with the interplay between what Lacan would call the symbolic, the imaginary and the real in the construction of that subject. The text plays with images of disintegration and doubling, images of the dissolution and dispersal of the individual subject, but what is striking about the text overall is its strong recuperative thrust. The story is concerned with the entry into the symbolic of the young boy Danny, and with the difficulties he experiences because of a disruption of the symbolic caused by his father. The whole project of the novel is to place Danny securely in the symbolic order and to insert him equally securely into the social world. The power of the text stems from the tension between Danny and his father, the tension between the nightmare images produced by the (joint) unconscious and the everyday world of narrative and action. Jack, the father, has been disturbed by dreadful images coming from the shadow world of the unconscious: these images must be 'mastered'; and Danny must take a different path from his father if he is, literally, to survive the story. The novel is concerned very obviously with an opposition between image and text: text, or language, must be preferred over the fatal image. In this preoccupation with language (which offers a direct road, so to speak, to the symbolic and the social order), in its concern to establish Danny in a particular (white, American, male) social and symbolic order, *The Shining* might be considered a 'conservative', regressive text. Yet, paradoxically, the strong drive to the symbolic in *The Shining* is of course founded precisely on the overwhelming power of those oppositional images which haunt reader, writer and protagonist.

The Shining follows a male journey through the Oedipus complex, the journey of Danny, who is endowed with supersensory powers of second sight and telepathy. These powers are, as it were, symbolic, and, rather like Carrie White's telekinetic powers, suggest the power of the collective unconscious. (One of the themes of *The Shining* is the way in which our lives, conscious and unconscious, interrelate and intersect with others; also the way in which we are doomed to double and repeat the lives of others. Here Danny's relationship to his father is particularly important.) Danny is locked in the Oedipal moment, unable to progress through it, and his situation is explicitly related back to the Oedipal position of his parents. We are told of his mother's inability to move beyond the 'blocked' Oedipal relation to her father which Freud described: we are told that she had been her father's from the beginning and that she, as the father's primary love object, was responsible for her parents' divorce. Jack at one point asks her whom she wants to marry, her father or him. Wendy is particularly sensitive to the threat of repetition patterning, and to the life-or-death dangers which surround children as they struggle to establish a free, stable self. She knows that 'to children adult motives and actions must seem as bulking and ominous as dangerous animals seen in the shadows of a dark forest. They were jerked about like puppets, having only the vaguest notions why'[6] – which makes them of course *like* us, an emblem of the vulnerability of humanity. Endlessly, restlessly, Wendy links her own past and Danny's past and future – 'Oh we are wrecking this boy. It's not just Jack, it's me too, and maybe it's not even just us, Jack's father, my mother, are they here too?'

It is, however, Jack's inability to free himself from *his* father which poses the greatest threat to Danny. Jack's early closeness to his father ended when his father (associated repeatedly with phallic emblems: a gold-headed cane, an elevator) 'suddenly' and for 'no good reason' beat his mother, his cane whistling through the air. From that point on Jack exists in an ambivalent relation to his father, who still has power over him despite (or perhaps because of) his alcoholism: after his father's death he is haunted by him, as an 'irrational white ghost-god'. Through all this we can detect a repeating pattern going back from Jack to his father and so on, in which feelings of social insecurity combine with or give rise to irrational behaviour and drunkenness. The father, in other words, seems to be insecure in his place in the symbolic/social order, and this seems to be obscurely linked with a revulsion from the feminine or more specifically from the wife as *mother*. So Jack thinks of the relations between his mother and father with a kind of savage black humour:

The thing he'd never asked himself, Jack realised now, was exactly what had driven his daddy to drink in the first place.

And really . . . when you came right down to what his old students had been pleased to call the nitty-gritty . . . hadn't it been the woman he was married to? A milksop sponge of a woman, always dragging silently around the house with an expression of doomed martyrdom on her face? A ball and chain around Daddy's ankle? . . . Mentally and spiritually dead, his mother had been handcuffed to his father by matrimony. Still, Daddy had tried to do right as he dragged her rotting corpse through life.   (p. 355)

What threatens Danny is *Jack's* insecure hold on the symbolic: this insecurity is expressed through his rejection of his wife, Wendy, and his failure to hold down his job as a teacher, to fill his appointed social role. Jack resists what Sartre would call the 'thetic', the 'real' world of propositions and action. Almost consciously he embraces the unreal, the irrational, the 'sleep of reason' which, as Goya says, 'breeds monsters'.[7]

Significantly, Jack has been a writer, but as *The Shining* progresses he literally begins to lose his hold on language. He finds it increasingly difficult to write, daydreams, becomes overinvolved with a kind of degraded text, a scrapbook full of old newspaper cuttings through which he searches for some kind of lost meaning. As he declines in this way, be begins to *act* the part of the father in an overstated way rather reminiscent of Carrie's mother: this hollow acting is reflected in Danny's nightmare dream-visions, in which he is pursued by a mysterious 'shape' or 'monster', wielding a mallet which echoes with a 'great hollow boom'. Meanwhile Danny works, patiently to master the symbolic: he is desperate to learn to read in order to decipher the riddling words which have flashed before him in his dreams:

He hunched over the innocuous little books, his crystal radio and balsa glider on the shelf above him, *as though his life depended on learning to read*. His small face was more tense and paler than she liked. . . . He was taking it very seriously, both the reading and the workbook pages his father had made up for him every afternoon. Picture of an apple and a peach, the word *apple* written beneath in Jack's large, neatly made printing. . . . And their son would stare from the word to the picture, his lips moving, sounding out, actually *sweating* it out.   (p. 117)

As his hold on language becomes stronger, Danny becomes better and better able to confront the nightmares which pursue him. At first he represses the meaning of his dreams – 'It's like I can't remember because it's so bad I don't *want* to remember' – but gradually he is able to confront the dreams and relate them to through the symbolic. At the crisis of the book it is through language that he overcomes his father. As the father, transformed into a maniac figure with a swinging (phallic) mallet, looms above him, Danny has only words with which to oppose him – but words are finally enough and everything as Danny brings to the surface and into speech that which his father had forgotten:

> (*you will remember what your father forgot*)
> . . . Sudden triumph filled his face; the thing saw it and hesitated, puzzled.
> 'The boiler!' Danny screamed. '*It hasn't been dumped since this morning! It's going up! It's going to explode!*'   (p. 400)

Danny is now through, so to speak, his unbearably fraught passage through the Oedipus: he has, unlike his father, established a proper relationship between the pre-symbolic (imaged in the typography of the novel through everything in 'the basement' – including the boiler), and the symbolic. He achieves his place in the symbolic at great cost because his father has offered no stable or proper model for him. As a result, he has to split his own image of his father, blending all the beneficent aspects of his father into an image of the good father which can be split off from the crazed maniac who faces him in the final scene. The split father guarantees the healing of the split(s) in Danny, guarantees the establishment of a stable and unified self.

The Shining has a complex and shifting meaning which 'is' more than the sum of its parts. Much of the power of the text derives from the fact that the images of death in it – images which form the stock-in-trade of most horror fiction – function precisely *as images*. King sees that their power lies in their ability to evoke our most secret and fundamental terrors, terrors which are *not* of death itself, but of the extinction of personality, of which death itself is an image. We may never overcome these terrors; we may remain always 'overlooked' ('The Overlook' is the name of the vast hotel in which the main action of the novel takes place) by forces beyond our control, which continue to threaten our fragile, vulnerable constructions of self.

MISERY: TEXT

Misery is a highly sophisticated and self-conscious text. It constitutes an exploration of itself and an exploration of the genesis of all King's fiction, of the origins of what he calls his 'Gothic' horror. The novel's protagonist is a writer (compare Jack, in *The Shining*). Paul Sheldon has written a string of best-selling detective novels featuring an aristocratic nineteenth-century Englishwoman, Misery Chastain (the name itself is a little image complex, combining the words 'misery', 'chastise', 'chain', 'stain', etc.). After a bad car accident in which he is nearly killed, Paul finds himself, by a series of bizarre coincidences, not in hospital, but locked up in the isolated house of his 'number one fan', an ex-nurse, Annie Wilkes. Annie holds him as a prisoner, 'caring' for him by splinting his legs in an amateurish fashion and dosing him up with illegally obtained pain-killing drugs. She then strikes a strange bargain with him. In his last 'Misery' novel Paul has finally, and to his great relief, killed Misery off – he wants to get on with more 'serious' writing. Annie has been waiting to read this particular 'Misery' novel, and does so just after Paul has come into her power. Finding that Misery has been killed, she accuses Paul of 'murder', and dictates that he shall write another novel, immediately, bringing Misery back to life. Paul is in no position to argue: he senses that the underlying threat is that of a different murder, of himself by Annie, if he does not 'restore' Misery to her. Paul is thus placed in the position of literally writing for his life, a latter-day Scheherazade; all the time he is needed to write this text and tell this story, he will live – but he understands that he will die when 'his tale is told' (the closing lines of King's 'real' novel).

The text thus explores the relation between 'misery' as a common noun (defined by King as 'pain, usually lengthy and often pointless') and the generation of texts, stories. The access to misery must be there, King seems to suggest, in order for the text to be: indeed, it is indicated in the second half of the novel that Paul actually needs (and perhaps courts) the hellish circumstances in which he finds himself in order to write well, convincingly. The worse his situation becomes, the better he writes, and so, ironically, he colludes with Annie in his captivity. The writer too is a 'borderline' case in the Kristevian sense, not so fixed in the symbolic as would appear – he has to have or to generate access to the pre-symbolic too, to forms of feeling which in this case are acutely painful. King's writing would seem to suggest that the production of a Gothic/horror text is connected with an ability to reach down to experience before the symbolic, 'stirring up', so to speak, some of the horrors which (can) attend the birth of the self: the text works in this way as an exorcism.

The central opposition in *Misery* is between Paul and Annie: an opposition between masculine and feminine, between writer and muse. Annie *is* the mother; she is the monstrous feminine, the castrating female. At the very beginning of the novel we are told of her 'maternal' feelings for Paul: we hear of her 'maternal love and tenderness'; she is 'Annie the mom'. She is presented as monstrous from the opening of the novel too. She is described as an idol, and this image is developed through the novel, her implacability being stressed. She has a curious sexual quality: she is at once very feminine in the obvious physical sense, having large breasts, for example, and yet she is at the same time 'defeminised' in the social-sexual sense, unsubdued and unsubduable to the feminine as it is viewed/constructed by man: 'Her body was big but not generous. There was a feeling about her of clots and roadblocks rather than welcoming orifices or even open spaces, areas of hiatus.'[8] She operates as the castrating female in the most horrifying scene in the text, when she amputates Paul's foot, wielding an axe and a blow-torch. The castration image is under-scored: we are told that Paul is sure, in this scene, that Annie will castrate him, and later Annie coyly confesses that she had thought of cutting off Paul's 'man-gland'.

There could hardly be a clearer image, then, of the feminine as monstrous. Annie is to Paul an image prompting only one response, 'a feeling of unease deepening steadily toward terror'. Yet Annie, like the mother, *must* exist in order for the self/the text to begin to be born, in the primary movement of abjection. Like the mother she must be there in order that she may be abjected: in *Misery* that is the role of woman; she has no other function. There are *no* positive images of the feminine in this misogynistic text.

Annie is particularly closely associated with the pre-symbolic and the movement of abjection because she is herself a 'borderline' case, one whose problems are situated on the borderline between neurosis and psychosis. Paul describes her in this way:

> Because of his researches for *Misery*, he had rather more than a
> layman's understanding of neurosis and psychosis, and he knew
> that although a borderline psychotic might have alternating
> periods of deep depression and almost aggressive cheerfulness
> and hilarity, the puffed and infected ego underlay all, positive
> that all eyes were upon him or her.[9]

Her psychosis leads her towards self-mutilation, i.e. to a breaking-
down of the divisons between self and world, and her hold on
language is also weakened; she speaks a kind of nursery English
which is frighteningly at odds with the realities of her situation
and actions.

Annie and Paul have in common a skewed relation to language.
Overall they exist in a close, symbiotic relationship in which Annie
acts, as we have seen, as Paul's hellish muse, leading him back
into the past and his personal prehistory *in order that he should
write*. For, although Paul has fantasies about a miraculous escape
from Annie, he knows that the only way out of the situation he is
locked in is through writing: he must, as it were, write himself
into the symbolic. In this way he will gain control not only over
language, but also over plot. For 'writing', in the widest sense,
does not just give us control over language as *understanding* – the
kind of control Jack is seeking in *The Shining*. 'Writing' also gives
us control over plot, action, endows us with the power to intervene
in the life and destiny not just of ourselves but of others too. Paul,
in bringing Misery back to life, has to find a parallel way of
writing/plotting himself back to life, away from Annie. The connection between the plotting he undertakes for *Misery's Return* and
the plotting of his own escape is underscored in the text; also,
when Paul first realises that *Misery's Return* is turning into a better
novel than any of his others, a 'Gothic' novel, he notes that the
book was 'thus more dependent on plot than on situation. The
challenges were constant.'

Paul's successful completion of the new novel occurs immediately
before the successful completion of the plot to murder Annie, the
'Dragon-lady'. We may thus read our text *Misery* as signifying this:
Paul, a writer, has tried to kill 'Misery', to banish misery in the
sense of 'lengthy pain' from his life. He had thought that this would
lead to better writing. Yet Annie's intervention, her insistence that

he should bring 'Misery' back to life, and her production of 'lengthy pain' lead Paul to write a book which is better than any of his other 'Misery' novels. Paul begins to wonder whether Annie may not have done him a favour in insisting on the resurrection of Misery, and he reflects on his astonishing productiveness as a writer under the stringent, painful conditions she has imposed. It is thus as though Paul is driven to master the symbolic when he is impelled by fear, when he is in flight from images and situations which recall painful experiences (usually repressed) from the pre-symbolic, semiotic world. The text *Misery*, opening with Paul's 'second birth' after the car accident, thus has a double dimension. On one level is the apparent text, telling of Paul's incarceration with Annie and his eventual escape. On a second level the text constantly comments on itself, drawing attention to the processes of its own production as a horror text as Paul moves from the darkness of his first awakening after the accident (analogous to the 'darkness' of early infancy) to the daylight clarity of his final vision and production of text and situation at the close of the book. Annie, the monstrous feminine, has acted as the necessary catalyst to bring him from the darkness of infancy (Latin *infans*, 'unable to speak') to the wielding of textual power.

FEMINIST AFTERWORD: GENDER AND GENRE

Horror fiction is, primarily, produced and consumed by men. Why should this be? It would seem that the experience derived from horror fiction (as opposed to the experience of horror in 'real life') is peculiarly fascinating to men, or rather to the masculine subject, i.e. the subject constituted as masculine through the particular nature of his/her experience, particularly in early childhood. For the masculine child, the movement away from the mother, expressed as it is through abjection and the passage through the Oedipus complex, seems to be more traumatic than for the feminine child. For the feminine child there remains at least a possibility of reunion with the mother through *identification*; also, the feminine subject is actively encouraged to retain links with the maternal semiotic through the cultivation of such qualities as 'intuition'. The masculine subject by contrast depends for his very identity on the effectiveness of his repression of the maternal semiotic and of desire for the mother.

Horror fiction is constituted of images designed precisely to stir 'memories' of the early abjection of the mother and of the later traumatic passage through the Oedipus to the symbolic. As we have seen in the work of Stephen King, images of the monstrous feminine are common in horror fiction, as are images of castration, and fearful phallic power. The 'horror of horror' overall, however, seems to lie in the (r)evocation of the experience of abjection. Horror fiction is dominated by those images of waste, putrefaction and decay which Kristeva associates with abjection: these are, so to speak, the staple of horror. When we think of 'the horrid' we picture blood, corpses, the violation of bodily limits. Via these images horror fiction returns us to the scene of primary horror in the abjection of the mother, a scene which, however, *particularly for the masculine subject*, possesses fascination, the power of the taboo. Images of abjection lead the *masculine* subject back not only to the movement away from the mother but also to the original repressed desire for the mother, which returns with all the force of the repressed, of that which can be allowed no place in adult life.

Horror fiction thus seems to be designed to work for the masculine subject as an exorcism: it offers a way of repassing through abjection and of distancing oneself once again from the power of the mother. Horror fiction works in this sense as a kind of obverse of romance. For the feminine subject, the most painful aspect of early development is not the abjection of the mother but the movement into the masculine symbolic. It can and has been argued that romantic fiction exists precisely in order to 'cover up' the painful nature of the female insertion into the symbolic/patriarchal order. Romantic fiction offers a way of 'repassing' that insertion, 'tricking it out' with compensatory fantasies which are gratifying to the (feminine) ego. Horror fiction, we might argue, has a similar compensatory function, giving the *masculine* subject the opportunity to revisit and to 'repass' the crisis points of his early development. The masculine subject is thus allowed, via horror, to revisit forbidden realms in recompense for the day-to-day repression of certain desires. Horror fiction is, no less than romance, a genre which is tied to gender: awareness of its gender bias and of the role which it plays in social–textual terms as what Kristeva would call a 'rite of defilement' is long overdue.

Notes

1. Julia Kristeva, *Pouvoirs de l'horreur* (Paris: Seuil, 1980).
2. Julia Kristeva, 'Approaching Abjection', tr. John Lechte, in *Oxford Literary Review*, 5, nos 1–2 (1982) 125–6. (See *Pouvoirs de l'horreur*, pp. 9–10.)
3. Ibid., p. 127. (See *Pouvoirs de l'horreur*, pp. 11–12.)
4. Stephen King, *Carrie* (London: New English Library, 1974) p. 13. Subsequent page references are given in the text.
5. Kristeva takes the term from psychoanalysis: it denotes patients whose problems are on the borderline between neurosis and psychosis. The 'borderline', according to Kristeva, has 'foreclosed the Name of the Father' and thus remains in an alienated relation to language and the symbolic.
6. Stephen King, *The Shining* (London: New English Library, 1977) p. 18. Subsequent page references are given in the text.
7. One of the epigraphs for *The Shining* is from Goya: 'The sleep of reason breeds monsters.'
8. Stephen King, *Misery* (London: Hodder and Stoughton, 1987) p. 17.
9. Ibid., p. 59.

10

De-fanging the Vampire: S. M. Charnas's *The Vampire Tapestry* as Subversive Horror Fiction

ANNE CRANNY-FRANCIS

The Vampire Tapestry[1] is an innovative exploration of the horror genre by Suzy McKee Charnas, American author of the feminist dystopia *Walk to the End of the World* and its disturbing and ambiguous sequal, *Motherlines*. Horror literature, like all fantasy,[2] has the potential to be either a radical exploration of contemporary definitions of the 'real' or a conservative affirmation of that 'real', via the political ideologies (of gender, race, class) operative in the text. In this essay I analyse Charnas's textual inflections of these ideologies, principally through her characterisaton of the vampire. This characterisation is remarkable for Charnas's sophisticated manipulation of textual polyphony, characteristically foregrounded in the fantasy text. Accordingly, her characterisation of the vampire is subject to neither humanist reductionism nor generic stereo-typing. Instead Charnas constructs him as a fragmented conscious-ness, the decentred subject, characteristic of the fantastic in its most radically interrogative mode. By tracing Charnas's textual strategies and their ideological consequences, I present a case for *The Vampire Tapesty* as an example of the use of generic fiction by a politically committed writer to raise fundamental debate about social and political ideologies within a popular and accessible fictional format.

The Vampire Tapesty describes a period in the life of a vampire, currently masquerading as eminent anthropologist and academic Dr Edward Weyland. Charnas's story is not a chronologically direct narrative, but is told as five separate narratives; hence the 'tapestry' of the title. In each narrative Charnas describes a crucial episode in the life of Dr Weyland. In the first, 'The Ancient Mind at Work', Weyland's identity as a vampire is detected and he is shot and seriously wounded by his discoverer, Katje de Groot. In part II,

155

'The Land of Lost Content', the injured Weyland has been found by a group of petty criminals who, in collusion with a pathetic satanist character, put him on display. Part III, 'Unicorn Tapestry', sees Weyland free again, bargaining for the restoration of his academic position by agreeing to psychoanalysis for his delusion that he is a vampire. His analyst is Floria Landauer, and through her Weyland begins to discover some empathy with humans, who, until then, he had regarded merely as a food source. In part IV, 'A Musical Interlude', Weyland has moved to a university in New Mexico, significantly without killing Floria Landauer, who knows his true nature. Here Weyland attends a performance of Puccini's opera *Tosca* and is aroused by it to blood lust. He kills needlessly and indiscriminantly. In the final episode, 'The Last of Dr Weyland', the vampire is threatened with possible exposure and decides to end his masquerade as Dr Weyland.

I   'THE ANCIENT MIND AT WORK'

Charnas's novel works very well as an example of the vampire sub-genre of horror. She employs a number of the conventions associated with vampire novels since *Dracula*. And she employs them sensitively and intelligently; this is not a splatter text. The first of these conventions is the interrogation of the possibility of the vampire – the absurd notion that such a creature can have a real existence. This convention does not have its origins in *Dracula*, where Jonathan Harker's discover of the vampire nature of his host, Count Dracula, is preceded by very little knowledge of the topic. Certainly Harker experiences the fear of Transylvanian peasants, but this is not the learned scepticism of twentieth-century Americans. The reason for this modification of the convention is audience familiarity with the story of *Dracula* and other vampires, in literature and film. For modern audiences horror that such a creature can exist is replaced by a kind of second-order scepticism. No longer does such a creature seem so extraordinary. His feeding-practice is relatively fastidious and his motivation is rational and almost acceptable compared with the butchery most contemporary audiences witness night after night on their television screens. The vampire is no longer horrific because of his nature; in fact, his nature renders him understandable, explicable, in human terms. He sucks blood in order to live, not as a sexual thrill. He is not a psychopath; he is a human mutation, and a relatively civilised one.

For modern audiences, then, the vampire is a curiosity – a dangerous curiosity – but not quite the monster he once was. Modern audiences are not learning vampire lore; they know that already – garlic, crucifixes, wooden stakes, and so forth. The fun for contemporary audiences is in discovering how many of these elements of lore the urbane, modern vampire will reject. Movie audiences especially are familiar with the scene of a modern vampire laughing scornfully at the crucifix- and garlic-wielding human combatant, accusing her/him of belief in superstitious nonsense.

And, or course, fundamental to this play with the fictional-vampire knowledge is the question of the *reality* of the vampire. This is an investigation which operates simultaneously on a number of levels. In the modern story, the world of the narrative, contemporary characters are assumed to be familiar with the notion of the vampire. The major difficulty they face is accepting that such a creature, so familiar from late night TV reruns, is not purely fictional. The biggest obstacle they face in their battle with the vampire is not her/his monstrous nature, but their own scepticism. Only when they can accept that the vampire is *real* can they begin to fight her/him on informed ground.

Then comes the process of discovering how much of that information is superstition, and how much of it is effective against the creature – how much of the fiction is fiction and how much of it is real. The reader of contemporary vampire novels is thus caught up in a debate about the relationship between fiction and reality at the level of narrative. The 'hesitation' which Todorov described as the distinguishing characteristic of the fantastic has a structuring function in the narrative itself.

This narrative hesitation has a reflexive function, positioning us as readers to question our relationship to the text we are reading. What about *this* text is real and what is fictional? How is the 'real' signified/represented/discursively formulated in a fictional text? Does the 'reality' have to do with the responses of people just like ourselves to a creature so utterly different from ourselves? These questions are fundamental to the narrative of part i, 'The Ancient Mind at Work'. They are fundamental also to the sexual politics of the text, to Charnas's investigation of the ideology of gender which is implicit in this text, just as an affirmation of conservative gender relationships is implicit to most other vampire texts.

In part I Katje de Groot, expatriate South African Boer and widow of a university professor, discovers that the distinguished academic Dr Edward Weyland is a vampire. De Groot discovers this because she is at the university at a time when most other people have left, and that is because she works there as a domestic. With Katje de Groot Charnas constructs an unusual vampire-hunter. Politically conservative in the best traditions of vampire literature, de Groot is, however, a woman and she has no respect for the politics of either class or race. De Groot learns much from her interaction with the vampire and the mechanism of her education is crucial to Charnas's investigation of gender politics.

In choosing to work as a domestic Mrs de Groot shows her contempt for the class politics of the university, a point Charnas drives home by linking her work ironically with that of a black maid. Charnas has the black handyman Jackson made this connection: '"Yeah. Well, you sure have moved around more than most while you been here; from lady of leisure to, well, maid work." She saw the flash of his grin. "Like my aunt that used to clean for white women up the hill. Don't you mind?"' (p. 33).

Mrs de Groot also declares herself immune to race politics. Unlike her husband, she did not take part in the Black Majority Movement as an exile. She wants to return to South Africa, to buy her own house, and ignore the politics:

> Her savings from her salary as housekeeper at the Cayslin Club would eventually finance her return home. She needed enough to buy not a farm, but a house with a garden patch somewhere high and cool – she frowned, trying to picture the ideal site. Nothing clear came into her mind. She had been away a long time. (p. 17)

Eventually, however, she realises that it is not possible to ignore the politics of South Africa, and it is because of her interaction with Weyland that she comes to this realisation:

> Reluctantly she admitted that one of her feelings while listening to Dr Weyland talk had been an unwilling empathy: if he was a one-way time traveller, so was she. She saw herself cut off from the old life of raw vigour, the rivers of game, the smoky village air, all viewed from the heights of white privilege. To lose one's

world these days one did not have to sleep for half a century;
one had only to grow older.   (p. 44)

Mrs de Groot recognises the identity of difference, of alienation,
between herself and Weyland; each feels like 'a stranger in a strange
land'. This identity between female protagonist and vampire is
a crucial element in Charnas's analysis and is pursued throughout
the novel.

Gender politics are also discussed overtly in this section of the
book. Students have been raped on campus and Mrs de Groot's
co-workers worry about her vulnerability. Her response to the
rapist is characterstically conservative, as is shown in her scornful
rejection of the concern expressed by female academics: 'Katje
wasn't interested. A woman who used her sense and carried
herself with self-respect didn't get raped, but saying so to these
intellectual women wasted breath. They didn't understand real
life' (pp. 27–8).

Again de Groot has to change her ideas. In the final showdown
with the vampire, symbolically the attempted rape, she only
survives because she protects herself, abandoning her dignity to
do so. Only when she identifies wholly with the vampire is she
able to fight on familiar ground:

In her lassitude she was sure that he had attacked that girl,
drunk her blood, and then killed her. He was using the rapist's
activities as cover. When subjects did not come to him at the
sleep lab, hunger drove him out to hunt.
    She thought, *But I am myself a hunter!*   (p. 50)

The identification between the woman and the vampire is
also an identification of power, of strength. Having made that
recognition de Groot is able to defend herself:

She jerked out the automatic, readying it to fire as she brought
it swifly up to eye level in both hands, while her mind told her
calmly that a head shot would be best but that a hit was surer if
she aimed for the torso.
    She shot him twice, two slugs in quick succession, one in the
chest and one in the abdomen. He did not fall but bent to clutch
at his torn body, and he screamed and screamed so that she was

too shaken to steady her hands for the head shot afterwards. (p. 51)

This identification is interesting in that de Groot is not only a Boer
and a trained hunter, but also a woman. The race politics of the
Boer, of white supremacism and of exploitation, can be read as
having close parallels with the predatory behaviour of the vampire –
but women in our society are conventionally disempowered.
Which leaves the reader to ponder the significance of this dual
identification – as Boer, as woman.

The ending of this first narrative is unconventional on a number
of grounds. First, the vampire is shown to be vulnerable to bullets.
Even if they do not kill him, they stop him in his tracks. Fictional
vampire lore maintains that the vampire, being an undead, a
vivified corpse, cannot be bodily injured by normal human means.
Secondly, the vampire is shown to be a natural, rather than
supernatural, being. He is a great predator, a great hunter – in
Weyland's own terms, 'living . . . off the top of the food chain'
(p. 37). Charnas develops this theme in some detail by means of
the public lecture that Weyland gives during this narrative. The
'ancient mind' of the title (of the lecture and of part I) refers in the
first place to the unconscious mind which Weyland explores in his
sleep research. As question time continues, however, the topic
turns to vampires and, with the conventional hubris of the vampire,
Weyland describes his true nature to his unsuspecting audience.
The ancient mind becomes the mind of the vampire, the mind of
Weyland himself. And, of course, this episode is part of the fiction–
reality debate in which Katje de Groot (and the reader, in a different
way) is involved. Thirdly, the vampire is vanquished by a woman,
not a man – and by a woman who, via the identification process
described above, refuses her conventional role as victim. Instead
this woman acts as a hunter:

Then Scotty's patient voice said, 'Do it again,' and she was
tearing down the rifle once more by lamplight at the worn
wooden table, while her mother sewed with angry stabs of the
needle and spoke words Katje didn't bother to listen to. She
knew the gist by heart: 'If only Jan had children of his own!
Sons, to take out hunting with Scotty. Because he has no sons,
he takes Katje shooting instead so he can show how tough Boer
youngsters are, even the girls. . . . And to train a *girl* to go

stalking and killing animals like scarcely more than an animal herself!' (pp. 22–3)

The gender politics of this narrative had started conventionally enough, with the vampire identified as a sexually attractive man. De Groot's co-worker Nettie describes her encounter with Weyland at the sleep lab:

> He leaned over me to plug something into the wall, and I said, 'Go ahead, you can bite my neck any time.' You know, he was sort of hanging over me, and his lab coat was sort of spread, like a cape, all menacing and batlike – except white instead of black, of course – and anyway I couldn't resist a wisecrack. (p. 31)

The irony of this wisecrack is not lost on de Groot, of course. Weyland also becomes the subject of a T-shirt popular among the students: 'SLEEP WITH WEYLAND HE'S A DREAM' (p. 23). One of Weyland's academic colleagues notes, 'This T-shirt thing will start a whole new round of back-biting among his colleagues, you watch' (p. 24). Charnas here evokes the jealousy which male characters have traditionally displayed towards the vampire. This is how *Dracula*, for example, has often been read, with the male characters' pursuit of the vampire an attempt to destroy his great sexual potency, an Oedipal hunt after the *Ur*-father. Yet Weyland is vanquished not by his male colleagues, but by a female housekeeper. He is ousted by a woman who realises her strength through her identification with him, the 'other', the biologically different, the victim/hunter.

II 'THE LAND OF LOST CONTENT'

This identification between woman and vampire is implicit in part II, 'The Land of Lost Content'. Again Charnas exploits a familiar vampire convention – that the bloodsucking of the vampire is erotic. In vampire novels the bloodsucking conventionally signifies sexual intercourse, and so the vampire's attack on (usually) women signifies rape. This rape fantasy is a continuing preoccupation of (politically conservative/reactionary) horror fiction. Subsequently the female victim is often either made to feel guilty for putting herself in the vampire's power, no matter what struggle he has to go through to get to her (an example is Mina Harker in *Dracula*), or transformed by her own rape into something disgusting and repulsive, an undead – in other terms, reading the semiosis of the novel, a sexually assertive woman (Lucy Westenra in *Dracula*). The disgusting potency of the latter type of victim has to be destroyed by a group of marauding males, sometimes by the kind of symbolic pack rape to which Lucy is subjected.

In 'The Land of Lost Content' Charnas shows the vampire stripped of his power, a victim to the greed and voyeurism of others. In this section the identification process is reversed: what is revealed is not the monster, the biologically different, the 'other', in the woman, but the woman in the monster. Bereft of power, Weyland is placed in the traditional female role. Restrained in a cell-like room, he is put on display, an object of gaze, his subjectivity denied. Weyland points out to the boy, Mark, who has helped him, 'Have you noticed, Roger never refers to or addresses me by name? He is preparing himself to be indifferent to my death' (p. 105). And Roger himself confirms this when he tells Mark, 'Reese said absolutely not to feed the animal . . .' (p. 109).

Reese is the pathetic satanist who intends to use Weyland to consolidate his own power, a kind of ultimate macho man. When introduced to the weakened and helpless Weyland, Reese immediately manhandles the vampire:

> There was nothing silly in the scene anymore. Dr Weyland's fear touched Mark like a cold breath.
> Reese bent and clamped the vampire's head hard against his thick thigh with one arm. Seizing him by the jaw, he wrenched his mouth open.   (p. 77)

Reese goes on to examine the vampire's mouth:

> 'It's true there are no fangs, but here – see that? A sort of sting on the underside of the tongue. It probably erects itself at the prospect of dinner, makes the puncture through which he sucks blood, and then folds back out of sight again.
> 'Sexy', Roger said with new interest.   (pp. 77–8)

The language used in the description confirms the association between sexuality and bloodsucking. Accordingly, the vampire's mouth is synonymous with his genitals. Reese's brutal exposure of Weyland's mouth, together with the identification established between woman and vampire, can thus be read as a displaced representation of the exposure of female genitals to male gaze which characterises, signifies and defines the gender power relationships in our society.

The helpless vampire is humiliated by Reese and Roger, to the disgust of the boy Mark: 'Reese gripped and twisted the passive body of the vampire brutally, like a guy wrestling an alligator in a movie about the Everglades'; 'Roger looked high, as if exhilarated by the defeat of someone who had scared him' (p. 78). After this episode Weyland is forced to feed in public, for the voyeuristic pleasure of Reese's followers. The connection between sexuality and bloodsucking is a constant theme. When Bobbie, a female follower, allows Weyland to suck her blood, she responds sexually to him: 'She put out her hand as if to push the vampire's head away, but instead she began to stroke his hair . . . "oh, this is so far out, this is real supernova, you know?" Until he finished she sat enthralled, whispering, "Oh, wow", at dreamy intervals' (p. 71). Later, when another woman becomes distressed, yet another remarks, 'If she'd just relaxed and rolled with it, I bet she could have got off on that' (p. 92). Mark is not entirely sure of the significance of what he is seeing and questions Weyland about it. When Weyland responds that eating in public is common, Mark responds, 'It isn't just eating to the ones who come here. They make it dirty' (p. 98). Towards the end of the episode Mark feeds the vampire to save him from further exploitation by Reese, a situation which enables Charnas to present a naïve and innocent view of patriarchal sexual relationships: 'To have someone spring on you like a tiger and suck your blood with savage and single-minded intensity – how could anybody imagine that was sexy? He would never forget that moment's blinding fear. If sex was like that, they could keep it' (pp. 116–17).

When powerless, the vampire is a victim motivated by fear. His only weapon is the exhibition of that fear, that vulnerability, to someone young and innocent enough to be affected by it. Through that innocent character the vampire regains his strength and power. That scenario can be followed through in the vampire–woman identification, though not so simply. Children are often the only source of power, of strength, of identity, that women have in a patriarchal society. But that power is never so immediate, so focused, so controllable, as the vampire's power, centred as it is in his own body, his difference, which is also superficially a male body. Perhaps Charnas is suggesting that women do have an enviable power inherent in their difference – that of reproduction – but that that power is controlled by men who humiliate and degrade women by defining them purely in terms of that biology (a cunt) and/or in terms of difference: from them, from men, from humanity. This is the chain of significations in which normality, humanity, is defined in terms of masculinity; the feminine is, therefore, both abnormal and inhuman ('cattle'). Women are denied subjectivity because of their otherness and because of the frightening (to men) power it engenders. Interestingly, fictional vampires are often also assigned that power, of reproducing by transforming their victims into undeads like themselves.

'The Land of Lost Content' is an exploration of the subject–object relationship which defines the gender politics of our (contemporary Western) society. In a land of lost content, only form remains. Charnas reveals the formal or structural characteristics of gender relations isolated from particularising detail. The dominant gender ideology of our society, sexism, is described in this narrative as essentially a power relationship in which masculinity is identified with dominance and control, femininity with passivity and submission.

Just as Reese uses the paraphernalia of satanism to control his followers, so men in the past have used charges of witchcraft to control women. Who are the peasants with torches – the mob hunting the vampire, or witchburners?

III   'UNICORN TAPESTRY'

In part III Weyland encounters what he considers a modern form of the 'screaming peasants with torches', the psychological examination. Where the peasants would dismember him physically, the psychologist dismembers him emotionally: the result in both cases may be the same. If the psychologist destroys his distance from his victims, his food, his cattle, he will be unable to hunt. His identity, his subjectivity, will be destroyed.

The interest in this section for Charnas's analysis of gender relationships is that here the *difference* between women and vampire is explored. This difference is a function of power. At the end of part II it became clear that the identification woman–vampire only holds fully when the vampire is powerless. In 'Unicorn Tapestry' Charnas explores the other side, the vampire in control, the predator hunting his victims. This is the more conventional representation of the vampire, exploiting his erotic power to hypnotise his victims. Again, however, Charnas uses the convention innovatively, to deconstruct the gender ideology of Western society. Weyland's victims are identified as those without power in our society – women and gay men. While sexual attraction is an element in both cases, the power relationships involved simply confirm the powerlessness of both groups in patriarchal society. Weyland explains,

> Yet no doubt you see me as one who victimizes the already victimized. This is the world's way. A wolf brings down the stragglers at the edges of the herd. Gay men are denied the full protection of the human herd and are at the same time emboldened to make themselves known and available.
>
> On the other hand, unlike the wolf I can feed without killing, and these particular victims pose no threat to me that would cause me to kill. Outcasts themselves, even if they comprehend my true purpose among them they cannot effectively accuse me.   (p. 144)

Women too are accessible to him because of the social conventions governing gender relations, because he fits a particular social role which permits him to approach them, in that identity, in suitable places – 'galleries or evening museum shows or department stores' (p. 136). Weyland prefers men mainly because the encounter is likely to be brief and inexpensive.

So, in identifying the vampire's victims, Charnas exposes what traditional texts hide: the collusion of patriarchal ideology in the violent repression of large sections of the population – women and gay men. Both groups are denied the right to fulfil their sexual desires openly and honestly, and so are prey to a being who seems to embody patriarchal respectability. Women are attracted by the image of that lonely, handsome, ageing scholar; gays by the gentle closet gay who picks them up on a beat. Weyland uses the gender ideology of patriarchy to facilitate his bloodsucking/fucking, and that ruthless bloodsucking/fucking characterises the gender ideology of patriarchy. Charnas uses his story to expose that ideology.

Problems arise for Weyland when his psychoanalyst, Floria Landauer, begins to disrupt that relationship. Landauer asks Weyland to picture his relationship with the victim from the victim's viewpoint. Weyland responds, 'I will not. Though I do have enough empathy with my quarry to enable me to hunt efficiently. I must draw the line at erasing the necessary distance that keeps prey and predator distinct' (p. 146). When Landauer questions him about his sexuality, Weyland responds with the arrogance of Dracula: 'Would you mate with your livestock?' (p. 150). Weyland used this identification of human beings with cattle early in the book: 'Stop staring, cattle' (p. 51). It is used throughout Bram Stoker's novel, and is explored further by Charnas in this section.

As I noted earlier, in vampire texts bloodsucking signifies sexual intercourse so consistently that genital intercourse comes to seem an appalling aberration. Hence the reader's incredulousness at Mina Harker's conception of a child in *Dracula*. If the vampire was to have genital intercourse voluntarily (other than as a hunting-strategy), it would be a betrayal of his identity as a vampire. And in his role as an archetypal representative of patriarchal gender relations – an exploiter/oppressor of women and gays – it would signify his rejection of patriarchy.

So far Weyland's only encounter with a less unequal sexuality has been through watching ballet. Landauer records his response in her session notes:

But when a man and a woman dance together, something else happens. Sometimes one is hunter, one is prey, or they shift these roles between them. Yet some other level of significance exists – I suppose to do with sex – and I feel it – a tugging sensation, here – touched his solar plexis – 'but I do not understand it'. . . . W. isn't man, isn't woman, yet the drama connects. His hands hovering as he spoke, fingers spread towards each other . . . 'We are similar, we want the comfort of like closing to like.' How would that be for him, to find – likeness, another of his kind? 'Female?' Starts impatiently explaining how unlikely this is – No, forget sex and pas de deux for now; just to find your like, another vampire.

He springs up, agitated now. There are none, he insists; adds at once, 'But what would it be like? What would happen? I fear it!' Sits against, hands clenched. 'I long for it.'   (p. 165)

Weyland expresses the longing of many in our society for an equal sexual relationship, a longing abrogated by the patriarchal ideology which dominates so many interactions.

Later Weyland states, according to Landauer's notes, 'Your straightforwardness with me – and the straightforwardness you require in return – this is healthy in a life so dependent on deception as mine' (p. 165). So Weyland begins the process which will be his undoing. If Weyland is able to meet his victim face to face, without the mask, he will begin to empathise. If he empathises, as he explained earlier, he will no longer be able to hunt. In the same way, if those who conduct their sexual relationships in traditional patriarchal terms begin to empathise with their partners, they will no longer be able to operate. Once emotional engagement occurs, rather than emotional manipulation, equality results. But patriarchy is not based on equality; it is based on dominance–submission, hunter–victim relationships. Under patriarchy women are barely recognised as human (vampire–woman); they are the not-men, the 'other', 'cattle', 'livestock' (woman–victim). Landauer's examination of Weyland becomes an examination by Charnas of the function of patriarchal gender relationships. When Landauer and Weyland make love, a fundamental change in Weyland occurs. Once again he fails to eliminate someone who knows his true identity. Emotional engagement has taken place. Weyland is no longer a vampire; Landauer is safe.

The peasants with their torches are banished – but not for very long. Patriarchy is a powerful ideology.

IV 'A MUSICAL INTERLUDE'

Weyland leaves Landauer and heads for New Mexico. He cannot cope any longer with the challenge she poses to his identity. However, the disintegration continues, and again it is bound up with Weyland's new-found empathy – and also with a woman named Floria. Here the Floria is a character in Puccini's opera *Tosca*.

Weyland attends the opera at the request of colleagues at his new workplace. At interval Weyland feels disturbed by the effect on him of the music:

the music had been powerful; even he had felt his hackles stir.

Why? Art should not matter. Yet he responded – first to the ballet back in New York, and now to this. He was disturbed by a sense of something new in himself, as if recent events had exposed an unexpected weakness.

As the opera continues, Weyland's emphathetic response continues and increases:

Now the pattern of the hunt stood vividly forth in terms that spoke to Weyland. How often had Weyland himself approached a victim in just such a manner, speaking soothingly, his impatience to feed disguised in social pleasantry . . . a woman stalked in the quiet of a bookstore or a gallery . . . a man picked up in a park. . . . Hunting was the central experience of Weyland's life. Here was that experience, from the outside.   (p. 213)

Now Weyland has to face his nature from the role of the spectator, the victim, the role he refused to adopt for Floria Landauer. The opera reminds Weyland of his past and his whole identity starts to press in on him – not just Weyland the academic, the hunter, the vampire, but also the outcast, the stranger, the 'other':

More than once in such an office he had stood turning in his hands his tradesman's cap, or rubbing his palms nervously on the slick front of his leatherwork apron, while he answered official questions. When questions were to be asked, Weyland, always and everywhere a stranger, was asked them.   (pp. 214–15)

Finally Weyland recognises himself in Scarpia:

Resonances from the monster's unleashed appetite swept Weyland, overriding thought, distance, judgement.
    The lady in the snakeskin-patterned dress glanced at the professorial type sitting next to her in the aisle seat. Heavens, what was wrong with the man? Sweat gleamed on his forehead, his jaw bunched with muscle, his eyes glittered above feverishly flushed cheeks. What was that expression her son used – yes: this man looked as if he were *freaking out*.   (p. 216)

Weyland's empathy is now so intense that his knowledge of artistic form, of genre, is eradicated. Weyland empathises with the dynamics of the narrative, but without the 'civilised' control which allows him to see it as a performance rather than a reality. Now it is the vampire who confuses the status of fiction and reality. And yet maybe also the naïve response of the vampire tells us some fundamental truth about our acceptance of fictions imbued with ideologies which we might rationally reject, just as Mark's response to bloodsucking as eroticism constitutes a fundamental interrogation by Charnas of patriarchal sexual relationships.

When Weyland experiences a former, murderous identity under the stimulus of the opera, perhaps Charnas is suggesting that we as readers/viewers are insufficiently critical of similarly murderous (physically, emotionally, intellectually, spiritually) ideologies which structure the fictions of our society – from 'high' culture such as opera to 'popular' forms such as the horror novel.

Weyland is appalled to find that he has killed 'without need, without hunger' (p. 220). So the ideologies which structure our fictions are operative in our lives. We consume them uncritically and they structure our actions, our beliefs, or values. We act out desires 'without need, without hunger'. Charnas follows this questioning of the ideological function of art with an interpretation of the opera which ties it to the preceding narrative section, through the character of Floria Tosca/Landauer.

When the art-dealer McGrath rejects the opera as rubbish, a character, identified only as an art-collector, responds negatively:

> 'Other people do, too; they honestly feel that *Tosca*'s just a vulgar thriller', she observed. 'I think what shocks them is seeing a woman kill man to keep him from raping her [shades of Katje de Groot]. If a man kills somebody over politics or love, that's high drama, but if a woman offs a rapist, that's sordid.'
>
> McGrath hated smart-talking women, but he wanted her to buy another bronze; they were abstract pieces, not easy to sell. So he smiled.   (pp. 226–7)

Effectively Floria Landauer has done the same thing, destroyed Weyland the vampire, the rapist. Charnas seems to be working hard to ensure that we, the audience, make this connection: she has already had Weyland call attention to the name Floria – 'I knew someone in the East who was named after Floria Tosca' (p. 197). Floria Landauer's assault on the vampire/rapist is not physical, but psychological and ideological. By inducing in him an empathetic response to her, engaging him emotionally, Landauer began the deconstruction of the ideology and subjectivity that sustains Weyland. Now he feels an empathetic response to the opera and he resents its ability to touch him, to make him one with his prey:

> He feared and resented that these kine on whom he fed could stir him so deeply, all unaware of what they did; that their art could strike depths in him untouched in them. . . . But was he growing more like them, that their works had begun to reach him and shake him? Had he somehow irrevocably opened to the power of their art? (pp. 235–6)

In the first sentence Weyland also expresses his dismay that this art should touch him as it does not touch humans, though we know that the young artist Elmo has also been severely effected by his first night at the opera. Charnas seems to be making a number of points here, summarising the analysis presented in this narrative and again attempting to position the reader reflexively in relation to this and any other text. Weyland's literal empathy with the opera, set in a time he has experienced in a past life, calls into question our 'sophisticated' tendency to ignore textual politics for the sake of some aesthetic norm. Weyland's anger that he has been more affected emotionally than those around him corroborates this point, questioning the distancing-effect of atistic convention. How are we, as audience, affected by an artwork? How is empathy constructed in/by a text? The second part of the quote follows up this point. Weyland feels that his response to the artwork is an indication of humanness. Exactly how does response to art or culture of any kind define our humanness, our subjectivity? What are the crucial aspects of the spectator–artwork interaction which assist in or produce the effect of individual subjectivity? And is Charnas also making a case for the subversive potential of the artwork? Is the art-collector's interpretation of *Tosca* part of a strategy of rereading which will open up textual politics to intense scrutiny – as *The Vampire Tapestry* scrutinises vampire literature? Is Weyland's fear of the subversive effect of the artwork the cry of a patriarchal ideology under attack, from subversive writers of popular fiction as well as rereaders of traditional texts?

Perhaps one element of Weyland has met the peasants with torches and recognised himself among their number.

IV 'THE LAST OF DR WEYLAND'

Once the defining practices of an ideology are exposed, it is difficult for a practitioner to operate unself-consciously. And, once the practitioner empathises with the situation of those victimised by those ideological practices, it is unlikely that she or he will be able to persist in that victimisation. The hunter can no longer hunt. The hunt looks less like a heroic struggle than like a witch-hunt.

In the final narrative Dr Weyland is laid to rest, again by the agency of a woman. Charnas is concerned here not so much with the woman–monster identification as with the more traditional characterisation of the vampire as patriarch *par excellence*. As his latest lover tells him as she ends their relationship, 'this would be a lot easier if you weren't – you have the face of everybody's dream-father, you know that?' (p. 245). But this patriarch has begun to feel. Formerly a brilliant rationalist, a hunter, a manipulator, an exploiter, the patriarch is beginning to be troubled by his own identity, by the practices which make him what he is. The memories which begin to plague Weyland are fragments of his consciousness, his subjectivity. As I noted earlier, in characterising Weyland in this way Charnas avoids the simplistic humanist model of consistent subjectivity, representing instead a fragmented consciousness, the decentred subject, which is characteristic of the fantastic. It is this fragmentation of the subject, this process of continual formation and renegotiation, that produces the possibility for change. But Weyland does not change – at least, not in this life.

Once again his difference, his otherness, is recognised, this time by a female artist, Dorothea. As both artist and woman Dorothea recognises the insubstantiality of Weyland, his disguise which masks no substance: 'In the lecture hall in January I tried to draw you with my eye, but I saw that you do not draw. You have a stylized, streamlined quality, as if you were already a drawing rather than a man' (p. 270). Dorothea confirms Weyland's loss of contrived cohesiveness, contrived identity.

In this section, too, Weyland has his last encounter with Reese, the victimiser – the torch-bearing peasant – and he defeats him; he kills him. The narrative dynamics of this final encounter are fascinating to tease out. Weyland is by this time in a highly unstable state and calls on his former selves to help him:

If he could release his grip on his human surface and sink back into the deeper, darker being at his core, his root-self . . . this was not so simple as in simpler times. He suffered a frightful moment of imbalance and disorientation. Then something hot and raw began coiling in his body.

I am strong, I am already bent on departure, and I am hungry; why should I not hunt the hunter in my own house tonight?   (p. 287)

As a capitulation to that 'hunter' identity, Weyland's transformation can be read as a rejection of the empathy which had undermined the (patriarchal) ideology by which he operated – and which formed him as a subject. He hunts Reese on grounds they both understand, as representative of a violent patriarchy. Like Harker, Godalming and Van Helsing of *Dracula*, Reese has come to subdue the vampire to his will (the former by death, Reese by imprisonment). The Oedipal conflict is once more enacted, but in this text the vampire wins. Charnas here rejects one of the most prominent conventions of the vampire text, the ritual and savage killing of the vampire at the end of the narrative – the triumph of the peasants with torches. The peasants are vanquished, but so, in a sense, is Weyland: he wins, but also loses. His killing of Reese is his last feeding as Weyland. The disintegration of that character is now complete.

But how does the killing of Reese interact with that other level of signification whereby there is an identification between woman and monster? As I noted above, Weyland does summon up his former selves, reject his empathetic responses, in order to confront Reese as an equally ruthless member of a patriarchal order. In this guise the woman–monster identification perhaps does not operate. However, there is a kind of pleasure, a sense of justice, in his confrontation with Reese which seems to be related to more than the reassertion of patriarchy and/or Charnas's modification of vampire convention. And, in fact, this non-destruction of the vampire is now becoming a convention of the genre, particularly in film, in which the final scene often shows one of the heroes or heroines lunging at the other's jugular. Rather, it seems that, on some level, the woman–monster identification continues to work and that Weyland's destruction of Reese is an assertion of female opposition to patriarchy. And perhaps that is supported by Weyland's final conjectures, as he prepares for hibernation:

He had cared enough to preserve when it was no longer secure his Weyland identity and all its ties and memories. Tonight, in deadly jeopardy because of that recklessness, he had owed his fury only to past pain or the promise of future suffering at Reese's hands. He had burned also at the thought of Floria Landauer caught unknowing in Reese's net; of young Mark flying into a fugitive's perils from the net flung after him; of Reese obscenely alive and Irv dead. . . .

Now he knew with bitter clarity why in each long sleep he forgot the life preceding that sleep. He forgot because he could not survive the details of an enormous past heavy with those he cared for. . . . I am not the monster who falls in love and is destroyed by his human feelings. I am the monster who stays true. (pp. 300–1)

Weyland deliberately destroys a representative of oppressive patriarchy, and in so doing destroys a part of himself, the part that enables him to survive. As Weyland drifts into sleep, his personality as Weyland, that subjectivity, is secured in terms of his empathetic responses:

Then for a time came an unexpected gift. The voices of people returned vividly to him, their faces, gestures, laughter, the swirling brightness of the opera crowd, the jingle of coins in Irv's pocket, Mark's warm, bony shoulder under his hand as they walked towards the river, the scent of Floria's skin. Intense pleasure filled him as he yielded himself to the mingled ache and joy of memory, as he gathered in his Weyland life. (p. 302)

The ending of *The Vampire Tapestry* is unconventional in that the vampire is neither destroyed not left active (though in a different body); instead he is rendered harmless, his identity destroyed. The patriarchal order as represented by Reese is shown defeated by an even more ruthless member of that order, Weyland acting out his former self, as hunter. But that Weyland also contains the empathetic monster, the woman-identified subjectivity, who rejects that patriarchy and the victim role it offers him and woman. In this sense Reese is destroyed by the deconstruction of the ideology which engenders him. This ending is not simply a victory for patriarchy: it is also, simultaneously, a victory for those who reject that ideology. On the most subversive level, it is a victory achieved by the enemies of patriarchy, using the strategies of patriarchy.

And that perhaps is a fitting description of Suzy McKee Charnas's achievement in *The Vampire Tapestry*.

I noted at the beginning of this essay that horror, like other forms of the fantastic, has the potential for either criticism and subversion or conservatism. *Dracula*, the text which is the most obvious literary antecedent of *The Vampie Tapestry*, is an extremely conservative text. The gender ideology of that text is extremely repressive, with active female sexuality singled out for particularly brutal punishment. *Dracula* is, among other things, a patriarchal response to the strong and vocal Women's Movement of the 1890s.[3] The rape fantasy fundamental to the text is the correction rod applied to the psyche of assertive women of that time. *The Vampire Tapestry* can also be read as a response to the Women's Movement, of the 1970s and 1980s. However, this text demonstrates that other potential of the fantastic, for criticism and subversion.

Charnas uses generic conventions established in *Dracula*, such as the sexual attractiveness of the vampire, the vampire's pride, his classification of humanity as cattle. She also uses more recent modifications of the conventions, such as the scepticism of contemporary character towards the existence of such a creature. And in each case her use of generic convention is extremely self-conscious. As my analysis of the text shows, Charnas is always acutely aware of the ideological consequences of those conventions. Accordingly she modifies her text so that her use of the conventions focuses reader attention on their ideological function. *The Vampire Tapestry* is not only a text about the gender relationships of contemporary society; it is also a text about the way that contemporary texts, including horror novels, position readers as patriarchal subjects, reinforcing the repressive gender ideology of patriarchy.

Charnas's characterisation of the vampire is a crucial strategy in her textual politics. Instead of presenting him as a unified subject or melodramatic villain, she gives him the complexity and contradiction of the decentred subject, a strategy facilitated by the discontinuous narrative in which he operates. The vampire is thus able simultaneously to function conventionally as *Ur*-patriarch and unconventionally as woman-identified subject. Through the negotiation of this contradiction Charnas focuses on the gender politics of contemporary society, along with their textual representation and reinforcement. The text thus operates not only as an exploration of gender relations, but also reflexively as an interrogation of textual politics.

The subversive power of *The Vampire Tapestry* resides in these two textual functions. Charnas subverts the conventional vampire novel by using its own generic conventions to reveal its textual politics. In so doing she challenges the continuing operation of those texts, positioning readers to perform radical rereadings of the more traditional texts. She also, nevertheless, produces an entertaining vampire novel, effectively transforming the conventional political function of those texts, changing the genre from within in a classical subversive move.

The peasants with torches suddenly feel rather foolish. Who has put them in such an embarrassing position, chasing over the countryside after some poor damned creature/woman/victim? After all, what kind of thugs do they think we are! As torches are lowered and put out, dawn appears over the horizon.

Notes

1. Suzy McKee Charnas, *The Vampire Tapestry* (London: Granada, 1983). Page references are given in the text.
2. For valuable discussions of fantasy literature and the horror genre, and their conventions, see Rosemary Jackson, *Fantasy: The Literature of Subversion* (London: Methuen, 1981); David Punter, *The Literature of Terror: A History of Gothic Fiction from 1765 to the Present Day* (London: Longman, 1980); and M. M. Bakhtin, *The Dialogic Imagination*, ed. M. Holquist and C. Emerson (Austin: University of Texas Press, 1981).
3. See my essay 'Sexual Politics and Political Repression in Bram Stoker's *Dracula*', in Clive Bloom, Brian Docherty, Jane Gibb and Keith Shand (eds), *Nineteenth-Century Suspense: From Poe to Conan Doyle* (London: Macmillan, 1988).

Select Bibliography

Atlebury, Bruce, *The Fantasy Tradition in America* (Bloomington: University of Indiana Press, 1980).

Axelrod, Alan, *Charles Brockden Brown: A Collection of Critical Essays* (Austin: University of Texas Press, 1983).

Bassett, John (ed.), *William Faulkner: The Critical Heritage* (London: Routledge and Kegan Paul, 1975).

Cannon, Peter, *H. P. Lovecraft* (Boston, Mass.: Twayne, 1989).

Carter, Lin, *A Look behind the Cthulhu Mythos* (London: Panther, 1975).

DeLamotte, Eugenia C., *Perils of the Night: A Feminist Study of Nineteenth Century Gothic* (New York: Oxford University Press, 1989).

Jackson, Rosemary, *Fantasy: The Literature of Subversion* (London: Methuen, 1981).

Kerr, Elizabeth M., *William Faulkner's Gothic Domain* (Port Washington, NY: Kennikat Press, 1979).

Kerr, Howard, with Crowley, John W. and Crow, John (eds), *The Haunted Dusk: American Supernatural Fiction 1820–1920* (Athens, Ga: University of Georgia Press, 1983).

Lee, A. Robert (ed.), *Edgar Allan Poe: The Design of Order* (London: Vision Press, 1987).

Lovecraft, H. P., *Supernatural Horror in Literature* (New York: Dover, 1973).

Penzoldt, Peter, *The Supernatural in Fiction* (London: Peter Nevill, 1952).

Punter, David, *The Literature of Terror: A History of Gothic Fictions from 1765 to the Present Day* (London: Longman, 1980).

Ringe, Donald A., *Charles Brockden Brown* (Boston, Mass.: Twayne, 1966).

Rosenthal, Bernard, *Critical Essays on Charles Brockden Brown* (Boston, Mass.: G. K. Hall, 1981).

Schweitzer, Darrel, *The Dream Quest of H. P. Lovecraft* (San Bernardino, Calif.: Borgo Press, 1978).

Schweitzer, Darrel, *Speaking of Horror: Interviews with Writers of Weird and Supernatural Literature* (San Bernardino, Calif.: Borgo Press, 1989).

Sedgwick, Eve Kosofoky, *The Coherence of Gothic Conventions* (London: Methuen, 1986).

Symons, Julian, *The Tell-Tale Heart: The Life and Works of Edgar Allan Poe* (London: Faber, 1978).

Todorov, Tzvetan, *The Fantastic: A Structural Approach to a Literary Genre* (Ithaca, NY: Cornell University Press, 1975).

Underwood, Tim, and Miller, Chuck, *Kingdom of Fear: The World of Stephen King* (London: New England Library, 1987).

Warren, Robert Penn (ed.), *Faulkner: A Collection of Critical Essays* (Englewood Cliffs, NJ: Prentice-Hall, 1966).

Index